Lost Sols

Book Three

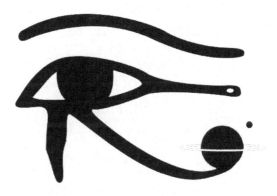

The

Awakening

James Kirk Bisceglia

Copyright © 2018 by James Kirk Bisceglia

Edited by Jennifer Koth
Cover design by Barbara Vallejo Francis

Visit my website at www.JamesKirkBisceglia.com

First Printing: August 2018

ISBN-13: 978-1986513609
ISBN-10: 1986513602

Chapter 1

All life finally left the felled alien leader. The strange alien sat motionless for ten minutes and was past the point of revival. No longer the leader of a nation, President Louis was lucky to be alive. When the guard turned his back for a moment, Louis made a fast escape out of the Bellagio Casino. Running to the point of exhaustion, the deposed President of the United States eventually ended up in a slave encampment by the airport. He sat on the ground exhausted as light penetrated the early morning darkness. "Aren't you President Louis?" a boy asked. "I was the President. I just killed the Annunaki leader and suspect the invaders will be looking for me. When they come, I want you to kill me and hide my body. Don't tell them where I am for at least ten minutes. I've already died many times and they keep reviving me," President Louis replied. "I will hide you, but if the people in this camp find out who you really are they'll kill you themselves. You're not very well-liked, Mr. President. Did you know a woman named Sandy?" the boy asked.

The President wondered how this boy could have known Sandy. "Yes, I did. How did you know her?" Louis asked. "She stopped here briefly and told me she was on her way to kill the alien leader. Is she still alive?" the boy asked. "She sacrificed her life making the attempt. I completed her mission," President Louis replied. "Let's get you somewhere safe, Mr. President. I know where there's a safe hiding spot. It's not much, but it might work for a while. By the way, my name is Leonard," the boy said.

President Louis was led from the small congregation of people to a remote scabland covered in rocks, dirt and sagebrush. Leonard wiped dirt off a piece of plywood lying on the ground. He moved the hidden door revealing a small hole dug into the ground. "There's some water down there and a little bit of food. I built it in case they decided to attack us from the air," Leonard said. "It's a spider hole just like the one where Saddam was hiding. I hope my fate is better. Thank you very much and remember what I said; I'd rather be dead then become their prisoner again," President Louis reiterated. "You're welcome Mr. President. Good job killing their leader. It's too bad you couldn't have done more before we were invaded," Leonard stated sincerely.

Buxare seethed with anger. She was urgently summoned to the hotel. Upon arrival, she found her mother dead. The human somehow managed to kill the Annunaki leader of Earth. "What are your orders?" one of the guards asked. Buxare was rocked with emotion. She was suddenly the new leader of the invading force.

"Find out where they're hiding and kill every human on the outskirts of the city. We'll imprison the humans inside the city. They will live in misery and exist only to serve us. Get our ships in the air and wipe out everyone else. If the human assassin is found, bring him to me alive," Buxare ordered grimly.

Leonard returned to the encampment. "Who was the stranger?" someone asked. "The dude was another crazy person scavenging for food. It will take the aliens time to wipe out all the stragglers, so I sent him to the north," Leonard replied as he suddenly noticed multiple lights in the distance. "They're coming!" he screamed and ran toward his hiding spot. Explosions rocked the camp as the invaders opened fire. Leonard was thrown to the ground and blood ran out his broken nose. He rose shakily, wiped his face, and ran as fast as possible.

The water was warm and brown but he needed it. President Louis was dehydrated after the events of the day. He dropped the canteen when an explosion rocked the area. The screams of wounded and dying people could be heard in the distance. More human casualties due to his actions. He was tired of failing humanity and being responsible for so many deaths. The moon appeared as someone quickly removed the plywood roof. Leonard jumped inside and slid the piece of wood back into place covering the opening. "The aliens aren't questioning anyone; they're killing everyone on sight. Apparently, you really pissed them off," Leonard said. "We'll be next. Kill me now," President Louis replied. "I'm sorry Mr. President. I planned on joining the Air Force, so I'm your last line of defense. We need organization to fight these bastards. You need to pick yourself up and fight these assholes."

President Louis and Leonard listened for the next hour as alien ships decimated the outskirts of Las Vegas. "What should we do now Mr. President?" Leonard asked. "We get the hell out of here. We need to find others in hiding who can help inflict damage on the aliens. We will leave when it's safe to do so, but for now, we'll stay here until we know they are gone for good. If there aren't any new attacks, we'll leave in the morning," President Louis asserted.

After a night underground, President Louis and Leonard left the safety of their hiding spot and ventured out on foot. "I've heard it's safer in the north. The aliens are apparently having trouble with resistance in the Cascade Mountains," Leonard said. "The Cascades are hundreds of miles away and we need to stay off the roads. Our ancestors traveled by horseback and we should do the same, so look for farms and horses," President Louis replied. After walking for an hour,

Leonard spotted an old, red barn and horses in a corral. "There's our ride. We will travel at night and sleep under cover during the day. I'm not the President anymore; I'm an ordinary citizen just like you fighting the alien invasion." "Mr. President, you are much more than that and we need organization. If nothing else, you need to inspire and organize any people we encounter." With a sheepish grin, Leonard added, "You're also a horse thief now."

"Captain, we've received the battle plan. Our orders are to drop back and protect the two ships firing quantum torpedoes at the gate," Isabella said. Vincent didn't like it. After learning who the Annunaki really were, he wanted to be on the front lines fighting the enemy as their ships passed through the gate. "Why are these two ships so special?" Vincent asked. "According to the battle plan, they will effectively shut down the gate. Enclosed within the quantum torpedoes are specific amounts of dark matter as well as exotic matter with positive energy density. According to the plan, the gate will be shut down when we believe forty-seven percent of their ships have passed through. The gate will be closed when it's estimated the enemy forces on our side of the gate can be defeated easily. Heavy damage will still be inflicted on their military," Isabella relayed.

"We will follow orders and do our duty. Set course for the ships. We must trust the plan is well thought out. Are the quantities of dark matter and exotic matter in the report? It would be nice to have the knowledge if we ever need to shut down a gate ourselves," Vincent asked. "The information is classified Captain. If all Alliance ships could access the information, there is a risk it might fall into enemy hands," Isabella replied. "Well then, how long until we reach the coordinates?" "We will be in position in approximately ten minutes and three seconds," Monique answered.

"Captain, Annunaki ships are traversing the gate," Isabella reported urgently. The monitors onboard the ship displayed tactical information and audio from the commanding officer of the fleet. Annunaki ships of various designs were breaching the gate at tremendous speeds and gathering at a single point. "Tactical information shows the Annunaki have traveled a quarter of the way to Rabanah and have stopped. We are receiving new orders. We are to proceed with the other two ships to a point taking us out of the line of sight of the gathering Annunaki force. Navigation is no longer under our control and has been fed into the computer by the Alliance," Isabella said.

"We are inexperienced in battle and the Alliance isn't taking any chances. Let's see what we can learn today. We will do what is necessary," Vincent said. "Captain, the quantum torpedoes will be fired in approximately twenty seconds. This should be interesting; an open gate has never been shut down until now," Julia reported.

Empress Zovad was still in the Vandi system near the outskirts of the gate in her command ship. She was satisfied with the execution of her battle plan. The invasion was proceeding precisely as planned. Her massive invading force would soon overwhelm the weak Alliance. After claiming the home planet of the Alliance she would be truly invincible. "Empress, a probe has returned with a tactical update. The Alliance has responded and fired torpedoes, but they will miss our forces completely," the tactical officer reported. "It's astounding how incompetent their leaders are. They can't even hit a stationary target," Empress Zovad smiled as she watched the tactical display. The torpedoes were projected to miss her invading force and travel aimlessly toward the gate. When the torpedoes arrived at the entrance they exploded at equidistant locations.

"Empress, we are receiving strange and unstable fluctuations at the gate," the tactical officer reported. "Show me immediately," Empress Zovad commanded as a three-dimensional image of the gate appeared before her. She watched as the gate to the Rabanah System suddenly collapsed in a blinding flash. The ships traversing it at the time were destroyed.

The crew of the Santa Maria watched as the torpedoes travelled toward the gate. After the massive explosions, the gate suddenly closed. "Fire at will!" The Commander of Alliance Forces ordered. The Annunaki ships which successfully traversed the gate were now under attack. All Alliance vessels converged and attacked the Annunaki fleet. Any damaged ships were ordered to immediately retreat to avoid destruction.

"Captain, navigation is no longer under Alliance control. We are clear and free to navigate," Isabella reported. "Get us in the battle. Fastest speed possible," Vincent barked. Isabella quickly guided the Santa Maria to the closest enemy ship. Two other Alliance vessels were present as well. "Firing missiles!" Julia reported. The enemy ship was quickly destroyed by the trio of Alliance vessels. Vincent punched his fist into the air as the explosion faded. "Let's go find another one," he ordered. A second heavily damaged Annunaki ship was quickly destroyed. "Move on to the next target," Vincent shouted.

"Captain, the battle is essentially over. The Annunaki ships that made it through have been defeated. There are only a few Annunaki vessels left and those remaining are surrounded by Alliance forces. The Commander is ordering all ships to cease fire and disable the weapons on the remaining enemy ships. He demands prisoners in order to gather intelligence," Isabella reported.

Vincent watched as Alliance ships targeted the weapons and engines of the Annunaki vessels. "The Commander reports the ships have been disabled. He's sending in boarding parties. We've been ordered back to Rabanah," Isabella said. "It's nice to see those assholes die; they've had it coming for a long time. The plan from the Tactical Council worked very well. I will speak to any prisoners myself. We need to know what we'll be facing when we get to Earth."

Two hours later, Vincent was in the office of Chief Administrator Kizak. "I want to be part of the interrogation team," Vincent demanded. "This is a delicate process. The team I've assigned to interrogate the Annunaki prisoners has spent years perfecting their techniques and have been trained to gather maximum intelligence. You simply don't have the required training. I'm sorry, but you will not be allowed to participate," Kizak replied.

Vincent was angry and knew he needed to channel his anger properly. "Goddamn it. The Alliance is supposed to be about honesty, morality and trust. Chief Ambassador, you are now the leader of the

Alliance which owes a debt to humanity as well as the Martians. We should have been told from the beginning that Mars was the ancestral home world of the Annunaki. The true nature of the Annunaki was hidden from the people of Sol by the Alliance you now lead. Give me the opportunity to speak to the Annunaki prisoners. You owe us that much," Vincent angrily replied.

Kizak didn't like the idea of diverting from established standard operating procedures, but the human did make a compelling argument. The Sol System had always been the long-term target of the Annunaki. The information never should have been withheld from the citizens of Sol. "I will allow you to question any and all Annunaki prisoners we have captured. You will be allowed to question the prisoners only after the interrogation team has completed their duties. Will that be satisfactory?" Kizak asked. "Thank you, Chief Administrator; I appreciate your consideration in this matter. Please let me know when your team is done. I would like to speak with the Annunaki as quickly as possible," Vincent replied diplomatically.

Alixias was tired, irritable and worried. She could now feel their child moving inside her body. The reality of the situation scared her. "Why are we bringing a child into this world? It's very likely we will soon be slaughtered by the Annunaki," she lamented. "We must not give up hope. As long as we're alive, we have a chance. Our family will live together or die together," Patrick replied. "We will likely die together and sooner than you think. You heard the message from the Alliance. The Annunaki will be here soon to reclaim their home world. We will be annihilated," Alixias said. "We're not dead yet, so cheer up. Anyway, it's time to meet with Dalton and give him an update on your pregnancy," Patrick replied. "I'm tired of Dalton and his never-ending questions. The man is a nuisance and we give him the same information every time. You can meet with him alone today. I'll stay here and rest," Alixias said. "As you wish. Is there anything you want Dalton to know?" Patrick asked. "I have no additional information for him. Bring back more food; I'm eating for two." Alixias testily replied.

"Where is Alixias?" Dalton asked. "She is resting and very worried about the future. I try to stay positive, but she has a point. Our child will likely die before it's even born. There's little to be hopeful for," Patrick said forlornly. "We received a communication today; Salkex's discovery enabled the Alliance to close the gate to the Vandi System. Nearly half of the total Annunaki force was destroyed after the gate was shut down. The

Alliance suffered very few losses and will now attempt to retake the Sol System in the near future. The fight near Rabanah was a complete success and a battle plan is being prepared, but we do not have a timeframe yet. Your child might very well live a long and prosperous life. The child Alixias carries is unique. There is an unknown and ancient reason why humans and Martians were meant to reproduce. The child must live and grow old. I will inform everyone on Mars of this latest information when we're done here, so tell Alixias there is hope. The good news will help reduce her stress," Dalton assured Patrick.

Patrick didn't realize how demoralized he was until he heard of the Alliance victory at Rabanah. "Alixias will be happy to hear the news. I think her maternal instincts are already taking hold. Our child hasn't been born yet and she's very concerned about its future. She will be an excellent mother," Patrick said. "The two of you don't need any additional pressure; just focus your efforts on bringing your unique child into the world safely. We have no control in the battle for the Sol System," Dalton replied. "You make a good point. I will return to Alixias and tell her the good news. Do you have any extra food? She's apparently quite hungry," Patrick asked.

Chapter 2

Strithu filled the sky once again. Vandi was a beautiful planet and it was a shame the Alliance had to abandon the gorgeous world. Tony parked his ship far from the capitol among destroyed Annunaki vessels. He retrieved his bullak and set the vessel ablaze. He wouldn't use the ship again and didn't want the Annunaki to use it for any of their purposes. If he ran quickly, the trip to the capitol would take about three hours.

He lofted the bullak into the air and watched sunlight reflect off the four dangerous blades. It was a weapon he was growing attached to. The run would help clear his mind and help him focus on what he was preparing to do. The strange energy he felt after the transformation was affecting his decision making. He knew returning to Vandi was most likely a suicide mission. As he picked up speed, two Strithu appeared on either side of him. They were flying just a few feet off the ground. Tony felt reenergized and picked up his pace as more Strithu joined. He was at the apex of a V-formation gracefully swinging the bullak high through the air as he ran. The Strithu bellowed with each swing of the weapon. The strange and helpful birds were welcome. Suddenly the sky grew dark. He glanced up at the two suns and was overwhelmed. Strithu filled the sky blotting out the light. The birds bellowed in unison with each swing of the weapon as he led them to the destroyed city.

When he arrived, the capitol was eerily silent. After the healthy run with the Strithu, Tony felt a new sense of purpose. One of the largest birds laid down directly in front of him as the remaining Strithu formed a perimeter around the courtyard that extended for miles. His adrenaline subsided; he was tired and sat down next to the large bird. He always felt safe around the Strithu and they served as his guards.

Day turned to night and someone or something tapped him on the head. He looked up into the massive beak of the large Strithu he fell asleep next to. As his vision adjusted, he noticed thousands of lights on the horizon traveling toward the capitol. The Strithu looked at him quizzically. Tony pointed at the bird and then to the sky. The Strithu leader shook its head from side to side. "I am not here to fight today and there will be no battle. I appreciate you more than you'll ever know, but you must leave now and take your companions," Tony said and pointed to the sky again. A loud call emanated from the massive animal. The area abruptly cleared as Strithu flew off in all directions. The Strithu leader hovered in the distance observing the proceedings. Tony was suddenly alone in the courtyard and cut off from the Alliance and his friends. He watched as Annunaki ships descended.

Escorted by a dozen other vessels, the largest ship landed last. A security team cleared the area before a solitary Annunaki female exited the ship. She was dressed in all red regalia and led her crew to the courtyard. When she arrived, Annunaki exited the surrounding ships. Tony watched as the Annunaki leader walked in his direction. Tony wasn't wearing clothing and was completely camouflaged, still there was no point in taking unnecessary risks. He retreated a safe distance as the Annunaki and Krace gathered around their Empress. Thousands of Annunaki formed ranks around their leader and her second in command. The Krace were furthest from Empress Zovad. It was obvious she didn't trust them. All Annunaki and Krace kneeled as she began to speak.

"An unprecedented event has occurred. The Alliance has somehow managed to shut down the gate to the Rabanah System," she said. "Empress Zovad, how could this have happened?" her second in command asked. "I've barely spoken and you have the audacity to interrupt me? You do ask a valid question however. The Alliance has discovered something you should have known about and anticipated. You will now answer to me for failing to gather proper intelligence for this battle," Empress Zovad said as she quickly pulled a weapon from her side and shot her second in command. The weapon produced a horrific result. The woman let out a shriek as her skin took on an eerie glow and her body burned from the inside out.

"This is what happens when you fail your Empress! We will remain on Vandi until we discover what has happened with the gate to Rabanah. You will stay on alert and if the gate reopens, we will resume our attack," Empress Zovad ordered with severity. She was preparing to order her forces back to their ships when she unexpectedly felt an alien presence within the assembled group. It was something she hadn't experienced in a long time. She closed her eyes, took a deep breath and focused on the mind of the alien intruder. The intruder was not far away.

Tony was relaxed and at ease as he listened to the Annunaki leader's speech. The murder of the second in command was not surprising but it was a waste of life. There was no way the dead woman could have known how the Alliance shut down the gate. The speech was winding up and Tony was preparing for the next phase of his mission when a presence suddenly entered his thoughts. Empress Zovad stared right at him. He felt a consciousness enter his mind. The assault was surprising and unexpected. His thoughts were no longer his own and he began to panic. The Annunaki leader invaded his mind with overwhelming intensity.

He attempted to fight the intrusion and quickly lost consciousness.

Empress Zovad knew she touched the mind of the one called The Shadow. She'd seen the human's thoughts and knew another encounter was likely in the future. The connection was suddenly broken and she didn't know why. She considered ordering an immediate search for The Shadow, but if her search failed, some would doubt her leadership. Empress Zovad decided she would torture and kill The Shadow herself. Any alien with the audacity to get so close to her needed to be studied.

It was dark and Tony was in the air. He looked up into the face of the Strithu leader. She was flying as fast as she could and he was in her pouch. A brief time later, the bird landed. The attack on his mind by the Annunaki leader left him confused and disoriented. Tony found himself in the presence of the Volmer once again. "Why have you returned, human? You gave your word you would not come back," Gly inquired. Tony didn't know how to respond; he wasn't thinking clearly and was trying to recover. "I was attacked unexpectedly and I'm trying to regain my focus. Please give me a moment," he replied. Gly observed the human. Tony helped liberate Vandi, yet here he was, helpless and disoriented.

Gly studied history and never forgot the tales he was taught in his youth. He had experience with Empress Zovad himself. The Annunaki slaughtered thousands of his people until his ancestors eventually learned how to block out the mind probe from the Annunaki leader. This human was special and Gly decided to help him. "I will teach you how to fight the mental intrusion, but first you must rest," he said.

Tony wasn't sure how long he slept, but it was needed. His head ached and he was still confused. Someone left him food and water which helped. After eating his meal, Tony went in search of Gly and found him conferring with other Volmer. "You must have luck and many lives human. You should be dead many times over," Gly said as he walked away from his companions toward Tony. "There have been many times I've thought I'd be dead as well. The mind probe was invasive and very unsettling. Please tell me everything you know about the Annunaki and their leader; I must learn about our enemy," Tony implored.

"Until recently, we've only had sporadic, individual interactions with the Annunaki. Our species has the ability to communicate telepathically, yet we seldom use our ability as it is considered highly immoral and an invasion of privacy. It's very personal and primarily a tool used during mating rituals. We rarely use against an enemy as it is exhausting and additional rest is required afterward.

When the Annunaki initially invaded Vandi, their leader believed we would easily become their prisoners. Due to our ability to retreat to the sea and fight on various fronts, the Annunaki were unable to enslave us. Their leader believed a decisive battle with massive forces would overcome our resolve and she planned on leading the battle personally. I felt her presence when she arrived in the north and I'm sure she felt mine as well. I alone visited her encampment. We shared our thoughts and minds and after the sharing, she knew it would be impossible to overcome our unique advantages and abilities. I willingly shared the thoughts I wanted her to know and blocked out her attempt to overcome my mind. The battle never took place and she immediately withdrew her forces and left us alone," Gly explained.

"I felt as if my mind was not my own when she invaded my thoughts. How are you able to block the intrusion?" Tony asked. "It takes practice and discipline. Your species lacks this capability right now, but the ability lies dormant in most humans. It's likely humanity will begin to understand how to use telepathy at some point in the future. We will practice and you will learn how to protect your thoughts. In time, it's possible you can learn to read and communicate with the minds of others, but you must avoid the mind of the Empress. You are incapable of overcoming her mental powers," Gly replied. "I will do my best to learn what you can teach me. I will do whatever it takes to kill Empress Zovad," Tony humbly avowed.

The remoteness of the safe house in Trundle ensured short term survival. There hadn't been any contact with the invading force for several months. It was also very boring. Randy found Enzo just waking from another nap. Everyone seemed to be sleeping more than normal. "A spotter has located another group of aborigines about a mile away," Randy reported. "That's the third group in the last couple of months. Has anyone figured out what they're doing and why they are traveling around the countryside?" Enzo asked. "We can't figure it out. You would think they'd want to bunker down in a safe location like us," Randy shrugged. "I'm going stir crazy. Would you like to go for a walk with me and meet some aborigines?" Enzo asked. "Wouldn't that be dangerous? How do we know they wouldn't attack us?" Randy wondered aloud. "They are simply trying to survive just like we are. I don't believe the stories that all aborigines are dangerous. I'll be leaving in five minutes if you want to go. Maybe they've learned something," Enzo said as he pulled on his jacket.

It was an hour before sundown as Enzo and Randy approached the area where the group of aborigines was last seen. "I wonder which direction they went?" Enzo asked. As Randy was about to respond, a group of ten aborigines suddenly appeared out of the brush thirty yards away. Enzo heard something behind him and turned to see another group emerge on the path. All held weapons of some kind. A few held spears, but most were holding rifles and guns. Both Enzo and Randy placed their rifles on the ground. "We're not a threat to you. Does anyone speak English?" he asked.

A tall and skinny male stepped forward. "Jesus Christ, it's not the eighteen hundreds. Of course, we speak English. I am Mowan. What are you doing here?" he asked. "I came here to ask you the same question. A group of us live in a safe location not far from here. We have recently seen your people in the area and I decided to make contact. What are you doing wandering the countryside?" Enzo asked. "We are hunting the invaders. What else would we be doing?" Mowan asked.

Enzo was astonished. "Why would you bring attention to yourselves? The aliens will decimate you," he replied. "We've killed a dozen and only lost three of our own. It's simply a matter of getting them out in the open," Mowan stated matter-of-factly. "How have you managed to kill our enemy?" Enzo asked. "Come with us and I'll show you." "Let me discuss it with my friend. If we go, we'll need to go back and get supplies," Enzo said. "Discuss it if you must, but there will be no time to return for supplies. If you stay with me and my people you won't need any," Mowan stated. "Please give us a moment to discuss your offer," Enzo turned and walked away with Randy.

"What do you think? Do you want to go?" Enzo asked. "I think it's way too dangerous; I'm not going," Randy replied. "I need to know how they're killing the aliens. Mowan says he's killed some and we need to learn how to do it. Why don't you return and take charge at our base? I don't know how long I'll be gone, but with luck, I'll make it back shortly," Enzo said. "Take care, my friend and remember you don't have any allies in the outback." Randy waved and headed back toward the base.

The first few weeks with the aborigines was not easy for Enzo. He wasn't in the best of shape and no longer a young man. It was difficult trying to keep up and to understand what the tribe was attempting to do. During the day the aborigines traveled in what seemed like random directions. Rotating crews worked at night digging massive holes in the ground. By morning the holes were large and deep with dirt stacked precisely on two of the four rectangular sides.

Enzo awoke when the sun breached the horizon. He was tired and decided he could no longer keep up with the tribe. As he set out to find Mowan, a sound pierced the morning calm. He looked up and saw an alien airship approaching their location. Suddenly, many of the aborigines began to whistle and everyone began running. Enzo quickly spotted Mowan and yelled to the man. "What should I do?" he asked in a panic. "The ground vehicles will be here soon to capture us. Run as far and fast as possible!" Mowan yelled. Enzo took off alongside Mowan. "We must scatter; do not run next to me! We've got to spread out!" Mowan exclaimed.

Adrenaline kept Enzo moving at a good pace for about two minutes. But ultimately he put only a minimal amount of distance between himself and the encampment. He hoped it would be enough as he approached the base of a small hill. Exhausted, he decided if it was his time to die, then so be it. He slowly clambered up the hill and gingerly sat down at the top as events of the attack unfolded below. Two alien ground vehicles chased members of the tribe. The tribe members spread out and didn't travel together. He watched sadly as one of the aborigines was brought down by weapons fire. The aliens immediately found a

25

new target nearby. Enzo recognized the area where the aborigine was running. It was close to one of the holes they dug and camouflaged. The man ran over the piled dirt and stopped defiantly on the other side of the camouflaged hole. The ground vehicle accelerated as the aliens were going to simply try and run him over. Enzo watched in fascination as the ground vehicle plunged into the hole. The tribe member put his fingers in his mouth and a moment later Enzo heard a faint whistle. Aborigines quickly descended on the location and began refilling the hole. Weapons fire emerged from the hole and the tribe members were careful to stay out of the line of fire. The second ground vehicle eventually suffered the same fate as the first. Enzo continued to watch until both holes were completely filled. The aliens were buried alive. Members of the tribe made their way back to the encampment except for one person at each location where the aliens were buried. He decided it was time to speak with Mowan and began heading back himself.

The early morning attack left Enzo tired even though he'd only been awake for about three hours. Mowan sat by the fire enjoying a meal. "How do you know the aliens won't escape?" Enzo asked. "They never have in the past. I post a guard to make sure. The guard stays for ten days. The aliens have never recovered from being buried. We cannot fight them in a traditional sense, but we can bury them alive," Mowan replied. A nearby explosion suddenly interrupted the conversation. "What was that?" Enzo asked. "It was the alien airship. Once the ground vehicles leave, the airships are unmanned. We destroy them as soon as possible," Mowan explained. "Why don't the aliens attack you by air?" Enzo asked. "They used to and we lost many of our people. They only began using ground vehicles when we scattered and ran. It is our only way to survive," Mowan replied.

Enzo knew the alien airships were a valuable commodity. Randy would have a field day examining one. It was imperative to bring a ship back to the base if possible. "Mowan, I am not a young man and cannot keep up with you and your tribe. Can we travel back to my base? I would like to invite you and your people in for some rest and a few decent meals," Enzo offered. "You have fought alongside us and I accept your invitation. We will be back at your base by nightfall."

Randy hated camping and he didn't like being outdoors. He was becoming so stir crazy he regretted passing at the opportunity to go with Enzo. Any change would have been welcome. Gail approached. "A lookout has spotted another aboriginal party traveling in our direction. It appears Enzo is with them. "Follow me, we're going outside," Randy said. Enzo and the aborigines approached slowly. "Tell the guards to stand down. I will go meet them," he instructed Gail. He walked out and met the tribe. "It's good to see your still alive my old friend. It looks like you've lost a few pounds," he said as Enzo approached. "Only thanks to our new friends. What they've managed to accomplish is remarkable. Prepare quarters and food. We will have guests for the next few days," Enzo smiled as he motioned his guests towards the base.

Enzo wanted a private audience with Mowan and Randy. After resting he shared what happened with Randy and arranged dinner in a small room with the two men. "Mowan you are to be congratulated. The invading force is massive and the aliens are almost impossible to kill. You have found a primitive yet very effective way of killing our enemy. There is more at stake, however. You destroy their airships, but we need the airships to understand the alien technology and to possibly use the ships in a future attack. When you leave, I would like to send some of my people with you. I would like to bring at least one of the alien airships to this location. There is a lot to learn if we are to win this war for mankind," Enzo said.

"The airships must be destroyed as quickly as possible. More follow if we don't destroy them," Mowan countered. "I will go with some of our people and fly the airship away from your location immediately. We must understand and use the alien technology," Randy interjected. "You have been gracious hosts. I will agree to your request; however, it's important for you to understand that if the airships aren't removed immediately, I will destroy them," Mowan said pointedly. "I appreciate your cooperation. We must work together to defeat these bastards. Randy and I will select a small group to travel with you when you leave. For now, let's enjoy this victory you have provided. I have transmitted your method of killing the aliens to anyone on Earth who is listening on the ham radio network."

Four days later, Mowan and the aboriginal tribe were ready to leave. Randy selected five others from the base to accompany him on the journey. Only two were somewhat familiar with flight operations and none had any experience with an alien aircraft. "Recover the alien technology. We must educate ourselves; we can only defeat our enemy if we have the knowledge to do so. You must find any tracking devices and remove them," Enzo instructed Randy. "I understand and would like to use these airships to fight our enemy in the future. Do you have any last-minute advice?" Randy asked. "Yes, I do. If you have to run, run like hell."

The training was proving fruitless and frustrating. Tony was not receiving any telepathic information from Gly. They tried for two days without any progress whatsoever. Gly instructed Tony repeatedly to open his mind, but he didn't know how to do it. The mission he wished to conduct would not work if he couldn't figure it out. The Empress read his thoughts and discovered his plans. It was time for a break; he needed to clear his head. Tony climbed a nearby mountain and sat meditating at the peak. Deep into his meditation he felt a consciousness. It was gentle and not invasive like that of the Empress. He felt the consciousness asking permission to enter his thoughts and Tony gave permission. "You are at peace. Only at peace with yourself will you be able to communicate in this manner. I present no danger. Accept this form of communication and grow accustomed to it. This is the first step. Maintain your serenity. Breathe deeply and maintain the link," Gly spoke into his mind.

The Empress and the remaining Annunaki forces remained on Vandi. Empress Zovad instructed her scientists to try and figure out what happened with the gate. The Empress was irritable and demanded immediate results. She needed the gate reopened as quickly as possible. There was little doubt her forces that made it into the Rabanah System were quickly destroyed. She would keep the military in a constant state of readiness. Empress Zovad wanted nothing less than swift vengeance.

Chapter 3

Gly patiently trained Tony to control his mind and communicate telepathically. When other Volmer were nearby, Tony was able to sense their presence. He respected their privacy and never tried to enter their thoughts. Gly was impressed with how quickly Tony learned. He was now able to block any attempts by Gly to enter his mind and read his thoughts. "I think you've learned all I can teach you. What are your plans now?" Gly asked. "I will travel to the Annunaki home world. I will kill the Empress or die making the attempt," Tony replied with conviction. "You do not fully understand the Annunaki or the Empress. It's likely she will try to increase her mental powers. You have more to learn if you are to be successful. There are always two in a position of power, the Empress and her daughter. You must kill them both to create chaos and ensure a power vacuum exists within their society. Can you kill the young daughter of the Empress in cold blood?" Gly asked. "I will do what I must to bring down the Annunaki."

"You need to understand that even if you kill the Empress and her daughter, a new Empress will take power within weeks or months. The Annunaki will immediately begin a process of emergency Empress rearing. Ten to twenty young female Annunaki will be fed royal jelly. The female who outlasts and kills the others will emerge as Empress," Gly stated. "So, there will likely only be a few weeks or months to mount an attack against the Annunaki while they're disoriented?" Tony clarified. "Yes, the best chance for the Alliance to defeat the Annunaki is immediately after the death of the Empress and her daughter," Gly responded. "How do you know all this?" Tony asked. "My mental abilities are currently stronger than that of Empress Zovad. I took the information from her mind," Gly said slyly.

A Strithu appeared in the sky and landed nearby. Gly translated a message from the large bird. "The Annunaki are beginning to depart the planet, but the Strithu do not know where they are going." "Then it's time for me to leave as well. Thank you for all you've taught me, Gly. I will always be a friend to you and your species," Tony said. "Best of luck to you Tony. You are a brave human traveling into the soul of our enemy." Gly held up his hand as Tony climbed into the pouch of the Strithu. The bird graciously ascended into the sky. Gly wondered once again if it would be the last time he'd see the crazy and unique human.

The interrogations conducted by Alliance specialists were complete. Vincent, Monique, Julia and Dominic arrived for a meeting with Chief Administrator Kizak. "Very little useful information was gained from the captured Annunaki. We essentially learned what we already knew. The Annunaki were planning to take this system and immediately invade the Sol System as well. Empress Zovad planned to lead the ground attack on Mars personally. You may now proceed with any interrogations you would like to make, but it is unlikely you will learn anything new," Kizak stated. "It's important for us to meet the Annunaki and understand what we're fighting against. We still wish to interrogate the Annunaki prisoners," Vincent replied. "So be it. They will be moved off planet when you are finished. There will be a guard posted at all times and your interrogations will be recorded in the event you uncover something new. Good luck."

A guard brought a shackled Annunaki prisoner into the large conference room where Vincent, Monique, Julia and Dominic were waiting. "He's been given medication to elicit truthfulness," the guard said as he placed the prisoner into a chair. "What is your mission?" Vincent asked. "My mission is to serve the Empress," the prisoner responded. "And how do you serve your Empress?" Monique asked. "By killing you, everyone like you and anyone who is different from us. The Empress must be defended at all costs. This is only a minor setback; you will all die soon." "Your Empress is dead. I fucking killed her myself!" Dominic suddenly screamed at the prisoner.

Vincent didn't know where Dominic was going with his outrageous lie. He watched in fascination as a look of panic and fear appeared in the eyes of the Annunaki prisoner. The prisoner closed his eyes and breathed deeply. "You lie. My Empress still lives and I will serve her until my death," he said calmly. "How do you know the Empress still lives?" Julia probed. "I can feel her consciousness and lifeforce. If you could feel her power, you would join with her."

"Are you aware you will be defeated and you will never reclaim the fourth planet in the Sol System?" Vincent asked. "Empress Zovad will reclaim our home and destroy any species who dare oppose her. You are foolish for trying to resist," "Your Empress is mentally unstable and you should rebel against her wishes if you wish to survive. If you refuse to rebel against the Empress, the Alliance will have you put to death," Monique said. "My allegiance to the Empress will never waver. You may kill me now," the prisoner responded placidly. Vincent stared down the prisoner. "Your Empress will never retake the Sol System. The Alliance will defeat you." "The Empress will retake Mars. It's our ancestral home world and she will not fail. Perhaps one of you will receive the ultimate compliment. If you're truly special, the Empress will kill you herself," the prisoner informed the group.

Five additional Annunaki prisoners were questioned and the results remained the same. There was no new valuable tactical information. "Should we request another prisoner?" Vincent asked. "I don't want to repeat this questioning over and over. I think we've learned all we can," Monique replied. "I agree. Dominic, why do you continue to tell the prisoners their Empress is dead?" Vincent asked. "I do it to gauge their reactions. All six of the prisoners briefly panicked when they were told the Empress was dead. The Empress is everything to the Annunaki. If she could be killed, we'd have a tremendous advantage. I wanted to know how they'd react," Dominic replied. "Unfortunately, we don't really have any chance of killing Empress Zovad," Vincent said grimly.

Immediately after the interrogation, Kizak summoned Vincent. "You humans continue to surprise me. Our interrogation team hadn't thought to tell any of the prisoners their Empress was dead. Our teams were focused on gathering intelligence-based information. Killing the Empress simply isn't feasible at this time. She is well protected, and we can't get anywhere near her unless we destroy her military and her personal guards. Only then, can the Alliance depose the Empress and restore peace to all Alliance worlds," Kizak said.

"I believe the tactical council should prepare for a strategic attack on the Empress. We've seen the

Annunaki panic when they think their Empress has died. If we can actually kill the Empress, we will win the war," chimed Dominic. "It's time for us to focus elsewhere. I admire your ambition and will forward your request to the tactical council. In the meantime, I will reconvene debate among member worlds. We will soon establish a timeline for retaking the Sol System and I will make sure you are part of the invading force," Kizak concluded.

Alliance member world representatives once again filled the Great Chamber. Vincent, Monique, Julia and Isabella were present as Dominic's guests. "I really hope the representatives are ready to take action. If there's any more of this waiting for months, years, or decades bullshit I'm going to lose my mind," Isabella said. "Stay positive; let's hear what the Chief Administrator has to say. There are always alternatives if we don't like what the Tactical Council recommends," Vincent retorted.

The chamber lights dimmed and a spotlight illuminated Kizak. "The Tactical Council has reached a decision. It's a scientific fact that the gate to the Vandi System cannot be repaired by the Annunaki. Our scientists have determined the gate will reopen naturally in approximately eighty-three years. The agreements with the Osarians and the Cardonians are still in effect. It's expected the Osarian fleet will arrive in eleven days and the Cardonian fleet in fifteen. The Tactical Council is recommending an invasion of the Sol System in seventy-nine days. It is estimated the Annunaki will be quickly overwhelmed by the Alliance armada. Voting will take place in four hours," Kizak announced.

Vincent took his crew to a local restaurant. It was busy as there weren't many places to get food so close to the Great Chamber. Two aliens were on a stage performing an intricate dance while singing a very high-pitched arrangement. The arrangement suddenly ceased at times as the range of voices sporadically exceeded human range.

"Seventy-nine days. Not as quick as I would have liked, but for the Alliance it's damn near a miracle," Vincent said. "I can't wait to get back to Earth and fight those bastards. I hope my father is still alive," Dominic said. "Unless we appoint a new representative, you will be required to stay on Rabanah," Vincent said with conviction. "Does anyone want to replace me? I'd like to get back to Earth," Dominic asked. An uncomfortable silence followed as the musical arrangement went out of range and nobody said a word. "I need some time for myself. Please excuse me," Dominic said and sulked off.

"I feel bad for him. It's hard being away for so long. I'd take his place, but I want to liberate Earth and Mars just as bad as he does," Monique said. "I think we all feel that way. He made the choice to be the representative for Earth, so I guess he's stuck with it," Vincent replied. Isabella watched as Dominic sat at a different table, put his head in his hands and ordered a drink. "Why can't he act in absentia? Communication is now possible through the gate. There's no reason he needs to be present for all the debates and votes. He should have the chance to see if his father is still alive," Julia queried. "It's one of the rules. All member planets must have a representative present during all Alliance proceedings. We simply don't have a choice," Vincent replied somberly.

"How are we going to get back to Earth so quickly?" Julia asked. "I asked Chief Administrator Kizak to have a faster than light drive installed on the Santa Maria. It's similar to the Alcubierre warp drive NASA was working on. The drive can only be used infrequently as it requires tremendous power, so it's useless in battle. When space time is folded, an exact exit location is impossible to pinpoint.

Isabella listened to Vincent and Monique discuss the Sol invasion for the next hour. She also watched Dominic order more drinks. She excused herself and joined him at his table. "It might surprise you to know that I've spoken with Enzo in the past." Dominic's head snapped up. "How do you know my father?" "That's not important. What would he say to you now? You are the first ambassador for Earth. There will never be another. What you are doing is historic and your father would be proud of you. So what if you won't be able to return to Earth as quickly as you'd like? Your job here is far more important," Isabella said. "Would you like another drink?" an automated attendant asked. "Bring him a coffee," Isabella responded. "I must return, find my father and defend Earth," Dominic asserted stubbornly. "Goddamn it! You will stay here and fulfill your requirements as the Ambassador for Earth. You must vote in thirty minutes on the recommendation from the Tactical Council. Pull yourself together!" Isabella spelled it out to him forcefully .

The coffee was served and Isabella worried as Dominic contemplated what she said. "How are you two doing? It's about time for us to go back. Chief Administrator Kizak will call for the vote soon," Monique said. "Let's go. I will of course vote in favor of the recommendation," Dominic stated.

As they approached the Great Chamber, Dominic stopped. "Come on Dominic, it's nearly time for the vote," Vincent said. "Go on without me. I'll be there in time for the vote." Dominic noticed the curious look on Vincent's face as his friends entered the Great Chamber. He stared at the Eye of Horus on the outside of the pyramid trying to comprehend the meaning. It was a symbol, but what did it represent? He hoped it represented morality, peace and acceptance of others. As the Ambassador for Earth, he decided that was what the symbol would mean to him.

"Where is he? The vote is in two minutes," Monique asked. "He'll be here. Don't worry about it," Isabella said. "I hope so. It's a pretty damn important vote," Vincent replied. Kizak reappeared. "It's time for the vote. You have one minute to submit your response regarding the recommendation from the Tactical Council." Dominic slowly sat down. "Jesus Christ Dominic, you sure are cutting it close!" Vincent growled. "I'm well aware of my responsibilities. I wouldn't have missed the vote," Dominic said placidly as he voted in favor of the recommendation from the Tactical Council. The announcement came quickly afterward. "All votes have been submitted. The resolution for the invasion of the Sol System has passed," Kizak pronounced.

"Thank God. I hope Earth and Mars will be able to hold out for that long. I'm sorry you must stay Dominic. I'll try to find someone to replace you as soon as possible," Vincent said. "That will not be necessary Captain. I'm here to serve the best interests of Earth. I intend to fulfill my duties." "That's very gracious of you, but let me know if you change your mind. I'm sure once we defeat the Annunaki I can find someone on Earth to take your position so you can return home."

"Perhaps at some point in the future, but for now I will represent all people of Earth," Dominic said as he glanced at Isabella.

Annunaki ships were sporadically departing when Tony arrived at the courtyard. He instructed the Strithu to land next to one of the larger ships. The hatch was open and there wasn't anyone nearby. He quickly boarded the ship and immediately hid the bullak. In the next few hours, the ship filled with Annunaki. The engines roared to life and the vessel took to the skies. Tony found the command center and listened as the Annunaki conversed. "I hope the Empress orders us into battle soon. The quicker we can expand her realm, the more pleased she will be," one of the crewmembers said. Tony listened for another three hours finding that nearly all the conversation related to the Empress in one way or another. Her subjects were unrelenting in their desire to fulfill her needs.

The ship was large and there were some empty living quarters. Tony chose one and decided to sleep in a storage closet just in case someone suddenly decided to occupy it. Just as he was dozing off, the door to the quarters opened. He peered through a crack in the door and discovered it was an Annunaki female. She undressed and entered her sleeping chamber. After ten minutes, he heard loud snoring making sleep impossible. "Damn, I thought I was bad," he whispered quietly.

Tony inhaled deeply and concentrated on seeking out the mind of the sleeping alien. As he entered her mind, he felt no resistance. She didn't seem to be aware he was present. Perhaps only the Empress was trained in proper mind control. The female was dreaming as to how she could best please the Empress. Tony got the impression the female believed her life would be more valuable and satisfying if she could find a way to please her leader. He grew tired of observing the alien's dreams and tried a more intrusive approach. He steered the woman into dreaming about her home world. It was an overpopulated and nasty place where most of the population aspired to become members of the military. It was considered an honor and a way to truly serve the Empress. Fights to the death were not uncommon for those trying to impress military recruiters.

The home world of the Annunaki was not a place Tony wished to live. It was violent and deplorable. He steered the dream toward other worlds in the Annunaki System. There was a total of fifteen planets circling the star. After delicately guiding the woman's dreams for another hour, Tony found a suitable planet within the Annunaki System. He would live there until he figured out how to accomplish his task. It has been a long day and he needed some rest. He gently broke his link to the female and quickly fell asleep despite the loud snoring.

An alarm resonated throughout the ship and Tony woke quickly wondering if he'd been discovered. The alarm went silent and a voice was broadcast throughout the ship. "Your full attention is required. Our Empress has graced us with a message." Tony left the Bullak in another part of the ship and hoped he wouldn't need it now. The message began. "You must all improve and perform better. If you fail me, you will be put to death. The scientists who don't understand the workings of the gate now kneel before me for judgement. Learn what happens when you fail me," Empress Zovad snapped.

Tony watched the viewscreen as dozens of bound Annunaki were decapitated. The executioner was methodical and went down the line of bound Annunaki slowly. The spectacle was gruesome and Tony turned his head until it was over. Empress Zovad resumed her speech. "Replacements have been appointed and it is my expectation for all combat units to remain prepared for battle at any time. I am dissatisfied with all of you. We must expand and conquer. There are many on the home world available to replace you; therefore, if the goals I've set are too difficult for you to achieve, then you will be eliminated."

Tony was relieved he hadn't been discovered. He was curious how the Annunaki would respond to the message from their leader and travelled to the command center. The aliens were unusually silent. He waited for two hours, but none of the Annunaki said anything. Such behavior was unexpected from what he learned about the aliens. It was time for him to gather more information. He began to reach out to the aliens' minds individually. After probing a fourth Annunaki mind, he learned all he needed to. They all felt the same. Shame, sadness, fear and determination dominated their thoughts. Finding a way to please the Empress was all that mattered. The address from their leader affected all of them in the same profound manner.

Tony was about to leave the command center when a gate appeared on the viewscreen. The entrance to the Annunaki System approached and moments later the ship passed through the gate and entered the Annunaki System. Returning to Rabanah was no longer an option. The gate to the system was gone. The Alliance managed to close it completely. He was now in the heart of enemy territory. There would be no turning back and he didn't have any allies.

The viewscreen changed and displayed all vessels in the system. There were thousands of ships traveling between all the planets and the larger moons.

In the distance, Tony saw a grey world approaching. It could only be Tanas. For the first time in hours someone said something. "We are on schedule and will arrive as planned," the navigator reported. The approaching planet matched what he'd seen in the female Annunaki's dream. The atmosphere was barely breathable for the Annunaki and it wouldn't last much longer. There was very little color. It was a grey and overpopulated planet that left the Empress little choice. Everyone on the planet would die soon if they weren't relocated to a planet with sufficient resources.

The ship descended into the atmosphere and travelled toward a large city. Vessels of assorted designs were arriving and departing. It was a wonder none of them collided. The ship docked at a large hanger and Annunaki silently disembarked the vessel. Tony remained in the command center. After an hour passed, he engaged the engines and navigated the ship out of the hanger. After observing the pilot and navigator, he was confident he could pilot the vessel and set a course for the sixth planet. It was a vibrant green world that would suit his needs. The planet was ripe for exploitation. Tony didn't understand why the Annunaki left it alone. An answer to the question was not provided when he was guiding the dreams of the Annunaki female.

The approaching planet was beautiful and covered primarily by land. The computer indicated twenty-three percent of the planet was covered in water. Tony selected a landing location on an island in the north where the temperature was warm and the computer indicated the atmosphere was marginally acceptable for humans. The planet was similar to Earth but much smaller. Tony landed in a clearing close to the shoreline. The world seemed too good to be true. There was an elegance and peaceful nature which Tony enjoyed. The planet was surprising; it was in Annunaki space and abundant in resources. On approach to the world, he did not locate any Annunaki vessels or personnel on the planet. The atmosphere on Tanas was turning to poison and it appeared the Annunaki had no interest in the planet whatsoever. It didn't make any sense.

The sun began to set and Tony watched day turn to night. He was at peace on the beach watching a new set of stars fill the night sky when he heard something approach. Tony stood up, turned on his data pad and prepared to defend himself if necessary. A lone figure approached. The alien mammal looked like a cross between a capuchin monkey and a koala bear. The animal appeared to be quick and strong. "What do you want?" he asked as the mammal stopped its approach.

"You are alien. What are you doing on our planet?" his data pad translated. "I seek refuge, peace and tranquility. I'm not a threat to you. How can you see me?" Tony asked. "Due to the eccentric orbit of this planet, we see in many wavelengths. What is your purpose here?" the alien asked. "I will tell you my purpose, but first I must ask a question. Why haven't the Annunaki enslaved you and taken the resources from this world?" Tony asked. Slowly, the creature responded. "For many centuries, the Annunaki have attempted to claim this world. We will not allow it. Any resource that might prove beneficial to the Annunaki have been tainted and are poisonous to them." "How are the Annunaki poisoned?" Tony asked. "We have identified their genetic requirements and have introduced a substance into our food which is not harmful to our race; however, it is fatal to the Annunaki. I ask you one last time. What are you doing on our planet? I have many friends nearby and suggest you give me an answer," the mammal demanded sternly.

"I represent an alliance of alien species who are attempting to subvert the dominating rule of the Annunaki and establish a peaceful coexistence with all intelligent species. I welcome your friendship and any assistance you can provide. It is my intention to bring peace, prosperity and freedom to all lifeforms," Tony replied in earnest.

"It took our species hundreds of years to free this planet. Thousands of us died testing the formula which ultimately proved lethal to the Annunaki. We tried to fight them and failed. Our only success was in poisoning our own planet against them. We gained our freedom by killing our own kind. Why should we believe in you?" the alien mammal asked with skepticism.

"My name is Tony. I don't wish for you to believe in me. I only ask that you accept my friendship and allow me to live here for a brief time. I will share a potential future with you. It is a future without the oversight and rule of the Annunaki. It is a future in which all intelligent lifeforms are free. I believe in fate and in my unique abilities. Will you share what you know about the Annunaki with me?" Tony asked. "You are an outsider; we don't know anything about you. If you wish to gain our trust, you must live under guard amongst our people." "I accept your conditions and wish to learn as much as possible," Tony stated. "My name is Madroni. I am the leader of my village. Welcome to Olanion."

"Is the food on this plant safe for me to consume and am I free to explore your world?" Tony asked. "The food on this planet is safe for you to consume and we

48

will not restrict your travel so long as you abide by our rules. You will be followed and observed," Madroni explained. "What are your rules?" Tony asked. "You must respect our species and explain how you think you can defeat the Annunaki." "Will members of your species assist me in my mission against the Annunaki?" Tony asked. "No, we will not provide assistance. You're an alien trying to accomplish an absolutely impossible mission. A lone individual has no chance against Empress Zovad."

Chapter 4

Sleep didn't come easy. Alixias was becoming more impatient and uncomfortable with each passing day. She quickly grew tired and her back constantly ached. The last few months were surprisingly uneventful. Patrick was proving to be a good mate and she was optimistic about their future together. He was very supportive and made sure she was as comfortable as possible. Dalton even decided to leave her alone for the most part, only asking questions during her scheduled appointments and checkups. Patrick provided Dalton with daily updates in order to reduce her stress. Time was growing short and she was getting nervous. The child would arrive soon. "It's time to go. This is an important appointment. Dalton needs to check your vital signs and the health of our child. He will be waiting for us," Patrick said as he gently kissed Alixias.

The examination didn't take long. Dalton left the room briefly and returned with his report. "As far as I can tell, your pregnancy is normal. I don't see any problems right now. The child's heartbeat is strong, and my diagnosis doesn't show any issues for either of you. I believe the child will arrive sometime within the next forty days. With communication reestablished with the Alliance, I've obtained all information possible from their medical experts. We've manufactured any medication you might possibly need. I have recruited assistants and trained them for any contingency that could occur during childbirth. From this point forward, you could go into labor at any time. I am requesting your permission for the birth to be broadcast back to the medical professionals in the Alliance should their counsel and expertise become necessary."

In the past, Alixias often became annoyed by Dalton and his propensity to overthink every detail of daily life, but she was now grateful for his meticulous nature. "I appreciate what you've done. Regardless of the outcome, I know you're the best person for this task," she gratefully told Dalton. "It's my job to see to your safety and the safety of your child. Should you feel any unusual pain or any changes in your condition, please come see me immediately. I've studied the records of your anatomy and all possible treatments. The medical experts of the Alliance have been very thorough. I've extensively studied the information they sent and am confident we can overcome any possible issues which might arise. You may return home now. I recommend you continue to rest and eat well," Dalton replied. "I doubt that will be a problem. She's been sleeping and eating constantly," Patrick said with a smile. Dalton was still trying to learn Martian facial expressions, but it looked as if Alixias gave Patrick a dirty look for his comment.

"Patrick, if you don't mind could you stay behind for a moment? I'd like to speak with you about some of our recent discoveries," Dalton asked. "Sure, will you be alright getting back home by yourself?" Patrick asked Alixias as he kissed her head and rubbed her belly. "I'll be just fine. I'm not totally helpless quite yet."

"Can you make this quick? I should get back quickly and see to her needs. What are these new discoveries you speak of?" Patrick asked. "We are still in the process of deciphering the golden walls. What I need to tell you is not groundbreaking by any means, but I wanted to speak to you alone. The Martian civilization was amazing. From what I can tell they are an ambivalent, albeit somewhat introverted species. They were aware of the gate and never chose to pass through it even though they were a spacefaring species for a time. The Martians were focused on Earth, yet it appears they were waiting for humans or Neanderthals to advance as a species. They took the first steps and visited Earth," Dalton said.

"That's very interesting. I'm sure there must be more to it than that. Once our child is born, I will do everything I can to help you with your research," Patrick replied. "There is more. I keep coming across references about how important it is for Martians and humans to breed and to eventually become a singular species," Dalton added. "Why? I don't understand why it's so important for our species to interbreed." "I don't know the exact reason either, but I do have a few thoughts. So far, I have not uncovered any instances of Martians fighting amongst themselves and there are no recorded religious or political wars or interspecies hostility. As a species they were at peace with themselves. The Martians were spiritual, but not religious per se. There were no religious factions that fought over which God was the true God. On the other hand, the history of Earth is filled with senseless death. Endless religious wars and acts of cruelty litter our violent history. The Martians somehow avoided such a fate," Dalton replied solemnly.

"That's very interesting, but what does it have to do with Alixias and me?" Patrick asked. "I have people helping me and word has spread through our small community. The birth of your child is now widely anticipated, so you need to be prepared for the attention you will receive after the child arrives." "I appreciate the information. Please spread word to the community that we will raise our child as we wish. We will be a family and not some sideshow. What's most important to me is Alixias' safety and that of our child. I don't care what anyone else thinks and I'm sure Alixias doesn't either," Patrick testily replied. "I understand and will relay your request to everyone here. Please do not share this information with Alixias yet; I do not wish to cause her further stress at this critical time," Dalton replied.

When Patrick returned, he thought Alixias was asleep. He let out a heavy sigh. "Are you alright? What has Dalton recently discovered?" Alixias asked groggily. "He told me the history of your people is amazing. There were no wars and your ancestors were very peaceful. He also said he is completely prepared for the birth of our child. You should rest and not worry. Everything is going according to plan." "I'm very relaxed right now. Knowing our child is healthy puts me at ease. We should start considering a name for our child, but I could use a quick snack before I fall asleep," Alixias said. "You're right. We are running out of time. I will get you something to eat and then we will discuss a name, but let me give you a massage first."

Empress Zovad became increasingly worried. The Alliance was undoubtedly requesting additional ships and weapons from their member worlds. Her enemy was becoming stronger with every moment the gate remained closed. She counted on taking the Rabanah System quickly and the Sol System would then be within easy reach. Her entire plan was failing and falling apart.

In the history of warfare with the Alliance, a gate had never been closed and a new one had never been opened. None of her scientists could figure out how the Alliance managed the feat. She was informed by her military leaders that even if the gate to the Rabanah System could be reopened, the military no longer had sufficient numbers to defeat the Alliance. All her scientists were now in the throne room kneeling with their heads down. "Every last one of you has failed me! We can no longer defeat the Alliance in the Rabanah System. I'm now giving you a new task in which you will not fail. You will conceive a way to open a new gate directly to the Sol System and our true home planet. You will figure it out and find a way. My Kingdom is vast and there are many who would gladly replace you. I expect progress immediately. I will begin killing you and your families one by one if you don't produce immediate results. The future of our race is in the balance!"

Vincent, Monique and Isabella were watching a vintage movie featuring a friendly crew aboard a starship boldly exploring space when the door chime sounded. Isabella answered the door and summoned Vincent. "He says his name is Ekraq and claims to be one of the leaders of Cardonia." "I'll speak to him alone and will return shortly," Vincent replied. "Why does he want to talk to you?" Isabella asked. "I'm not sure; I'll find out." Vincent retrieved a jacket out of the storage area and wondered if his life was in danger. He surreptitiously retrieved an incapacitation gun and slipped it into his pocket.

"I'm Vincent, let's take a walk," he told Ekraq as he quickly left the building. The alien leader came alone. Perhaps he only wished to talk. "Why have you sought me out?" Vincent asked. "My contact within the Alliance has informed me you alone are responsible for the theft of our sacred Nalis. We were prepared to declare war against the Alliance once the sacred texts were returned, but we now understand the Alliance had nothing do to with the theft. Our vengeance will fall solely upon you," Ekraq stated ominously.

"I bear full responsibility for my actions. You've been in contact with your counterpart Olube?" Vincent asked. "Yes, we've arrived at a temporary truce and are working together to ensure the safe return of the Nalis," Ekraq replied. "It's illogical to fight over religion and whom should have custody over an ancient text. I, myself, am a spiritual man and believe in a higher plain of existence. It's a personal choice to force your beliefs on others, to commit acts of violence on behalf of religion, and it's also how wars begin. How many lives are saved daily because the fighting has stopped on your world? Your religious beliefs have brought your species nothing but death and destruction. War kills the innocent, their ideas and extinguishes the prospect of advancing as a species," Vincent said.

"It's of no concern to you. If I didn't need you, I'd kill you where you stand for your disrespectful blasphemy. My purpose here is to make sure the Nalis is safe and to ensure it will be returned when the battle is concluded," Ekraq responded angrily. "The Nalis is safe and will not be touched until the Sol System is liberated. It will be returned to you when my world is safe. Please consider the words I've spoken. As a leader of your world you have a responsibility to your people; you will not find spiritual peace by committing acts of savagery and senseless violence.

One more thing before we part ways. If you attempt retribution once the Nalis is returned, I have instructed The Shadow to steal the books again. If I die due to the action of a Cardonian, the Nalis will be stolen again and burned, so choose wisely," Vincent bluffed as he parted ways with Ekraq.

"What was that about?" Monique asked when Vincent returned. "He just wanted to wish us luck in the upcoming battle and hopes his species can help free Earth and Mars," Vincent replied. "It seems odd to make a personal visit for that." "Well, they are an odd species. I'm tired and going to bed," Vincent said.

"So, are you going to tell me what's really going on?" Monique asked as she entered the bedroom. "What are you talking about?" "The visit from Ekraq. What are you hiding?" she asked. He took a deep breath. "I guess you understand me pretty well now. I've been thinking about telling you anyway. Somebody else should know in case something happens to me." Vincent told Monique the entire story, including Tony's visit to Cardonia and the theft of the Nalis. "You're blackmailing the Cardonians?" she asked. "Yes, at the time we needed all the allies possible. Even with the Annunaki fleet stranded on the other side of the gate, we could still use the additional firepower. Dominic can never learn of what I've done. As the representative for Earth, he would become complicit in all this," he explained. "I understand and your secret is safe, but you're taking one hell of a chance with your life. I hope it pays off for all of us. I don't want to lose you," Monique replied as she undressed and joined her lover.

Gail made another entry onto her graph paper. Someone new managed to make contact. "How many does that make now?" Enzo asked. "We now have contact with eighteen ham radio operators across the planet. It's not much, but at least it's something. We have to start somewhere," Gail replied. "Make sure we keep sharing information and forward all vital information to the new contact." "Have any of the others tried the technique used by the aborigines?" Enzo asked. "Yes, a group in the United States has successfully done it, as well as a group in China. Details are still sketchy, but apparently a group in Afghanistan managed to kill some aliens using a landslide technique of some kind. Our enemy likely has thousands of soldiers. Do you really think killing a few here and there will help?" Gail asked. "They have devastated our home and killed billions. We will continue to find ways to fight and to take back our planet," Enzo replied as the sound of an airship approached.

"What the hell is that?" Gail asked. "Hopefully it's Randy; if not, we're in big trouble," Enzo replied as he ran toward the door. When he arrived outside he found an ominous alien craft parked next to the manmade lake. Randy was already instructing people to remove the tarp so the craft could be placed into the empty lake and covered immediately. Enzo quickly ran down to the vessel. "Were you followed? Are you sure it's safe?" he asked Randy. "I spent two days with the ship before we flew it here. I removed anything that was not directly involved with propulsion and weaponry and left it behind," Randy replied. "I hope you're right. If not, it's going to be a very short day," Enzo replied.

With the ship safely covered, Randy came inside to get clean. "I'm glad you made it back safely. How was it out there?" Enzo asked. "It's the hardest thing I've ever done. It was a real pain in the ass and I thought I was going to die about a dozen times. The aborigines are brave and fearless. We need their spirit and attitude if we are going to win," Randy stated. "What's your plan with the ship?" Enzo asked. "We don't have the manpower, technology, or materials to replicate or reverse engineer the design. We must try to find their weakness. It's simply figuring out what type of weaponry we need to attack the weakest point of their ships. Unfortunately, I've been delegating this type of research and development tasks for about the last twenty years. This will definitely be a challenge." Enzo smiled. "I have faith in you. With all your experience, I'm sure you'll figure it out,"

Olanion was a beautiful and sparsely populated world Tony explored as often as possible. The Olanions following him were having trouble keeping up. He approached a valley filled with vibrant vegetation and found it strange the colors were not interspersed but were grouped together. Seeking rest after his run, he slowly walked into the valley and took in all the vibrant colors and fragrances. He decided to lie down to meditate and take a nap when suddenly he smelled a hauntingly familiar and elusive plant from his past.

Tony jumped up quickly. It couldn't be, could it? Was it the alien plant which caused his transformation and his resulting quest for more? He smelled the fragrance again and began searching for the source. After ten minutes he fell to his knees in the center of the valley floor amongst thousands of the plants in bloom. There was no doubt it was the species he identified back on Earth. Blind luck graced him and he walked to the center of the blooming mass, careful not to destroy any of the precious growth. He inhaled deeply over and over again. His became dizzy and at the same time felt stronger and more determined than ever. He would return as often as necessary and take specimens when he needed to leave.

Madroni didn't trust the strange alien and joined the group following him, but it wasn't easy. He recruited a group of friends to assist and they all tried to keep up with the swift human. He knew regardless of species this alien was different and possessed traits associated with ancient prophesies. He hadn't ever met an Overlord and his suspicions about the unique creature were now confirmed. "He has the gift and has found the rastish as prophesized. He will become stronger and wiser. Tony is an Overlord. Perhaps he truly is the answer to our freedom and will conquer the Annunaki," Madroni stated to the group. "Are we to follow him blindly and await his guidance?" one of his friends asked. "The ancient scripture tells of those who have the gift. There were those who failed to follow the instructions of the Overlord and the results were disastrous. We will not blindly follow this Overlord, yet it is likely the words and actions he has planned will be wise and worth following. Let us go greet our new Overlord in accordance with the ancient scripture," Madroni replied.

Tony was breathing deeply when he sensed a presence nearby. He opened his eyes and found a group of ten Olanions bowing before him. "You cannot sneak up on me. How long have you been following me?" he asked. "We've been following you all day and we've been bowing here for quite some time. I believe you were preoccupied," Madroni replied. Tony laughed. "Perhaps my senses are a bit off right now. What are you doing here? Am I high?" he asked. "We would like to hear of your plan. All of us now consider you a legitimate threat to Empress Zovad," Madroni stated.

Alixias planned on being a good mother to her child. Dalton constantly provided her plenty of reading material. She studied the numerous ways humans raised their children and was currently reviewing information from the Alliance about how Martian parents raised their young. She was hungry and rose from her bed to find a snack. When she stood up, she felt a splash of water around her feet. She was perplexed for a moment before she realized her water broke. Patrick was working with Dalton deciphering the golden walls. She summoned the newly trained nurse Dalton posted outside her door. "I'm going into labor. I need Patrick and Dalton here now!" Dalton planned for every possibility and made sure a messenger was always on standby. The nurse sent the messenger to summon Patrick and Dalton. "Come with me. We must get you to the medical facility immediately," the nurse instructed Alixias.

"According to this translation, Martians were more advanced and slightly more intelligent than humans. Unfortunately, their introverted nature and lack of a military doomed them when the invading forces arrived," Dalton shared. "They were a peaceful species and too trusting. The Martians didn't expect such a violent and immoral attack upon their species. I'm surprised the Alliance wasn't more involved at the time," Patrick said. Dalton was about to reply when a messenger interrupted them.

"Alixias just went into labor. You are both needed immediately." Patrick and Dalton ran toward the medical facility as quickly as possible. When they arrived, the nurse was taking vital signs. "The time has arrived. Our child will soon join us," Alixias said to a nervous Patrick. "It's an historic day. Our two species will be intertwined for eternity from this moment forward," Patrick replied. "Our child will bring the best of both worlds together. The ancient prophesies will now be realized," Alixias said as she grimaced in pain. "As we discussed, Patrick, I'm going to need you to wait outside until the baby arrives. It's important for us to concentrate on the task at hand without any distractions. We don't know what to expect and there may be complications," Dalton said.

When Patrick exited the room, he was surprised to find a crowd gathering. He received good wishes from everyone, but the waiting was nerve racking and he wondered how long it would be before his child was born. Becoming a father was something he always thought he wanted. Now, he was nervous and a bit scared. He was grateful to have friends nearby offering support.

"We're going to give you some herbs to help you relax. They are completely natural and you shouldn't have any adverse reactions," Dalton told Alixias. "How long do you think labor will last?" she asked. "It's impossible to say. My best guess is up to about half a day," Dalton responded. "I appreciate your professionalism and care for my family. Let's get this baby out. I'm tired of being pregnant."

Nervousness quickly gave way to boredom. Patrick was thinking about the golden walls when the silence was pierced by the cry of an infant. Everyone in the room began cheering and clapping. A few moments later Dalton emerged from the operating room. "It's a healthy baby girl!" Patrick rushed into the room to greet his mate and their new baby.

Alixias was awake and holding their bundled child. "Oh my god, we did it! She is so beautiful," Patrick proclaimed as he looked at his daughter's beautiful face. Light orange skin covered the child and he'd never seen eyes so blue and bright. "We shall name her Zabu, if you still agree upon the name. The closest meaning of the name in your language is genesis," Alixias said. "It sounds good to me. I love you and look forward to our future," Patrick said as he kissed Alixias and picked up his child for the first time. In addition to light orange skin and blue eyes, Zabu had incredibly long arms and legs compared to a human child. Her nose was about half the size he'd seen on human infants. Patrick couldn't remember ever seeing a baby as beautiful as Zabu. He was proud and now it was time to share his joy.

He opened the door and held Zabu aloft for all to see as cheers and applause erupted. "Thank you, I'm so happy to be a father! Her name is Zabu." "What is the name of this new species?" someone asked. It was a question Patrick hadn't anticipated. "I don't know. Zabu is a child of Sol. Perhaps you should ask Dalton. He's the scientific expert. I have a beautiful daughter, for us that's what's most important," Patrick replied as he gently hugged Zabu.

Chapter 5

The occupation of Earth was not proceeding as planned due to unfortunate and unexpected problems. The Empress didn't arrive as scheduled and the humans managed to kill a handful of ground troops. Buxare was still mourning the loss of her mother, but she would not let the loss affect the expectations and requirements of the Empress. "Why and how are your soldiers on the ground being killed?" she asked Vixel. She hated the Kracian leader and for reasons unknown he was the leader of the Krace on Earth. "The humans in hiding are using primitive and barbaric methods. They spread out and set traps, so it's difficult to prepare for the unknown. Why hasn't the Empress arrived?" the Kracian leader asked. "She will arrive when she desires. Do not question the methods of the Empress. You will find a way to kill everyone in hiding. If it becomes necessary, I will find someone to replace you. It is our duty to follow the will of the Empress and to act according to her directives. I'm sure she has a valid and strategic reason for arriving later than scheduled. You are not to question our mission again. Have you forgotten that the function of your species is to serve the Annunaki?" Buxare asked. "My species understands how you've protected us and are grateful. It's unfortunate we must deal with complications and setbacks. I will comply with your request."

"I'm growing bored and require entertainment. I have been reviewing the amazing and varied animal species of this world. You will capture some of these creatures to do battle with humans. It will be a learning experience as well. Perhaps some of your soldiers will learn how to avoid these primitive and barbaric traps. Be sure to capture creatures from the sea; humans are capable of surviving in water," Buxare ordered.

It took four days to arrange the first battles. Ten humans were selected to fight in water against oceanic opponents. A massive inland lake was quickly manufactured in the Nevada desert. Buxare watched as each of the ten humans were easily defeated by the aquatic animals. "Is this the best these humans have to offer? Why are they being defeated so easily?" she asked Vixel. "Perhaps we should move to the other venue. Humans might be more effective on land," the Kracian leader replied. "You must do better. Is this the type of entertainment you will offer the Empress when she arrives?" Buxare asked.

Vixel prepared an event at a large stadium. "People filled this arena in the past. I've located many violent species and have prepared glorious combat. You will find this much more entertaining. We have given the lone human female enough resources to be victorious if she uses her supplies wisely," the Kracian leader said. "I have yet to be sufficiently entertained. Do not disappoint me," Buxare replied. A lone human female was escorted into the arena. At the opposite end seven animals entered. The animals walked on four legs. "Those are called wolves and they have not been fed in quite some time." "Shut your mouth and let me watch," Buxare barked. She watched as the human quickly started a fire with the resources she'd been provided. The wolves stealthily approached the female and stopped about twenty yards from her.

Buxare was transfixed as she watched the animals slowly creep closer as the fire began to fade. The human was given only enough resources for a quick and bright fire; no other fuel was available. Suddenly a wolf sprinted toward the woman and the others fell in close behind. The silence was pierced as a weapon rang out. The lead wolf fell not more than three feet from the woman who held a primitive weapon of some kind. The remaining wolves quickly scattered and retreated. "She only has one more shot from the antique pistol. She will then be forced to use more primitive weapons," the Kracian leader stated with pride. A brief time later, the wolves attacked again. The female managed to wound one of the predators and kill it with a spear, but the final attack was brutal. The remaining wolves converged and the woman didn't have a chance. The ravenous wolves quickly ravaged her and began to feast.

"That was better. You need to start adding more humans and additional weaponry. These battles need to be a contest where the humans have a chance to prevail. After what I just witnessed, it's amazing this species managed to prosper and conquer this world," Buxare commented. "Your wishes will be granted; I think you'll like this next matchup. It's an animal called a python against a large human male."

Madroni and his friends silently led Tony back to their town. "You will be relocated to a dwelling that hasn't been used in centuries," Madroni informed him. "Why hasn't the dwelling been occupied?" Tony asked. "It's high on the hillside and is reserved exclusively for an Overlord," Madroni replied. "I don't understand. Who is this Overlord you speak of?" "My species does not have a reaction to the rastish. Only a select few who have visited our planet have been affected. Intelligence, strength and all your senses will continue to improve. In our recorded history, there have been five previous Overlords. Our historical records tell us that none of the previous Overlords were affected until they reached our planet. You are different than the others. It appears you were previously affected," Madroni explained. "Yes, on my home world I was researching a rastish plant which recently bloomed. The experience changed my body and mind. It also brought me here. What happened to the previous Overlords?" he asked. "They all died attempting to kill the Annunaki Empress," Madroni said curtly. "The position of Overlord sounds like a temporary job," Tony replied dryly as he was led toward his new home. "As an Overlord, it's your duty to try and kill the Empress. Are you prepared to make the attempt?" Madroni asked. "Yes, I'm prepared. The Annunaki have grown too strong and if they grow any stronger the Alliance will cease to exist."

"You will be assigned an assistant who will bring you food and attend to your needs. In the meantime, it's critical you review the texts and add your input for any future Overlords. The texts are handwritten, so your aide will also serve as your translator. You are to review the words of every previous Overlord. Rastish will be brought daily," Madroni stated. "I understand, but there will be no need to bring me Rastish. Exercise is important to me and it helps clear my head. I will travel to the rastish field when I feel the need to do so." "As you wish. As a rule, you will be left here in solitude with your aide. You will be required to meet with me and any other representatives of this world when we request. Remember our agreement. You are here to kill the Empress." Tony nodded. "It's the reason I came here in the first place. My mission hasn't changed."

Tony felt strong, but the excitement of the day tired him. He took a nap and awoke to someone singing. He found an Olanion female preparing food. "Hello, I'm Tony. Who are you?" he asked. "My name is Tulari. I am your aide and your translator." "How is an aide to an alien Overlord so readily available?" Tony asked. "There are always two of us assigned and ready to assist an Overlord should one arrive. It has been many centuries since our services have been needed. I'm privileged to assist you, Tony." "I appreciate your presence, but it's unlikely you'll be able to assist me. What I must do I must do alone," Tony replied. "Your response is interesting. It's exactly what the previous Overlords said and they all were killed by an Empress. You are growing in many ways, but overconfidence is a weakness that will be your demise. It's important to understand that every Overlord before you failed. You must learn from their mistakes if you wish to be successful. It's my job to give you the tools to succeed. You have the unique and rare opportunity to be the first Overlord to defeat an Empress. If you wish to save your Alliance, you must study, plan and learn. After you eat we will begin reviewing the historical records left by the previous Overlords. My services are needed and will be quite useful," Tulari said.

The food was welcome and tasted good. Tony didn't know what he was eating and didn't particularly care. He detected both animal and plant life and it did the trick. "It is time for our work to begin," Tulari said as Tony finished his meal. The next eleven hours were spent reviewing information from the previous Overlords. There were very few details as to how the Empress was protected and how to infiltrate and defeat her defenses. Most of the information was dedicated to improving and increasing his ability to communicate telepathically. "That is enough for now. We still have ample time and I need to process the information you've provided today," Tony said.

Tulari retreated to her quarters. Tony briefly had an impure thought and went outside to the balcony. With his advanced vision he could see Olanions in the valley below. A large group congregated near a fire where they laughed and enjoyed companionship. Their spirits seemed to have improved since his arrival. Everyone on Earth lost their freedom and those on Mars were trapped. In time, Tony knew the same freedom would be taken from the Olanions. The Annunaki would either figure out how to overcome the poisoned world or would wipe the planet clean and terraform it to fit their selfish needs. The Annunaki were desperate for resources and Olanion was abundant. Tulari was right, he was overconfident. It was time to learn from the lessons of the past and for an Overlord to finally defeat an Empress. He would be patient, listen to Tulari and learn as much as possible before confronting the alien leader.

The exams were complete and both mother and baby were declared healthy. Dalton wanted constant video of Zabu and the family's daily activities, but Alixias refused. Patrick and Alixias made the short trip to his quarters and gave him the data for the previous week. Patrick notated how often Zabu cried, ate, slept and produced waste. "There are no current issues, but if something comes up, please inform me immediately. Thank you for the notes Patrick. You may leave now," Dalton said distractedly. Alixias sensed something was bothering Dalton. She needed to know what it was and if he was hiding something.

"Patrick, please return with Zabu. I wish to speak to Dalton for moment," she said as Patrick left. "You don't seem to be yourself. Normally you have many questions for us. Is there information you are withholding? Is there something wrong with myself or Zabu?" Alixias asked. "No, it's nothing like that. I've been studying the research of Salkex; he truly was a genius. The brightest minds in the Alliance couldn't figure out how to alter a gate, yet he managed to do it by himself." "What is upsetting you? Is it something we can help with?" Alixias asked.

"Salkex documented one of his astounding theories. He believed the extinct ancient species that placed the gates in their current locations had a grand plan. The gates appear to have been placed at locations making it possible for peaceful species to eventually make contact with each other and grow. Salkex believed the grand plan was for these peaceful species to coexist and advance eventually to their level of intelligence and technology," Dalton said. "Well that makes sense in a way. So, what's the problem?" Alixias asked. "Salkex theorized that the Annunaki were not part of the plan. He believed the ancients knew about Earth and the remainder of Alliance worlds. In his opinion, the ancients spread the seeds of life in all Alliance worlds. Salkex theorized that the ancients believed the Annunaki wouldn't survive due to their violent nature. The Annunaki became powerful and dominant naturally and didn't destroy themselves. The species might very well disrupt and ruin the plan entirely. Did you know the Annunaki wiped out a species on their current home world Tanas when they first arrived?" Dalton asked. "No, I wasn't aware there was an indigenous species on Tanas before the Annunaki arrived. What does it all mean?" she asked.

"The species on Tanas was supposed to eventually incorporate their intelligence, knowledge and morality into the Alliance before they were completely wiped out. Salkex indicated none of the species survived the Annunaki attack. They were preindustrial and hadn't achieved spaceflight when the attack occurred. The same thing happened on Vandi. At some point in time there was an indigenous species on the planet, but the Annunaki annihilated them before losing the planet to the Alliance. Vandi was never meant to be a safe haven for species of Sol, rather it was meant to produce a unique species capable of advancing the Alliance. It was part of the grand plan. The birth of your child was also part of the plan, but it was supposed to take place about one hundred and forty years ago according to Salkex. The Martians were supposed to intervene on Earth before World War One and bring civility to Earth. Instead we ended up wasting life and resources fighting each other. The grand plan did not turn out as expected. I believe it might not be attainable due to the setbacks. However, one thing is certain. If the Annunaki are not removed from the equation, there is no hope for the future," Dalton wearily explained.

"I understand why you are preoccupied, but the past cannot be changed. Our sole focus now should be on defeating the Annunaki. The Alliance will continue to grow once the Annunaki are defeated. It might not be planned, but we will advance. Patrick often tells me to have faith in the future and you must have faith that we can overcome any obstacles. I must return now. Zabu is likely getting hungry." Alixias headed toward the door. Dalton felt guilty. Perhaps he was too preoccupied and wasn't focusing properly on his patients. He watched as Alixias stopped briefly by the door. "Is there something else you wish to discuss?" he asked.

Dalton was a good human. She didn't completely understand herself what was going on. Perhaps it was time to talk about it. She shut the door and reentered the room. "I've never been a mother before. Maybe I don't understand what motherly instinct means, but when Zabu is hungry I can sense it. When she needs her diaper changed I can suddenly sense it. I don't know if it's motherly instinct or if it's something else." "Do you think it's possible Zabu is communicating telepathically?" Dalton asked. "Like I said, I'm a new mother and trying to understand how it all works." "We must begin testing this possibility immediately!" Dalton said excitedly.

Patrick was surprised when Alixias returned with Dalton. "What did I miss?" he asked. "Your mate believes Zabu might have telepathic abilities." "That's not what I said. I was trying to say I didn't know if it was motherly instincts or something else. To be honest, I'm very confused about it myself," Alixias replied. "It's time to find out. There are other telepathic species within the Alliance. I understand you don't want your daily activities recorded; however, I think it's essential for the upcoming tests to be well documented," Dalton said. "You can document these tests, but nothing else," Alixias conceded.

Dalton began testing the relationship between Zabu and her mother. Over the course of thirty days he separated Alixias and Zabu as often as possible. The child didn't cry. Instead, the child summoned his mother when she needed to be fed, or for any other issues. When testing was complete, Dalton determined without a doubt Zabu was telepathic. He informed Alixias and Patrick. "I'm her father, why don't I receive these telepathic messages?" Patrick asked. "I don't have the answers to everything, but my best guess is that Martians are more advanced and mentally open to telepathy. I will request additional information from the medical experts within the Alliance. Perhaps in time you will be able to communicate mentally as well.

Please keep me updated on even the smallest of changes with Zabu. There is nobody like her anywhere else and there is a reason why Martians and humans were meant to reproduce according to the grand plan. We must find out why. Zabu is the first step to attain the knowledge we seek. It's likely there will be more changes as she grows," Dalton said.

The balance he sought was finally achieved leaving Tony physically and mentally strong. Sleep was infrequent as he was energized and studied at night and exercised during the day. He always spent a few hours in the rastish field during his exercises as his analytical nature and his need for the rastish encouraged introspection. The argument on Earth over the use of marijuana was a situation like his. Both marijuana and rastish were organic substances provided by nature. Tony decided since rastish was available it must be utilized to make him as strong as possible. He would take full advantage of the plant. As an advanced lifeform, rastish brought him peace and balance. It was not a manufactured product and the medicinal benefits were tremendous.

Tony studied the historical documents extensively. As a student he studied for years to attain his position on Earth and his study habits were proving beneficial. Previous Overlords did not consider the Annunaki's ability to quickly replace an Empress. The Annunaki were constantly prepared for such an unlikely contingency. Supersedure was instantaneous. When the Empress died, the Princess immediately assumed the role. If the Annunaki were to be defeated, Tony would have to kill the Empress and her daughter simultaneously.

"Tulari, I require a ship. I'm making a visit to Tanas," Tony requested. "You are not yet prepared to visit Tanas." "I'm the Overlord. You will provide me a ship. There will be no combat or hostile action. Reconnaissance is required for the eventual defeat of the Annunaki. Previous overlords did not take the time to learn about the inner workings of Annunaki society. I must learn how the Empress is protected and what type of defenses she has. When the time comes to battle Empress Zovad, I must be fully prepared. I will return when my mission is complete," Tony instructed firmly.

Madroni was surprised the human wished to visit Tanas so quickly. He was summoned to discuss the human's plan. "The Overlords before you failed in their plans. I have a responsibility to my people to ensure your plan has a reasonable chance of success. Why do you wish to visit the planet of our enemy so soon?" Tony explained his reasoning and was promptly given the location of an old Annunaki vessel that would take him to Tanas.

Tony prepared the dilapidated old ship and made sure there was an ample supply of rastish onboard. He pointed the vessel in the direction of Tanas and accelerated. The ship creaked and groaned but somehow managed to stay together. He was looking forward to studying the species and trying to find any weaknesses. Tony piloted the ship into what appeared to be a salvage yard where the banged up vessel wouldn't seem out of place. He landed in the heart of the capitol and planned to move on foot to the palatial compound of Empress Zovad.

It took thirteen days for Tony to discover the underground facility where the Annunaki prepared for supersedure. The facility was well guarded and was in a constant state of readiness should a new Empress need to be anointed. Tony wanted to destroy the facility immediately and to continue his attack against the Empress and her daughter, but he knew he must wait and continue his surveillance.

Chapter 6

Her kingdom was vast. Empress Zovad controlled everything within her domain and knew something wasn't right. She sensed an alien presence. It could only be The Shadow. She was growing tired of the annoying human. She opened her mind and was prepared to dispatch soldiers to destroy the bothersome alien, yet as she prepared her orders her mind was suddenly overpowered by an invader. She tried to block the intruder, but her powers were not strong enough and an alien voice dominated her thoughts. "You will die. Your daughter will die, and your empire will be destroyed," the alien voice screamed into her mind. Empress Zovad gasped and quickly closed her mind completely. She couldn't understand how his mind grew so powerful in such a brief time.

Such an occurrence hadn't happened in generations. The invasion of her mind could only be accomplished by an Overlord. Empress Zovad felt great anger and knew she must take this new threat seriously. She blocked her mind from the Overlord and opened it again to all Annunaki. Her personal guard and only confidant, Quay, quickly approached. "What happened? Your presence disappeared from my soul briefly." "There is a new Overlord. I'm aware of the ramifications of closing my mind to my subjects, but it was necessary. Do not question my actions," Empress Zovad testily replied. She knew her response was harsh, but the invasion of her mind rattled her. It was extremely rare for an Empress to close her mind completely and it only happened on a few occasions throughout Annunaki history. She knew all Annunaki were affected and work ceased as her people attempted to comprehend what was going on. In those brief moments, her species was weak and vulnerable. She could not allow it to happen again. Empress Zovad explained the invasion to Quay and instructed him to recruit additional security. "You are not to speak of this to anyone. An Empress should never be questioned. We will continue to conquer our enemies. Inform me immediately if you or any of your personnel encounter the Overlord," Empress Zovad ordered.

"What did you accomplish on your mission?" Madroni asked. "I surprised the Empress and gave her reason to doubt her power. She now fears me and I gained valuable information on Annunaki operations," Tony explained. "The Overlords of the past were overconfident and failed in their mission. What makes you any different?" Madroni asked. "I'm not overconfident. Do you wish to succeed, or do you wish to ask me useless questions? I am the Overlord and I have a plan. Will you and your people follow me?"

"Our species abhors oppression. If there is any chance to defeat the Annunaki, we are with you," Madroni replied. "Then our mission depends on your cooperation and ability to follow my instructions precisely."

President Louis and Leonard traveled north for weeks. "We're getting close; I think I see it," President Louis said. "Why are we going to a training center?" Leonard asked. "It's remote and there might still be some military personnel on site," President Louis replied, but he didn't feel confident. The buildings were burned and the site was severely damaged, leaving very few structures standing. "Let's at least see if we can find some food and a place to sleep." President Louis said as he entered what was left of the facility. "I think this may have been a bad choice. It doesn't look promising," Leonard replied. After all the travel, President Louis hoped to find something or someone and didn't know what to do next.

"Put your hands up and lie down on the floor!" ordered an authoritative voice from behind. "Comply with the order. Don't do anything rash," he instructed Leonard as he laid down on the floor. A boot was forcibly placed on his back and his hands were quickly cuffed. President Louis was yanked to his feet and found himself looking into the eyes of a young soldier.

"I'm the President of the United States. Bring me to your commander!" The President insisted. The soldier laughed. "How disappointing, I was hoping to capture a supermodel today. I guess the President will do. Why do so many of you lunatics end up here?" the soldier asked.

President Louis and Leonard were brought to a small underground facility and isolated in a tiny room. A dirty soldier entered. "Good afternoon. I'm First Sergeant Mathers. I apologize for the uncomfortable accommodations. Mister President, your identity has been verified by both facial recognition and fingerprints. We are now under your command. What are your orders, Sir?" Sergeant Mathers stated. "Update me on our assets and the current condition of the occupation. I've not received any relevant information for months."

"There are twelve of us here. We were in the hills conducting training exercises and managed to avoid the initial attack. We're currently in contact with naval personnel near the Midway Atoll. A submarine in the area managed to surface after the attack and the captain established contact with the civilians on the island. We have contact through ham radio with several other groups on the planet. Some primitive methods have been successful in killing enemy combatants," Sergeant Mathers relayed his intel.

"Thank you for the update, Sergeant. For now, I need sleep. Continue your normal activities and patrols. We will reconvene in the morning and discuss the current situation and how to defeat these bastards."

The next morning, Louis awoke to a wonderful aroma, one he hadn't smelled in a very long time. He found a hot cup of coffee on the end table next to his bed. His raggedy clothes were gone and a suit and tie had been placed in the closet. He dressed and found a guard stationed outside the room when he opened the door. "Bring me to Sergeant Mathers. After that, you are relieved from guarding me. You will be assigned other duties more vital to the war effort,"

"Sergeant Mathers, please provide a list of all our contacts worldwide," President Louis stated as he entered the small office. "It's posted on the wall, Sir. There are not too many yet, but the list is slowly growing. One of our top priorities is to locate new groups to learn from and share information with," Sergeant Mathers replied. President Louis scanned the list and found what he was looking for. "Contact the people in Trundle, Australia. I need to speak with them immediately."

Enzo dreamt of a petty crime he committed in his youth when he stole a Salvation Army kettle to buy food for his brothers and his sister. His sleep was abruptly interrupted by Gail. "Please wake up, Enzo. You're needed at the radio. It's urgent!" "I'm awake. I'll be there in a minute. This better be damn important. Can you please get me a cup of coffee?" Enzo replied. "No problem. I think you'll find this interesting," Gail said excitedly.

Randy was present and the room was full of people talking. Enzo didn't get enough sleep and was tired and cranky. "It's President Louis," Randy said. "Bullshit. I don't believe it. He'd be long dead by now," Enzo replied as he sat down at the ham radio. "Who is this?" he asked. "Sorry for the early morning wake up call. It's President Louis." It sounded like President Louis, but Enzo was still skeptical. "If you're really the President, what did we discuss last?" he asked. "If my memory is accurate, it was something to the effect that Vincent would bring his alien friends back to kick my ass if I continued my evil ways," President Louis responded.

"That sounds about right. I'm amazed you're still alive. How did you manage to survive?" "I'd still be a prisoner or dead if it wasn't for Sandy. She died, but I finished her mission and killed the alien leader. Have you discovered any weaknesses we can exploit?" the President asked. "We are simply trying to survive. I'm sure you've reviewed our notes by now. We haven't found a way to kill the enemy in large numbers.

Actually, it appears impossible," Enzo said. "That's disappointing. There aren't many of us left," President Louis replied. "We've analyzed one of the planetary aircraft they use and there is a weakness that is likely to occur in all their vessels," Randy interjected. "Please forward all of your research and information to this facility. There is a highly classified and top-secret facility that might still be operational," President Louis replied. "We'll send what we have. I hope your military experience will help us. God knows your political bullshit didn't help anyone on this planet," Enzo said.

"Sergeant Mathers, once you have the intelligence from Enzo prepare all personnel to travel to Montana," President Louis ordered. Seven hours later, Sergeant Mathers informed the President it was time to depart. "Please climb aboard, Mister President," he said. "What the hell is this?" President Louis asked. "It's a Barouche, Mister President. The highest class of horse drawn wagon. You will be guarded constantly during the trip. We cannot travel by modern vehicles without being discovered," Sergeant Mathers responded. President Louis climbed aboard the Barouche. "I always admired President Lincoln. Now I get to travel as he did. Let's get to Montana as quickly as possible and don't stop by the theatre."

Monique woke up and Vincent was not in bed again. He wasn't getting enough sleep and was on edge. The visit from the Cardonians scared him and he recently began taking early morning walks. She got out of bed, made some coffee and began making breakfast. A half hour later, breakfast was ready, but Vincent hadn't returned. He was usually only gone for an hour or so. She called him and got no answer. She asked Dominic and Isabella if they knew where he was, but neither had seen him.

A sense of dread suddenly overwhelmed her. Perhaps the visit by the Cardonians wasn't just an idle threat. She quickly dressed and summoned Isabella. "Why are you in such a rush and where are we going?" Isabella asked. "Get ready as quickly as possible. It's best for you not to know what's going on, but I need your help right now. We're going to the Santa Maria and we need to get there as quickly as possible." Monique handed Isabella a standard Alliance paralyzing gun. "Jesus, we might need to fight? What the hell are you getting me into?" Isabella asked. "Just get moving. We don't have much time."

All appeared peaceful as the two women approached the Santa Maria. They were approximately one hundred yards away. "You stay here. I need to go onboard and get something. If anyone else approaches the ship you must stun them," Monique said as she ran toward the ship.

Once aboard, she entered the storage room and reached behind the supply of emergency drinking water and found what she was looking for. Inside a clear sealed pouch was the ancient Nalis. She quickly made her way to the exit and met up with Isabella again. "What do you have?" Isabella asked. "I cannot tell you. Your life would be in danger if you have knowledge of what's going on. You must trust me in this. We will go to the fifth level now and perform reconnaissance on the Santa Maria. There is still danger." "What are we looking for?" Isabella asked. "We are looking for Vincent. Cardonians will be escorting him. He is likely their prisoner," Monique replied ominously.

The wait was short. Within twenty minutes two Cardonians escorted someone in an electronic exoskeleton device toward the Santa Maria. "Is that Vincent?" Isabella asked. "It has to be. He's likely unconscious or heavily drugged," Monique replied. "We have to go get him now!" Isabella said with urgency. "No, we must wait and be patient. The Cardonians will make contact shortly. Vincent will soon tell them I have what they want."

The pain was excruciating. Vincent never felt anything like it. The Cardonians inserted nanobots into his bloodstream. He managed to hold out for two hours before he finally told them where to find the Nalis. The pain was too great and he could bear no more when he finally gave up. In retrospect, the habit of taking an early morning walk was a bad idea. Ekraq was monitoring his whereabouts and stalking him. He was captured far too easily. The nanobots were currently deactivated, but still in his body. He felt tremendous shame and failure as he ordered the computer on the Santa Maria to open the door. He waited and wondered if Earth and Mars were now doomed because of his weakness. The two Cardonians emerged from the ship and the immense pain suddenly returned. "You lied to us! The Nalis is not here! Your pain will increase tenfold." Ekraq stated in rage as Vincent was led away from the Santa Maria.

"They're leaving! I wish you'd tell me what's going on. Are you sure we shouldn't do something?" Isabella pled. "We are going to do something, just not quite yet. We will board the Santa Maria in a few minutes once we're sure they aren't coming back. Stay here, I'm going to see if they leave the area in a vehicle," Monique replied. A few minutes later Isabella received a text directing her to meet Monique aboard the Santa Maria.

"Prepare the ship for departure. We might need to leave at a moment's notice," Monique said as Isabella boarded. "We can leave whenever you want. Routine maintenance and resupply was completed a month ago. We're as ready as we need to be. Why are we on the Santa Maria and where are we going?" Isabella asked. "This is the safest place I can think of. If we need to leave, anywhere will be better than here. I'm going to try and contact Vincent and his captors now, so stand by and be ready for anything," Monique replied.

It shouldn't have been as hard to give up Monique as it was to give up Earth and Mars, yet somehow it was more difficult. He told the Cardonians she knew where the Nalis was located and now they would go after her. Vincent failed her and everyone still alive in the Sol System.

He wasn't sure how he managed to endure the pain. Perhaps his body was finally going numb. Mercifully, the agony stopped. "You have an incoming call. Activate your communication device," Ekraq demanded. Vincent answered the call and found Monique on his screen. "Are you alright? Where are you?" she asked. Before he could answer, Ekraq hit him hard in the face and took the device. "Who is this and what do you want?" Ekraq sneered. "I'm his mate. What have you done to Vincent and what do you want?" Monique asked. "If you're his mate, you know what I want. Vincent has been surprisingly stubborn. Where is the Nalis?" Ekraq demanded.

"Isabella, take us into orbit around Rabanah immediately," Monique ordered. She watched the ground fade away as the Santa Maria quickly climbed into the sky. She returned her focus to Ekraq and held up the Nalis. "I have what you're looking for. You will return Vincent to me immediately. If you fail to follow my instructions the Nalis will be destroyed. What is your decision?" Monique demanded. She watched as Ekraq quickly consulted with the other Cardonian. "Stand by. I will contact you shortly," he stated and disappeared from the screen. "Well, it looks like you got his attention. What exactly is a Nalis?" Isabella asked from behind. "It's best if you don't know for now."

"I need to help watch over Vincenzo. We need to look after each other, so it's time you shared what's really going on," Isabella replied. "Mind your own business and follow my orders. Since when is he Vincenzo to you? Only Enzo calls him that. I'll explain the Nalis to you later, but for now we must focus on the task at hand."

The Cardonians were in a panic. Vincent didn't have his translator, but it was obvious Ekraq was arguing with the other Cardonian. "My mate will destroy the Nalis if you fail to comply. She will not hesitate for an instant, so I suggest you do what she says. You will be held accountable by your people for the destruction of the Nalis."

The argument between the Cardonians subsided. "The safe return of the Nalis is the highest priority. We apologize and regret any inconvenience you've been subjected to," Ekraq stated in defeat.

Isabella was growing frustrated. "There are only a handful of Cardonians on Rabanah. Contact Dominic and have the Alliance arrest all Cardonians until we can get to the bottom of this," she offered. "That is not an option. Dominic can have no knowledge of what has happened, nor can any member of the Alliance. The battle for Earth and Mars hangs in the balance, so you must trust me. I'll explain everything once we safely recover Vincent., Monique said as her communication device accepted a call.

Ekraq appeared on her screen. "We agree to your terms. The safe return of the Nalis is of paramount importance. Vincent will be returned to you unharmed." Ekraq said. "Let me speak to my mate now!" Monique ordered as she heard static on the device. The signal suddenly returned, and Vincent reappeared. "Don't trust them. They placed nanobots inside my body to inflict pain," he said. "You will be safe soon. Stay strong. I need to speak to Ekraq again," Monique said. Ekraq appeared and Monique raised the Nalis into the air. "These ancient books has divided your people and resulted in the death of millions. Personally, I think your sacred books should be destroyed right now. Vincent promised he would return the Nalis and he thinks you should have it back. I do not. Return him now or I will burn these damn books. Bring him to the berthing dock of the Santa Maria after you remove the nanobots you've placed within his body. Depart immediately or face the consequences. If you don't follow my instructions I will make sure your world learns how the two of you failed in your mission."

"We will comply. There is no need for additional hostility. Please keep the Nalis safe." Ekraq ended the transmission. Vincent watched as blood was removed through his thigh. "What are you doing?" he asked. "We are removing the nanobots. Your pain is at an end, but we expect that you will uphold your end of our bargain," Ekraq responded. "The only way you will get the Nalis back is when Earth has been liberated." Vincent was released in the Santa Maria's berthing dock and his captors quickly departed. He was still confined within the exoskeleton suit and unable to move.

"Are you certain there aren't any Cardonians still in the area?" Monique asked Isabella. "Sensors indicate Vincent is the only lifeform, so we should be safe to land." Isabella replied. "Set autopilot to land and stand by on weapons. Prepare to fire on my order," Monique commanded. The Santa Maria descended, and a lone figure waited. Monique didn't detect any nearby threats. "Do you see any activity near the landing area?" she asked Isabella. "There is none." The Santa Maria landed and Monique rushed out and dragged Vincent inside. "Are you alright?" she asked as she kissed him on his forehead. "I'm fine. They said the nanobots have been removed. I'm sorry. I shouldn't have been so foolish," Vincent responded. "You're safe now. Let's get you out of this freakish suit."

"How is he?" Isabella asked. "He's fine. Just a little blood and a few bruises. I think the damage to his ego is the most severe," Monique replied. "We should get him to the medical center to make sure there isn't any permanent damage and that all the nanobots are really gone," Isabella suggested. "I'm fine, let's get the hell out of here," Vincent asserted as he entered the command center. "You were assaulted and kept prisoner by an alien race. I think a medical diagnosis is necessary," Isabella demanded. "Fine, if you insist, but I doubt it will do any good." Vincent said over his shoulder as he walked toward the medical center.

He felt fine and was ready to focus on the upcoming battle. "Let's get this over with; we have more important things to worry about," he said as he laid down on the diagnostic table. "Computer, please diagnose the patient," Isabella ordered. The computer's response was immediate. "The patient has minor facial damage which will be repaired in five minutes.

Nanobots have been identified within the patient's bloodstream. Do you wish for the nanobots to remain, be destroyed, or saved for future use?" the computer asked. "Vincent said the Cardonians removed the nanobots," Monique stated. "He also told us not to trust the Cardonians. He was obviously correct. Computer, remove the nanobots and save them for future use," Isabella ordered. "Are you sure that's a good idea?" Monique asked. "I think in the upcoming battle we need to have as many weapons as possible at our disposal. It's a valuable tool for causing pain and extracting information. The nanobots will be removed and stored safely," Isabella responded. "It's a horrible weapon. I sincerely hope we don't ever have to use it," Vincent winced as the computer began its work.

"Isabella knows about the Nalis, but she doesn't know why we have it. I needed her help and didn't have any other options. Dominic was not told about your abduction," Monique said. "I guess now that you know, you should know the whole story." Vincent explained Tony's victory and why the Cardonians were suddenly so willing to help the Alliance to Isabella.

Her father taught her to find close friends to trust. Isabella knew the situation could change at any moment and additional allies might be necessary. "Why are you here so late in the day?" Maxis said as he opened the door to his home. "I need to speak to you and Tissa," Isabella replied. "Please come in. I will wake Tissa and we will listen to what you have to say. Please keep your voice down as Zanther is asleep. My son sleeps well now that we're free. He even enjoys bedtime stories again." Maxis said. "What's this all about?" Tissa asked as she entered the room. Isabella told the tale of the Nalis and explained why Dominic couldn't know what happened. "Vincent is playing with fire. It's one hell of a gamble," Maxis stated. "Well, so far it's working. He's doing everything he can to liberate the Sol System. I agree with and condone his actions," Isabella replied. "We will assist Vincent should the need arise and you can count on our help. Tell him to be careful. He was very fortunate you and Monique were able to get to the Nalis before the Cardonians. Next time, he might not be so lucky." Maxis responded.

Promptly after Zabu's birth, nearly everyone on Mars wanted to take a picture with the infant. Alixias refused at first, but eventually set aside one day for pictures a week later. Three months passed and Zabu grew and remained healthy. Dalton made it a nightly habit to drop by at dinner time.

"I think it's time to for Zabu to begin her education. I've assigned her a data pad and programmed words and phrases associated with pictures as directed by the specialists within the Alliance. I think an hour each night before she falls asleep would be appropriate for now," Dalton said. "Actually I have already started. In the evenings I've been devoting some time to her education," Alixias replied.

"Will the displaced Martians from Vandi be relocated here?" Patrick asked. "Most of them will be, but some will be relocated to Earth. Alliance leadership has decided it's time for our two species to live together and reproduce as quickly as possible. In time, Chief Administrator Kizak believes the new hybrid species will strengthen the Alliance. I've been informed once the war is over, Mars will be terraformed within a year. The magnetic shield designed to protect the atmosphere has already been prepared and once it's in place, it will simply be a matter of increasing atmospheric pressure and getting the oxygen level dialed in correctly. Apparently, terraforming is something the Alliance is quite good at," Dalton replied.

"Zabu will be the eldest of her new race. She will be seen as a leader. It is an overwhelming and extraordinary responsibility," Alixias stated. "She will have two loving parents and all of the Alliance to assist her and will never be alone," Dalton replied confidently.

"Have you made any recent discoveries?" Alixias asked. "We're still deciphering the golden walls and we've learned much of it relates to the history of the Martian people. From a sociological point of view, it's very fascinating. We are continuing to document everything. The work is interesting, but it's becoming mundane. I think I'm going to begin further studies on Salkex's work; his discoveries are unprecedented and it makes me wonder if there is more yet to be uncovered," Dalton stated.

Chapter 7

The climb up the hillside was not an easy one. Tony watched Madroni slowly ascend. Prior to each meeting, the Olanion leader met with his advisors. Tony continued his daily trips to the rastish fields. He knew his transformation was continuing on a level he didn't quite understand. His plan was different than those of the previous Overlords. The door closed as Madroni entered the dwelling. "My people want to know how we can assist you and what part we will have in your plan. If we are to be involved, we must be given the opportunity to prepare as soon as possible," Madroni said. Tony remained silent and reviewed the plan in his head one last time. "Did you hear me?" Madroni asked.

"I did. I appreciate the offer of assistance, but your help will not be required." Tony replied. "As you know, every previous Overlord has requested our assistance. Why do you think you can defeat the Annunaki without our help? Are you so overconfident in your abilities that you think assistance isn't necessary?" Madroni asked. "Your species has assisted all previous Overlords. Every previous Overlord has failed. Thousands of your people died in vain. I have an affinity for you and your people. My emotional attachment has no bearing on the plan, however. If I thought you could help me, I'd ask for your help. The plans of previous Overlords were overly complicated. A straightforward and direct attack has the best probability of success. My enhanced abilities will be enough to defeat the Annunaki.

I have studied past attempts to kill the reigning Empress. The Overlords did not possess the same skill sets that I possess; I am both physically and mentally stronger than those before me. The rastish affects alien species in different ways. Its strong effect has changed me radically and I suspect the rastish wasn't as effective on the previous Overlords. According to my research, I'm the strongest and most intelligent Overlord thus far. There is no need for your people to sacrifice themselves unnecessarily."

Madroni took a moment to consider possible options. "At the very least we can create a diversion and attack the Annunaki in a vulnerable spot." he replied. "I see you have studied the historical records. The diversions didn't work in the past. If you and your people were to try it again, it would simply serve as notice that an Overlord is coming. Your attacks have always accompanied one by an Overlord. I will go alone and the Annunaki will not be forewarned. I've put much thought and preparation into this, and don't turn down your offer of assistance lightly," Tony replied with finality.

"Is there anything you require from my people?" Madroni asked. "I require a normal life with social contact. This is a beautiful planet and I would like to spend more time with you and your people. I miss my friends and would like to make some new ones. There will be times when I require solitude to prepare; otherwise, I'd like to enjoy your company and the company of your people. I have committed the information from the previous Overlords to memory, so I have no reason to remain here all the time." "I'm sure I speak for my people when I say we'd be happy to know you. Please share your knowledge about your home planet and the other worlds you've visited. We'd like to know what we're missing out on. Come visit us this evening and you can explain your crazy plan so I don't have to." Madroni said with an easy smile.

"President Louis, we are approaching the coordinates for the base," Sergeant Mathers reported. President Louis was not hopeful. All Earth defenses and military bases were destroyed as far as he knew. Travelling by horse carriage was ridiculous, but it gave the soldiers a purpose and raised morale. The soldiers believed there might be hope. "Continue to the middle of the airfield," he ordered. Sergeant Mathers obeyed the President's order, although there was no activity of any kind. "I'm sorry Sergeant, but it appears there is no one left at this base to provide support. Please have your people search for an underground entrance. We'll stay here for now and review our options," President Louis ordered.

The Montana air was cold and silent. President Louis looked on as Sergeant Mathers issued orders. The silence was suddenly interrupted by a humming in the air as a drone appeared in the sky above. The ground suddenly shook and the carriage began to descend. President Louis and his party were slowly lowered into a hanger on the military base. "Drop your weapons!" Commanded a voice from a loudspeaker. "Order your men to comply." President Louis instructed Sergeant Mathers.

The President was surprised to see the base functioning normally. The platform was normally used for aircraft. Sergeant Mathers and his men were surrounded as an authoritative figure approached. "If we didn't have facial recognition software you'd be dead by now," a familiar voice said. It was Brigadier General Elliott. "It's good to see you again General. Thanks for not shooting us. What's the status of the base?" "Our location has not been discovered by the enemy and we are adhering to radio silence. We are fully operational and are continuing to produce new ships as quickly as possible. Would you like to see the completed spacecraft?" General Elliott asked.

"Absolutely! Please give me a tour. We will need quarters and clean clothes for Sergeant Mathers and his men. The trip here was pretty rough and they have all earned some rest," President Louis stated.

General Elliott led the way to the hanger. The sight of the ships was staggering. There were four completed vessels with another three under various stages of construction. "My God, are they fully functional with weapons systems?" President Louis asked. "Yes, we've managed to arm the ships with the same weaponry we found on the alien interceptors. It took some time, but our engineers managed to reverse engineer the design just last month. The new weaponry was just installed a few days ago," General Elliott explained. "You've done a wonderful job here General, but I'm trying to think of a way these handful of ships can defeat their entire invading force," President Louis forlornly responded.

"We'd be slaughtered. If it comes down to it, we can try and mount a surprise attack, but we would be easily defeated and the ships would be lost. We don't have enough tritium to manufacture more than these seven ships." The President's initial excitement began to diminish. "We don't have any options except to wait. There will come a time when we'll be able to blow some of those bastards out of the sky. I do have a small research and development team in Australia. They've been examining the weaknesses of the enemy ships. I'll put you in touch with them."

Food was growing scarce and winter was in full force. Enzo looked down at his potato in disgust as Randy walked in. "It's hard getting used to winter in July. I'm not sure which is worse, eating potatoes or starving to death," he said. "It's a useful source of potassium and a bunch of other vitamins. Finish your potato and keep on living. Besides, I have a little good news for a change. Our evasive and unpredictable President is still alive and has managed to make it to a military base in Montana. The base currently has four tritium coated ships with three more in production," Randy said. Enzo took a bite of his potato which somehow tasted a little better. "At least we have a few ships that might be able to put up a fight. We need to share all of our information with the base in Montana to let them know everything you've discovered about the alien ship," Enzo said. "I already did. They're sharing research with us as well. Unfortunately, it doesn't do us much good since we can't produce anything," Randy replied.

The news of the functional ships was welcome, but Enzo was beginning to lose hope in the overall battle. "What's wrong?" Randy asked. "I'm not optimistic about the future. My son and the rest of the crew are still missing and we haven't heard from them in a long time. If the Alliance was going to invade, it should have happened by now. It's time to face the reality that they've most likely been killed by the same alien race that invaded Earth. I'm sure Randy and the rest of the people on Mars are all dead as well. I think we're on our own and the future does not look good," Enzo said as he glanced down at the last bite of his potato. It was food and couldn't be wasted. He took the last bite and had a thought.

"Do you know the range of the alien ship we recovered? Can we fly it to Montana?" he asked. "The ship has the range and we could fly it there now, but there is a real possibility we'd be discovered and attacked. The risk involved is substantial.

Don't give up on the Alliance just yet. I'm still optimistic. I think you're just growing bored and cranky because you don't have anything useful to do," Randy replied. "I think going to Montana is worth the risk. How many people can fit inside? Some of the people here might want to come with us," Enzo asked. "We could probably jam in about twenty people; it wouldn't be comfortable, but the flight would be short." "We'll have a meeting, explain the danger, and see who wants to come. Contact the Montana base and advise them of our plan. Tell them we'll be bringing an alien ship,"

Enzo directed as his energy and attitude began to improve.

The meeting didn't last long. Only a dozen chose to leave the safety of Trundle. "We will leave late tomorrow night. Bring only what's necessary. Anyone is free to change their mind prior to departure. This is a one-way trip and we won't be coming back," Enzo said. He approached Gail as she was about to leave. "I understand why you don't want to come with us. The danger is very real and we may never reach Montana." "The danger is not the reason I've decided to stay. I need to continue to teach the children and everyone else here. Times are bleak, but there's no reason the future of humanity can't be better than the past," Gail replied. "Of course. Take care of yourself and take care of these people. Help the aborigines if you can. I think it would be a good idea to take small groups of them in for rest from time to time. They live a hard life and work constantly," Enzo said as he hugged his friend. "Have a safe journey and do what you always do." "What do I always do?" Enzo asked quizzically. "You always survive and make those around you better," Gail said with a warm smile. "I only survive because I surround myself with good people like you."

Randy was in the pilot seat preparing for imminent departure. Enzo couldn't help but think of what Gail told him. For most people, her words would have inspired confidence. He'd been lucky his entire life and just careful enough not to have been caught by the government. As he gained wisdom, he understood justice and how to dispense it properly. His mother taught him morality and her message was simple. "Recognize evil and destroy it. Surround yourself with trusted friends. Be a strong and humble man." His previous doubt about the alien invasion and the future of humanity was gone; he was determined to make a difference. "What are the chances of making it to Montana safely?" he asked Randy. "There hasn't been any unidentified aircraft in the air for months. I don't think the Annunaki are looking for airborne vehicles anymore, but just to be safe we will fly by autopilot. I've spent the last day reviewing our course. We do not have a tracker and we will be flying the entire trip barely above the surface the planet. At no time will we more than one hundred yards above the ground or ocean. Our flight plan puts us in at 3:11 AM local time," Randy explained. "Let's go. They are waiting for us in Montana. It's time to actually do something for once!" Enzo was charged as the ship lifted off.

President Louis watched from the command center as base personnel prepared for the alien ship's arrival. "We have nothing on radar, General Elliott," a soldier reported. "Stay sharp and watch the airfield," General Elliott ordered. The infrared cameras located the ship first. "There it is. Once it lands, lower it into the hangar immediately," General Elliott commanded. President Louis left the command center and went to greet his longtime adversary.

Enzo was happy to be on the ground again. He stepped out of the alien craft and took a deep breath. "You look like shit, but it's good to see you," a familiar voice said. "I've decided I won't die before you, Mister President." "Where in the hell is Vincent? Why hasn't he returned with some allies?" President Louis asked. "I have a recorded message from Vincenzo. Gather your top military leaders and I'll share it with you," Enzo responded.

President Louis watched as Earth was granted membership into the Alliance and the tactical situation was explained. "We will maintain a constant state of readiness. With the arrival of the alien craft, we now have a total of eight ships. It isn't much, but in a large-scale battle we will fight like hell and help our new allies when they arrive," he said.

Enzo hoped recent events changed the President. Was the man a leader or still a politician? It was time to find out. "I'd like to speak with the President alone." Sergeant Mathers immediately intervened. "I'm sorry sir, but the President must be accompanied at all times." "It's alright, Enzo is an old friend. Everyone is dismissed," President Louis waved his hand. Enzo waited for the room to empty and the door to close.

"Are you battling for your political career or are you battling for humanity?" Enzo asked. "How dare you ask me such a question! I've literally gone to hell and back more times than I can count. I was a prisoner and would have gladly welcomed death. There will no longer be politicians if we manage to survive. You were the criminal. Your crimes against the government are well known. You'd be an outlaw right now if it weren't for your assistance with the aliens and your ongoing threat of retribution once Vincent returns," President Louis hissed. "Fighting governmental corruption and injustice is not a crime. Someone must fight for the people and the United States Government stopped fighting for the people a long time ago. Your government stole our freedom, our money and the ability for hard working people to live comfortable lives. It was all done to pad your wallet and your corporate sponsors. Your indignant attitude rings hollow.

With that being said, it's time for us to put aside our differences. For what it's worth, I believe you are ready to fight for humanity. Win or lose, our world will never be the same. We now share a common goal." Enzo said. "As a politician, I would argue against your points to save my ass, but I'm no longer a politician.

Your points are valid. The United States government has been corrupt for a long time. We were controlled by the corporations. I intended to make changes but ran out of time. My time to lead has passed, but I have one duty left. The remaining military needs a leader to inspire the resistance. I can be that person. You must believe in me." President Louis held out his hand. "We shall see. You've made it this far, so I guess you've earned the opportunity to try. We're in this together and must forget the past," Enzo said as he took the President's hand.

The information was overwhelming. Dalton tried to follow the research of Salkex. The Martian scientist conducted massive amounts of research and speculated on many subjects. None of the information appeared to be beneficial to anyone currently on Mars. Frustrated, Dalton reviewed the scientist's personal notes. On one of the pages he found a small map, but the notes didn't indicate what the map led to. After further review, he found it led to a chamber near the subway system. With his curiosity piqued, he went searching for the undiscovered chamber.

Repairs to the Martian transit system were nearly complete. Dalton wondered what other discoveries awaited once the remaining stops on Mars were discovered. When he arrived at the platform, the workers ignored him. After consulting the map, he found a small and well-hidden doorway on a back wall. It took him a few minutes to find the release in the top right corner. The door sluggishly opened after he pushed with all his strength. Dalton entered and closed the door behind him.

He travelled through a dimly lit corridor and emerged into a room filled with blinding light. Artwork of various designs adorned every wall. Neanderthals and Homo sapiens dominated two of the walls. The work depicted the Earth species in various activities and many different poses. The two remaining walls depicted Martians in similar poses. In the center of the room stood a statue of a small child. It wasn't Martian and it wasn't human, rather the child was a combination of both species. Dalton looked at the hieroglyph etched into the base and translated it. "A new level of consciousness and an end to oppression." The words took him by surprise. The statue could only be a hybrid child and the face was eerily similar to Zabu. The ancient war delayed the emergence of the hybrid species. Dalton hoped the purpose of the species could still be realized.

Motherhood was proving challenging for Alixias. Zabu rarely cried and was at peace most of the time. According to the information she read, Zabu should have been much more dependent upon her parents. Her daughter was now ten months old and learning at a rapid rate. The specialists from the Alliance were at a loss to explain how Zabu was learning so quickly and Alixias couldn't understand why Zabu's mental abilities were so advanced at such an early age. It wasn't an ability found in either humans or Martians. A knock on the door interrupted her thoughts. "Dalton, you were just here yesterday. Is there a problem?" she asked as Dalton entered.

"There is not a problem, but with the uniqueness and importance of Zabu, I've decided to check her progress daily. I apologize if this disrupts your family life." Alixias was about to reply when a new voice interrupted. "I'm hungry. Please bring me some food." Dalton looked at Alixias in awe. "It's the first time she's spoke coherent words. I'll be there in a moment, Zabu. Dalton, come back this evening when Patrick is home. We have much to discuss." Alixias showed Dalton to the door and returned to feed her child.

Empress Zovad was pleased. Eighty-four ships recently returned from the outer reaches of the galaxy. Many were heavily damaged and on autopilot, but thousands of Annunaki were alive in stasis tubes. She now had more firepower at her disposal and nowhere to send it. In her brief glimpse into the human's mind, she knew he was staying on Olanion. In the past, the Olanions attempted to assist the Overlords. She would not give them the chance this time. "Begin repairs on all damaged vessels. Revive all personnel in stasis tubes. All vessels currently prepared for combat are to proceed to Olanion. Attack every village and decimate the entire world."

Tony was resting in the rastish field feeling very relaxed and peaceful. He was confident he could accomplish his task as Overlord. In the distance he heard a ship entering the atmosphere. A lone vessel was not a threat. The Annunaki sent ships to Olanion on a regular basis to record any changes and to observe the species, but within a few seconds he heard more ships. The sound of weapons fire suddenly pierced the silence. Tony suspected the worst and sought out the mind of his enemy, but it was futile. Empress Zovad learned to block his intrusions. Tony ran to the village to find Madroni and fight the invaders. More ships arrived as he ran and the vessels in the sky were firing mercilessly. None were landing and Tony didn't have a way to fight the enemy.

The Annunaki ships destroyed every structure in sight. Fire bellowed across the landscape as massive bombs dropped from the sky. Smoke and the smell of burning flesh filled the air. Tony regretted having advanced vision. With perfect clarity, he watched as many Olanions were burned alive.

The bombing eventually stopped; as far as he could see there wasn't anything left to destroy. The smell of death was sickening. In the distance Tony heard a cry for help. He ran as fast as he could and found a small child alive but severely burned. The injuries were gruesome. Tony used his medical knowledge and did everything he could to save the child. An elderly Olanion woman hobbled in from the growing field. Tony handed her the injured child.

His thoughts quickly turned to Tulari and he felt a sudden sickness in the pit of his stomach. The attack left very little standing. Tony let out a scream of anger and ran toward home. When he reached the valley floor, he scanned to see if his home was still standing. He breathed a sigh of relief as it appeared undamaged. The cover of trees might have made it impossible to see from the air. He quickly clambered up the hillside and into his home. Tulari was on his bed crying.

"I'm sorry. I don't know what else to say. There are survivors and I will kill that fucking Empress if it's the last thing I do. Maybe I shouldn't have waited so long. I'll leave tomorrow and do what I must." Tony was shaking with anger. "I thought I lost you," Tulari wept. "The Empress wasn't targeting me; the attack on your people was retribution. I was audacious enough to enter her thoughts, so she decided to kill those she knew I cared about. I'm just another Overlord. You'll lose me someday, we don't seem to live very long,"

"You're more than an Overlord to me," Tulari replied as she stood up and hugged him. Tony spent the rest of the night holding Tulari as she wept for her people. "In the morning we will help the wounded on your world for as long as it takes. I care about you too, Tulari," he said as he held her tightly.

The artificial rings surrounding Rabanah were bright and beautiful. Vincent marveled as he looked past the rings into the night sky and found the golden moon. Monique joined him on the balcony. "It's amazing. Such beauty," Vincent breathed. "Well thank you; I wasn't sure you noticed my new negligée." Monique replied. After the incident with the Cardonians, Vincent decided it would be a clever idea to spend some time away. It was also a good excuse to be alone with Monique. "I really like the choice you made, but you don't need anything to enhance your beauty." "Nice try. I saw you looking into the sky. You're right, it is beautiful. I find what's going on below us much more interesting, however."

Vincent contemplated the scene on the street below. Aliens from various planets comingled without any unnecessary drama or violence. The species were comprised of every shape and color. He watched as a small, blue alien brought food to a massive four-legged green creature with eight horns spanning its massive head.

"I'm not sure we deserve to be here," he responded. Monique wasn't sure what Vincent was referring to. "We're not causing any problems. Did you kick someone else out to get this room?" Monique asked as Vincent laughed. "I was thinking that perhaps humanity shouldn't have been granted membership into the Alliance. The species below are so peaceful and have no issue with coexistence. What if there were fifty humans down there? There would be arguments and nonstop drama just like on Earth. Immoral and horrendous acts of cruelty, evil and violence have sculpted our home world since we could stand upright. If the species below were on Earth, they'd be attacked just for being different. Acceptance into the Alliance will not change our nature.

We use politics and religion as an excuse to slaughter our own brothers and sisters. Our earnings are taxed heavily and the truth is hidden from us. It's a perverted and sick system with no beginning and no end. Earth can never go back to the old ways," Vincent said.

"I'm glad you're being so romantic tonight. Should we discuss nuclear war next?" "I'm sorry. You truly do look amazing." Vincent sheepishly responded. "You're right; I can tell this has been bothering you and too be honest it's been bothering me as well. Perhaps humanity does not yet belong in the Alliance. Unfortunately, there are as many immoral people as there are moral on Earth. Humanity is an infant species and has no sense of purpose or inner peace. There is something we have been longing for and it's something we lack yet require. An amazing transformation can take place if we win this war. We can get past our weaknesses and gain the inner peace and balance we crave so desperately. Our species can slowly and irrevocably change."

"How will winning this war suddenly change the nature of humanity?" Vincent asked. "It won't. Humanity on its own is either a failed project or a very long-term experiment which might eventually be successful thousands of years from now. There is simply too much immorality and greed to overcome. Perhaps you haven't been watching the news feeds lately?" Monique asked. "I've been a little busy trying to stay ahead of the Cardonians. What did I miss in the news?" he asked. "On Mars, a human and Martian hybrid child has been born. Her name is Zabu. According to scientists from the Alliance, it's part of some grand plan conceived by an ancient species. It's what humanity has been searching for since our inception. Don't give up just yet, Vincent, we still have much to fight for. We can become what we've always wanted to be," Monique replied.

"That's amazing. Perhaps I should start paying more attention to what's going on. A child of both Earth and Mars is incredible. The invasion of the Sol System will begin in a few weeks. Are you ready to take back our home?" Vincent asked. "I am, but first I have a question for you. Are you ready for me tonight?" Monique smiled seductively as she led Vincent inside.

The most recent transmission from the Alliance contained some good news. Dalton began his walk to meet with Alixias and Patrick. It was surprising Zabu was speaking so early in her development. The door was open when he arrived. "It sure smells good in here," he said as he entered the home. "Don't worry, you'll get fed. What is the latest from the Alliance?" Alixias asked. "They're analyzing the latest information. For now, they've designed new learning modules for Zabu. They believe it's a promising idea to advance her training. The Alliance specialists will make a further determination when they arrive on Mars in a couple of weeks," Dalton said casually. "What did you just say?!" Patrick asked. "The invasion is scheduled to start in eleven days. Members of the Alliance will arrive on Mars shortly after the invasion begins. With any luck, all of Sol will soon be free again." Dalton was clearly excited. "The leaders wouldn't authorize an invasion without a reasonable chance of success. Has the Alliance provided an estimate on the chances of success for this invasion?" Alixias asked.

Dalton anticipated such a question; Alixias paid great attention to detail. In his research he discovered Martians were a result-oriented species. "The current estimate puts the odds of victory at approximately ninety-one percent. The key for the Annunaki was to take the Rabanah System and move on to Earth and Mars. The Empress was to merge with the invading force on Earth. If her plan succeeded, the Alliance wouldn't stand a chance of ever retaking the Sol System. Sol would have become the heart of the Annunaki; however, they failed in their attempt to take Rabanah and now their plan is falling apart. Unless something crazy happens, we will be liberated shortly," Dalton said as he watched Patrick and Alixias' faces brighten. "Has the child said anything else today?" he asked. "Not today, but I'm sure she'll say more soon," Alixias responded.

Tony's transformation meant nothing to him in the aftermath of the Annunaki invasion. He relied on his training as a medical doctor to save as many Olanions as possible. The Annunaki weaponry decimated the species. Tulari did what she could to assist him. After he could do no more, they returned to the rastish field. There were no buildings or structures in the area and the field was ignored by the Annunaki. Tony felt selfish relief as he inhaled the rastish. He focused his mind and sought out the Empress. He channeled all his power and hatred for the Empress into his thoughts. He made a brief connection. It lasted only a few seconds, but it was enough. He was able to see the audacious plan the Empress conceived. "I must leave soon; it's almost time," Tony said. "You must wait. There are more of my people to help first. We still need you for the immediate future," Tulari replied.

Chapter 8

As the Representative for Earth, Dominic listened as the invasion plan was presented by Alliance military leadership in the Great Chamber. The gathered assembly was required to vote on the plan which would liberate the Sol System if it was successful. There were no new developments with the Cardonians and the Osarians. Both species were sending ships to assist with the liberation of Earth and Mars. Dominic placed his vote. Chief Administrator Kizak announced the result quickly and it was overwhelming. Liberation of the Sol System would begin as scheduled by the Alliance military.

Dominic was pleased. Action was finally taking place, yet something didn't feel quite right about the sudden cooperation of the Cardonians. It didn't make any sense and Vincent was acting strangely. An early morning visit might catch him off guard. He knew something was being hidden.

"Why are the Cardonians helping the Alliance?" Dominic asked as his friend opened the door. Vincent was barely awake and needed more coffee. He retreated to the bedroom to get his cup and Dominic followed. "What the hell are you talking about? What's going on with you?" he asked Dominic. "The invasion of the Sol System has been authorized and will commence shortly.

I want you to tell me why the Cardonians are suddenly so eager to help. I think you're hiding something from me," Dominic demanded.

"Sorry Vincent, I was in the bathroom and didn't know Dominic was here," Monique said as she entered the bedroom. "Everything is fine. Dominic has expressed some concerns, but we're all family. Let's go have some coffee and listen as Dominic explains the good news about the liberation of Earth and Mars. Give me a moment to freshen up and I'll be there in a few minutes," Vincent replied as Dominic and Monique left the bedroom.

The early morning visit was unexpected and took Vincent by surprise. Dominic previously asked about the Cardonians and he offhandedly dismissed the question, but now it was time to be more direct and speak to Dominic in a way he would understand. He was Enzo's son and should be able to read between the lines. Vincent entered the living quarters and found Isabella was awake and had joined Dominic and Monique.

"You've brought good news, but before we discuss the Cardonians, let's hear about the liberation of the Sol System, please," Vincent asked. "As you wish. An armada of Alliance ships is gathering at the gate to our solar system. The invasion has been approved and will begin shortly. You will receive orders to gather with the rest of the fleet shortly, but I do not know specifically what your role will be. The military leaders will inform you of your mission and the chance of success is high. Now that I've told you about the liberation force, it's time for you to tell me about the Cardonians."

Vincent took a breath and prepared his reply. "There are times when information must be withheld to protect those we care about. Surely your father withheld information from you in the past? It's in the best interest for everyone involved that you ask no more questions. We don't want to see you hurt or your reputation damaged for being involved in something without Alliance approval."

"You can't be implicated for something you have no knowledge of," Isabella interjected. Vincent was speechless. He didn't understand where Isabella's sudden cockiness was coming from, but she was exactly right and said it better than he could have. "Isabella is correct. We are here to support you and more importantly to protect you. The liberation of our people is paramount and I cannot allow politics to interfere with the most pivotal moment in human history. The Cardonian's assistance will be instrumental to accomplish our common goal. Trust me, those bastards are vicious and will do whatever it takes to win," Vincent said.

Dominic wasn't surprised by the response from Isabella and Vincent. If they wanted him to know what was going on, they would have told him long ago. He was curious and wanted to understand exactly what was going on. Deep down he knew his friends cared for him and were doing what was best for him. "I don't like it, but I understand. As the Ambassador for Earth, I will remain behind and represent the interests of Earth and Mars. If you see my father, tell him he was right and that I love him. Be safe and fight for all of humanity." Dominic hugged his friends and left.

As a doctor, Tony hadn't ever seen so many horrible injuries and such complete devastation simultaneously. He used all his skills to keep as many Olanions alive as possible and those he saved were appreciative. Uninjured Olanions glared at him in anger, blaming him for the loss of their friends and family members. He cared for the species more than they would ever know and felt tremendous guilt. As he changed the bandage on the wound of an adult female, a child approached. "Will my mom live?" the terrified little girl asked. "Yes, your mom will be fine, she just needs time to recover from her injuries. You don't need to worry about her," Tony replied. "We spoke of you when we ate our meals. I believe in you. Thank you for helping my mom. I believe you are the Overlord and here to save us all," the girl said.

The child's words affected him more than he thought possible. There was little left to do and it was time to leave. He needed to refocus and continue with what must be done. Tony flew his ship to the rastish field and spent the next two days with Tulari. After his meditation, he loaded the ship with rastish and set a course for Tanas. "Kill her and come back to me," Tulari said. "I love you. The time we've spent together has been the happiest time of my life. If it's possible, I promise I'll return to you," Tony replied as he kissed Tulari.

The home world of the Annunaki came into view. Fittingly, it was a planet devoid of vibrant colors and covered almost entirely by grey skies and brown land. From his vantage point, Tony observed a dozen green, shallow lakes. Pollution littered the skies. Tony piloted the ship to dock with the flagship of the Annunaki fleet. He listened to the communication channels and learned the Empress relocated to the flagship. She planned to travel, but he didn't know why. The ship was ornate and massive; nothing less would do for the Empress.

He immediately destroyed the engines on the small ship after docking with the flagship. Before he did anything else he found a safe location to hide the rastish. He expected to confront the Empress on Tanas;

now he needed to adjust his plans. He would learn about the flagship and how to defeat Empress Zovad's defenses. He felt confident he could block all his thoughts from her. The ship was immense and Tony decided to sleep in the last place anyone was authorized to visit.

"I just don't understand it. Isabella has been acting strangely and asserting herself in such a brazen manner," Vincent said. "I agree. It's difficult to understand her sudden change. Everything she's done or said has helped us, but for some reason she's become more assertive," Monique replied as she watched Vincent answer a sudden alert on his data pad.

"We've received our orders and the Santa Maria is to proceed to Earth with the invading force. Our specific mission is to scan all known Earth communication channels and to assist any surviving humans on the surface," Vincent said discouragingly. "Any surviving humans. The words paint a bleak picture. I wonder how many survived the Annunaki invasion?" Monique asked. "I don't want to think about that right now. We will establish communication with any remaining forces on Earth and complete our mission. The Alliance will protect any survivors we are able to identify," Vincent responded.

"I'm sure many have survived. The Annunaki always maintain an indigenous labor force and it's likely others are in hiding. Humanity will recover from the Annunaki," Monique replied. "I hope so. Find Isabella and let's get to the Santa Maria. It's time to go home."

The human gladiators were a source of great entertainment for Buxare. She enjoyed watching the aliens battle each other the most. Their thirst for blood was most apparent when they fought amongst themselves. Occasionally, she ordered the humans to fight battles with other species of the planet. She knew of their early history and occasionally forced them to battle other native species. The nightly trips to the stadium to watch the inevitable bloodbath was a source of great pleasure.

Buxare reviewed the daily operation report; virtually nothing changed from the prior day. Eighty percent of her ships were still awaiting the arrival of the Empress and orbiting Earth. The remaining vessels were at the gate ready to accompany her to Mars when she arrived. Buxare focused her mind and felt the power and presence of her Empress. The link suddenly disappeared for a few moments. Instantly, she was bombarded with questions from her underlings. She told them the Empress was fine and to focus on their duties. However, the incident was upsetting to all Annunaki. A ship performing a routine docking maneuver crashed when the pilot panicked and lost concentration.

The Empress was overdue and the brief disappearance of the link was unsettling. Perhaps all was not well with her leader. Buxare decided to launch another probe through the gate into the Rabanah System. The last probe was sent six months earlier and didn't return with good news. Alliance ships were stationed outside the gate. The probes were programmed to enter the gate, record the surroundings and return immediately. The process lasted less than five seconds. She ordered another probe through to collect readings. Surely by now the Empress would have succeeded.

Vincent felt good and was in the command center of the Santa Maria. "Monique, set course for the gate. Let's get back to Earth." "We have been ordered to delay our departure," Isabella interrupted. "Why? We're ready to go." "The military experts believe our vessel is now understaffed, so they are sending two additional crewmembers," Isabella replied. "Goddammit, we don't need any aliens interfering with our operations. When are the crewmembers scheduled to arrive?" Vincent asked. "They are on their way and will be here in just a few minutes."

Vincent didn't like it. He was familiar with Monique, Julia and Isabella and knew he could count on them. They would follow his orders and tell him he was wrong if the situation warranted it. "The new crewmembers have boarded and will be here momentarily," Isabella relayed. "As soon as the new crewmembers have boarded, lift off and set course for the gate. We will rendezvous with the fleet and await our orders," Vincent replied.

"Do you mind if I take the pilot's seat?" a new voice asked. Vincent looked up and saw a familiar face. "My God! Azmune, it's good to see you. Are you fully recovered from your injuries?" Vincent asked. "I am fully healed both physically and mentally. Thank you for asking," Azmune replied. "I'd like to apologize again for what happened. We didn't have a way to get you home after you crashed at Roswell. I'm surprised you've been assigned this mission and are returning to Earth. Did the Alliance assign this mission, or did you volunteer?" Vincent asked.

"I volunteered. I would have died if the physicians on Earth hadn't managed to sustain and feed me. You returned me to Rabanah as soon as the opportunity presented itself and if it wasn't for the help of humans, I'd be dead. If I'm not intruding, I'd like to assist in the liberation of your people. The Annunaki shot me down in the first place, so I figure it's time for a little payback. If my memory is accurate, I believe you called me Andy when I first arrived aboard this ship. I would like to keep my Earth name while I'm in your company," Azmune replied.

Vincent smiled. The Alliance made an excellent choice. "Welcome aboard, Andy. Please take the pilot's seat. I'm sure your expertise will be invaluable. It's a pleasure and an honor to have you assisting us. Maintain course for the gate, please."

"In what capacity will I be most effective?" another familiar voice said. Vincent glanced at the second new arrival. "Maxis, what are you doing here? You're the representative for Mars. You have more important duties," Vincent said in shock. "Do you really think I'd let you go back to Sol without a Martian onboard? Tissa will fulfill my duties on Rabanah and I will accompany you to Sol. I want to make sure the Vandi refuges have someplace to go when this war is over, Captain," Maxis replied. "Welcome aboard. Your orders on this vessel are to observe and learn. Currently all stations are occupied, but you can provide support and backup should it be needed."

It was the middle of night and Patrick was exhausted. Zabu was talking again and repeating what she learned. She was still watching the educational videos in the evenings before falling asleep. He was changing her diaper and thinking fatherly duties weren't always fun when he received a text from Dalton. "Let me know when you're awake. I have vital information," the text read. Patrick put Zabu back to sleep and texted Dalton he would be there momentarily. Alixias and Zabu were snoring loudly when he left.

"You don't normally send messages in the middle of the night. What's so important?" he asked as he entered Dalton's quarters. "I'm just now sending out a message to everyone. The Alliance will invade tomorrow. We've been advised to gather any weaponry we have and prepare to defend ourselves should the Annunaki decide to land forces on Mars." "Do you think it will come to that?" Patrick asked. "I don't think it will and neither does the Alliance, but they want us to be prepared just in case. Once the battle begins, the Alliance computes there is a fifteen percent chance Annunaki forces will attempt to regroup and form a base on Mars." "Hmm, I guess they're covering all the possibilities. Send the message and we'll start gathering weapons. I hope we don't have to use them. We don't have very many," Patrick replied.

The Santa Maria approached the gate. The first Alliance vessel came into view and it was truly massive, but it didn't appear to have any weaponry. It was nearly the size of a small moon. "What the hell is that?" Vincent asked. "I've been studying the battle plan. That vessel will go in last and is destined for Mars. It is the magnetic shield that will allow the planet to be quickly terraformed. We will be in our assigned position in the armada in seven minutes. Approximately eighteen hours later, the invasion is scheduled to commence," Julia replied.

"Captain, our orders have changed. An Annunaki probe just emerged through the gate and couldn't be destroyed before it returned. All ships have been ordered through the gate immediately," Isabella stated. "The probe will report we've amassed an invading force at the gate. The decision to invade immediately is correct. We must invade now before the Annunaki can alter their defenses!" Andy said with urgency.

At long last he could finally say the words. "Set course for Earth. Fastest possible speed now!" Vincent commanded. "Course set and engaged, we're on our way," Andy replied.

Buxare was enjoying her nightly entertainment at the stadium; however, her spectacle was suddenly disrupted when she received a high priority alert. It was the first high priority alert issued since she arrived on Earth with her fleet. The probe at the gate identified a massive enemy armada waiting on the other side. The Sol System would soon be invaded by the Alliance. She immediately issued orders to have the vessels at the gate return to Earth to mount a defense. "Kill everyone on the field. My ship must descend to pick me up," she ordered. The eleven humans left in the current battle were quickly dispatched by her guards. The flagship descended and Buxare boarded immediately.

"Provide me an update," she demanded as she boarded. "The Alliance has entered the system with a large invading force. Our ships at the gate engaged the enemy before they received the order to return to Earth," the communications officer reported. "What are the results of the battle?" Buxare asked. "Six manned vessels were destroyed, two unmanned vessels were destroyed, and five other manned vessels were damaged and are retreating. It's been estimated the Alliance will destroy all five retreating ships before they can safely reach Earth. The enemy ships are expected to reach Mars in three days and will arrive at Earth in four," the officer reported.

Buxare was furious. There wasn't a contingency plan in place if the Empress failed to arrive as scheduled. Such a failure was completely unexpected. "We don't have much time. Advise the Commanders of all vessels to prepare for battle. I will send a message on behalf of the Empress and a battle plan shortly. Remind the Commanders that the Empress does not tolerate failure."

Rediscovering the history of Mars was an amazing and fulfilling project; it really was a dream job. Dalton filled in as an emergency doctor and assisted in many ways while on Mars. He was now free to continue his job as an archeologist and gathered his pupils. "The history of this planet was well documented. It's up to us to translate that history and uncover unknown secrets. According to the Alliance, victory will soon be at hand and Martians will be coming home. We must provide returning Martians as much information as possible about their heritage and the past. The Alliance has decided to allow me to continue to direct research once they arrive. We have impressed them with our discoveries and our meticulous attention to detail. Be prepared to abandon your work at a moment's notice however. If the Annunaki decide to come, we will fight."

"I listened to your speech; it was good. You should be proud of everything you've accomplished on Mars," Patrick said when Dalton arrived. "It was only good because it was true. It's always been a team effort and we should all be proud. Everyone has been professional and done their jobs despite the ongoing threat," Dalton replied.

"So, we are likely to survive and all of our friends as well?" Alixias asked. "Yes, for the most part. Unfortunately, Tony decided he needed to travel to Tanis to confront the Annunaki. Even with his enhanced abilities, it's unlikely he has survived," Dalton replied. "You never know. Tony has proven his resiliency on many occasions under the most difficult of situations. He is a passionate person who has always looked out for his friends. If it weren't for him, we would have died on Vandi. I would like to see my friend again," Patrick replied. Zabu listened to his father's words, closed her eyes and instinctively reached out.

He was an Overlord, but Tony didn't have any idea what such a bestowment meant. He only knew he failed the people who gave him the title and despite his plan, his friends died. He managed to stay hidden on the flagship of the Empress. The rastish sustained him, yet the recent loss of his friends was very painful. It served as a reminder of how much power the Empress possessed. The task suddenly seemed incredibly daunting. He had been confident the mission could be completed without any help from his friends. The bonds he forged with the crew of the Santa Maria and the companionship of the Olanions couldn't be replaced. He missed his friends and felt isolated and alone. Tony closed his eyes and tried to find balance.

Meditation helped, but Tony knew he wasn't mentally prepared to confront the Empress at the moment. Without proper balance he would likely make a fatal mistake. He would leave the ship tomorrow and return when he regained his confidence. As he was beginning to fall asleep, he felt a presence briefly make contact with his mind.

Tony thought he was able to block out any possible intrusions and didn't know how the new mind contacted him. It was definitely someone he didn't know. The sudden contact brought extreme emotion as he felt a confident and innocent alien reaching out to him for reasons he couldn't understand. The mind was moral and untainted, but he was unable to reach out and respond. There was hope and determination in the contact and the individual could feel his difficulties, his heartaches and pain. The empathetic contact lasted only a few seconds and was gone. Tony sensed there was understanding and support from whomever it was, something he needed more than he thought possible. His loneliness suddenly dissipated and Tony felt resolute.

The people on Mars were courageous and Dalton felt privileged to work alongside them. The courtyard containing passageways to various chambers and transportation hubs were cleaned and polished. One of the passageways led directly to the pyramid and was adorned with ancient Martian hieroglyphs. The restored fountains glimmered in the artificial light with fresh drinkable water. Everyone on Mars gathered in the courtyard and waited for the Alliance to make contact when they came within range. There was subdued optimism as everyone listened to the static broadcast on the assigned frequency. "Don't you think they should have made contact by now?" Patrick asked.

Dalton was about to reply when the static was suddenly interrupted. "...........Mars Colony...........status?" Patrick smiled as he listened to the incomplete message. It repeated. "This is Commander Evir. Mars Colony do you receive? What is your status?" the message asked. The courtyard erupted as everyone cheered and yelled. Dalton was forced to wait a moment to reply. "We receive you, Commander Evir. Everyone here is pretty happy to hear a friendly voice. Our status remains unchanged. We have not encountered the enemy," Dalton replied. "I'm glad we could make it. We have a small team ready to land and assist. They bring additional weaponry. Please be prepared to receive additional personnel to assist in all aspects of rebuilding and terraforming Mars," Commander Evir replied. "We are ready and your team is more than welcome," Dalton joyfully replied. "In a breach of protocol, one of my Captains has asked to speak with you. In this instance, I've decided to approve his request. Go ahead, Captain," Commander Evir stated.

"Hello again, old friend. I don't think Maria could have ever envisioned this. It's good to hear your voice and I'm glad you're alive and well," Vincent said. "The Alliance surprised me when they told me you were still alive. I didn't think you'd be able to survive without my help. Who knew our trip to Old Snowy Mountain would've brought us here?" Dalton replied. "I guess there's a reason for everything. We're going to Earth and have duties to perform to assist in the upcoming battle to liberate the planet. I will return and look forward to seeing what you've accomplished on Mars," Vincent concluded. "Stay safe. I will see you soon, my friend." Dalton wiped tears from his eyes.

"We were lucky to have survived," Alixias stated. "The Empresses is arrogant; she wanted to be the first Annunaki to set foot on Mars and reclaim the planet. If she would have redirected her forces from Earth, we would have been dead a long time ago. I'm going outside to meet our new friends," Dalton replied.

As far as he was concerned, the small team was massive. Dalton watched small ships converge around the pyramid. An alien figure exited the closest ship and approached. "Hello, my name is Teb; we are here to assist," she said. Dalton extended his hand to the alien. "Welcome to Mars, let's go inside and talk. Woah, what the hell is that?" Dalton asked as he watched a massive vessel suddenly obscure the sun. "That vessel is transporting the magnetic shield. Terraforming will begin immediately and the shield will protect the Martian atmosphere. My personnel will begin their mission and do their best to stay out of your way. We will discuss how to best coordinate and integrate our personnel for optimization," Teb replied.

Dalton felt a bit overwhelmed. He didn't expect such a massive force from the Alliance landing on Mars. "I appreciate you meeting me alone. I didn't think you'd have so many ships and personnel. We aren't prepared to house and feed so many visitors," he said. "We come prepared. Your daily activities will not be interrupted and you can continue your research. A vessel that can accommodate all our required housing and nutritional needs will soon be in place. I've been assigned the task of completing two missions on this planet," Teb stated.

Dalton knew what one of the missions was, but he wasn't sure of the other. "What are your missions?"

he asked. "Mars is to be terraformed as quickly as possible. The second mission is a bit more delicate and I have been assigned specialists to assist. The child, Zabu, must be observed, analyzed and tested. Our specialists will observe the child and the familial dynamics for the immediate future. We will offer guidance and advice as the situation warrants," Teb replied. "Alixias is going to love this," Dalton said.

Every conceivable battle plan was doomed to fail and Buxare was left with only one option. She watched as her message was broadcast to the fleet. "Our revered Empress entrusted me to command this fleet. She has been delayed and we will hold out until she arrives. All vessels are to immediately form around my flagship. We will remain in a stalemate until the Empress arrives. You are not to fire on the enemy without my prior approval under any circumstances. Biological weapons will be placed at various locations on Earth. If the Alliance fails to abide the stalemate or attempts to land on the planet, I will destroy every lifeform and make the planet uninhabitable. Mars is our home world. This planet is of no consequence to the Empress."

"Commander Evir, we have an incoming transmission from the Annunaki Commander of the occupation force," the communications officer stated.

The Alliance fleet would be in range and ready to commence the fight against the Annunaki within the hour. "Send it through," Commander Evir replied. There was no doubt the Annunaki would be defeated in the upcoming battle. It was unusual for the Annunaki to request communication. Perhaps the enemy understood defeat was guaranteed and wished to surrender. He watched as the Annunaki leader's image appeared on his viewscreen. "I am Buxare. Let it be known if you attack my fleet or attempt to land on Earth there will be grave consequences. Every creature on Earth will be killed and we will make this planet uninhabitable. If you fail to follow my instructions the biological devices on the planet will be activated. That is all."

"Well, she's not a very chatty gal. Forward her message to Rabanah and instruct the fleet to rendezvous at the moon. Inform all vessels to prepare to discuss this new development in two hours." Evir commanded.

"Captain, our orders have changed. We've been ordered to the moon. Commander Evir will address the fleet shortly," Isabella stated. "Damn, I wanted to blow those assholes to hell and back and get this over with," Vincent fumed. "Commander Evir is well respected and a very capable leader; I'm sure his reasoning is sound," Andy replied. "I know. He wouldn't make a change without a reason. I'm just impatient after all the waiting. Please set course for the moon Andy."

The Santa Maria was in orbit around the moon and the two hours were up. Commander Evir appeared on the screen and explained the threat made by the Annunaki leader. "I'm awaiting a response from the military council on Rabanah. Until we receive instructions from the Alliance, the fleet will conduct no offensive actions and will not approach Earth. Are there any questions?" Commander Evir asked. "Have the devices been located and can they safely be destroyed?" someone asked. "We are working on that problem now. Even if we can locate the devices, it's unlikely we'll be able to destroy them. The devices could be shielded and will detonate with any sort of tampering." There were no other questions and the meeting ended.

Vincent wanted to ask many questions, but didn't feel comfortable asking them in front of the entire fleet. "Isabella, please contact Commander Evir; I wish to speak with him." Seconds later the Commander appeared. "Hello Captain, what can I do for you?" "Commander, I would like to continue our mission. We were tasked with contacting any remaining people on Earth, but our fleet is not allowed to land. Perhaps we can make contact with someone on Earth who can provide intelligence about the biological devices the Annunaki have threatened us with. We can approach the planet when the Annunaki are on the opposite side of Earth. If we remain in the upper atmosphere we won't violate the terms outlined by the Annunaki as we attempt to contact anyone below. I will ensure we never land," Vincent explained.

He watched as the Commander considered the request. "I'm inclined to wait to hear from Rabanah before taking any action. However, your plan doesn't violate any of the conditions set forth by the Annunaki. You must keep in mind the Annunaki are very thorough and communication from the surface of your planet is unlikely. You saw what happened on Vandi, Vincent. It is likely the same has happened on Earth. If we can visually inspect one of the devices, your mission is worth the risk. Proceed with caution and send me an update if you learn anything important," Commander Evir ordered. "Thank you, I will be careful and will follow your orders."

"Andy, are we out of line of sight with the Annunaki right now?" Vincent asked. "Yes, we will be for the next three hours and fifteen minutes." "Perfect, set course for Earth and establish our altitude at forty thousand feet above the surface upon arrival. Monique, is the computer prepared to scan all known communication frequencies?" Vincent asked. "Yes, the computer is ready to transmit and receive."
"Computer, please record the following message and

broadcast the transmission on all frequencies," Vincent said. "This message comes from the Alliance. We are here to free Earth from your captors known as the Annunaki. If you can hear this message, please reply by any means possible. The Alliance requires information only you can provide to defeat our common enemy," Vincent said.

The Santa Maria descended into the atmosphere and the message repeated constantly. Vincent hoped for a quick response, but none was forthcoming. There were only forty-five minutes left before he would be required to return to the moon. The computer suddenly interrupted his thoughts. "Contact established."

Vincent listened as a voice pierced the silence. "Hello, my name is Gail. I'm in Australia and have received your message." Vincent was relieved. It was good to hear a voice coming from Earth. "Hello Gail, my name is Vincent. Thank you for responding. We are trying to gather information. Are you in contact with anyone else on the planet?" he asked. "Yes, we are. We've established contact with nineteen other groups via ham radio," Gail responded. "We must withdraw shortly. Please provide a list of your contacts and their locations as quickly as possible," Vincent replied.

Gail provided the information just as it was time to depart. "Return to the moon please, Andy. Isabella, please contact Commander Evir," ordered Vincent. The

Commander appeared on the screen. "Sir, we've established communication and have contact information for nineteen groups on the planet. With further communication we should be able to contact all groups and locate some of the biological devices," Vincent reported. "You've surprised me, Captain. I didn't anticipate a positive result. Continue your mission and do everything possible to find one of the biological bombs. The devices could be disguised as anything common. If a device is located, take no action. We have biological specialists and technicians specifically trained to analyze such horrific weapons. Find the devices, leave them alone and contact me immediately when they are found," Commander Evir ordered.

Chapter 9

Enzo wasn't knowledgeable about spacecraft, but Randy was excited and wanted someone to talk to. "The government reverse-engineered more than I thought they could. The propulsion unit is far more advanced than I thought possible," Randy explained. Enzo nodded his head in agreement and was trying to find an excuse to leave. Randy would have been better off speaking to a brick wall. His thoughts were suddenly interrupted as Sargent Mathers approached. "President Louis has requested your presence in the control center." "What for?" Enzo asked. "I don't know, but he said it was urgent. Please follow me."

"Jesus, I hope the base hasn't been found by the Annunaki," Enzo said. "If it has, we're in big trouble. Let's go find out," Randy replied. Upon entering the control center, the men were surprised to find President Louis smiling and drinking a beer. "What the hell is going on?" Enzo asked. "We received a message from your friends in Australia and have a new ally." "So, what? We've made contact with another group? How does that help us defeat these bastards?" Randy asked.

"Well, this new group calls themselves the Alliance and they are not from this world. We have aligned with a friendly alien force that is ready to liberate Earth and I believe it's possible Vincent might still be out there somewhere," President Louis happily stated as he handed Enzo and Randy a beer.

"Why aren't they here? Has a battle taken place?" Enzo asked. "All we know right now is that there is some sort of stalemate. The Alliance vessel abruptly departed. We were told it will return at some point to provide additional information. The Captain of the Alliance ship said they are in search of information that can only be provided by someone on the surface of Earth. I would like the two of you to remain here and wait for the transmission from the Alliance," President Louis replied.

"The information Gail provided us indicates the contact in Montana is a United States military facility. We will broadcast again on all frequencies and if we receive a response from Montana it is the highest priority. Begin broadcast of the recording," Vincent said as the Santa Maria descended into Earth's atmosphere again.

Enzo looked at the ham radio. It must have been a hundred years old, but right now it was the most important piece of technology mankind possessed. One of the indicators moved and a voice rang out. "This is the Captain of the Santa Maria. We are an Alliance vessel and are attempting to liberate this planet from the Annunaki. Please respond if you're able."

All three men recognized the voice. "I'll take this one Mister President," Enzo stated. "Santa Maria, this is Montana base. It's about goddamn time you returned Vincenzo! Tell us what we need to do to get rid of these sons of bitches!"

Vincent could barely keep his emotions under control and almost began to cry. Enzo somehow managed to survive. "I should have known you would survive the invasion. You're an old and tough son of bitch." "It's a trait I learned from your grandmother. Now, tell us how we can help," Enzo said.

"The Alliance has overwhelming firepower and the ability to defeat the Annunaki. For all intents and purposes, Earth is being held hostage. The Annunaki have placed biological weapons across the planet and have threatened to detonate them if the Alliance attacks or attempts to land. The stalemate will continue unless we can find one of the bombs. The Alliance needs to know what to scan for and what type of weapon to use to destroy the devices," Vincent said. "What should we be looking for?" President Louis asked. "Anything unusual or out of place. When you find it. Don't take any action. Specialists from the Alliance must come down to inspect the device and make sure it doesn't detonate prematurely. We cannot make contact with everyone on your list, so you must spread the message.

Remember, you must not approach any suspect devices. The life of every animal on the planet is in the balance."

"What happened? Did we lose contact?" Vincent asked. "Yes, Captain. The rotation of the planet required a course correction, but I believe your message was received before we lost contact," Andy replied. "Thank you, Andy. Continue broadcasting the recorded message and let's see who else might be listening," Vincent ordered.

President Louis knew he wasn't a good president, but he also knew he was a good military leader. "Intelligence wins wars. Touch base with everyone across the planet we have contact with. Explain the Alliance's message precisely and accurately. Patrols from this base will begin immediately. We will find one of these devices. Our future depends on the actions we take today."

For a lucky few people on Earth, life hadn't drastically changed. Somehow, the Annunaki forgot or ignored the Midway Atoll in the Pacific Ocean. Fifty-three people inhabited the small island. Fifty-two were United States Fish and Wildlife employees. Lieutenant Navin was conducting historical research for the Navy when the Annunaki arrived. After the invasion she didn't have much to do. When the transmission from

Montana arrived she began exploring. Nothing seemed out of the ordinary until she arrived at the Doctor's Cemetery. The cemetery remained undisturbed for decades. She now found a shiny silver coffin in the center of the graveyard. It wasn't there the day before and there weren't any recent deaths. It could have only been brought in overnight from the invaders.

Enzo found the situation amusing. He was now the de facto second in command of the United States Military. President Louis ordered his military commanders to follow Enzo's orders when he was unavailable. "How does a heathen like you become Vice President of the United States?" Randy asked as he entered the control room. "Trust me, it's a position I don't want and will renounce as soon as possible." "Sir, we are receiving a message from Midway Atoll. A Lieutenant Navin from Midway is standing by," a soldier stated. "Please put it on the loudspeaker. Lieutenant Navin, we are listening; please proceed with your information," Enzo said.

"I came across something that doesn't make any sense. There was a coffin in the middle of a cemetery," Lieutenant Navin stated. Enzo rolled his eyes and looked at Randy befuddled. "That seems like an ordinary occurrence. What seems odd in your judgement?" Enzo asked. "Six gravestones are in the cemetery and the last person was buried in 1950. There have been no recent deaths and nobody on this island has seen the coffin before. It's definitely out of place."

The information was unsettling. Knowing the devices could wipe out all life on Earth made him nervous. "Lieutenant, do you have any knowledge as to when the coffin was placed in the cemetery and have you seen any evidence of alien visitation on the island?" Enzo asked. "It must have been placed in the cemetery overnight. It wasn't there yesterday. I suspect the Annunaki placed the coffin in the cemetery and it is the only evidence of visitation. I think they've left us alone for now because we are small community completely surrounded by water. We don't have any weapons, can't get off the island and don't constitute a threat of any kind. I fear they will get to us eventually after the important targets have been eliminated," Lieutenant Navin replied.

"Thank you for the valuable information, Lieutenant. I think you've found one of the devices. Instruct everyone to keep their distance from the coffin; no one is to approach it for any reason. We'll send updates and further instructions when we have a plan in place," Enzo ended the transmission. "What did I miss?" President Louis asked as he entered the room. "We've found one of the devices and have valuable intelligence to give to the Alliance."

The crew of the Santa Maria was in good spirits and departed for the moon ahead of schedule. The new information from Enzo could change everything. "Captain, Commander Evir is on the viewscreen awaiting your report," Isabella stated. "Commander, our contacts on Earth have located one of the devices. The exact coordinates of the device have just been sent," Vincent reported.

"Excellent work, Captain. We will send our most experienced biological weapons specialist to the location as soon as possible," Commander Evir replied. "Won't landing a ship be in violation of the Annunaki conditions?" Vincent asked. "We won't be landing a ship. A very unique individual will descend alone. Alert your personnel at Midway to expect a lone visitor within the next twenty-four hours. For their own safety, tell them to leave the visitor alone. This will be a one-way trip for the specialist. The personnel on Midway will need to sustain our expert until we can liberate the planet."

Tony didn't enjoy feeling hatred; he felt the emotion was self-destructive and poisonous. He was spending a second day in the corner of the opulent yet gaudy chamber. Empress Zovad was guarded constantly and her personal needs were tended to around the clock. At no time were there less than twenty Annunaki in the room catering to her every instruction and need. Multiple forcefields protected the Empress and only a select few were given permission to remain inside the forcefield with her. Tony wanted to unleash his mind. Anger, hatred and the need for vengeance consumed his thoughts. He watched as the Empress stood up and admired herself. Two days were enough. He learned everything there was to know about the defenses in her chamber.

Tony retreated to the top of the vessel where there was a solitary, isolated viewport. Here he gathered his thoughts. There were always too many servants and soldiers surrounding the Empress. He knew the mission could be accomplished if he could breach the security forces. He counted five separate forcefields surrounding the Empress and technology was not one of his strengths. Tony decided it was time to leave his comfort zone and brush up on the skills he would need to win. Knowledge was power and it was time to understand as much about the Annunaki as possible. He decided to dedicate the majority of his time to learning. Educating himself about the forcefields and turning his weakness into an advantage would give him the best chance at success.

Lieutenant Lee Navin was told a visitor would be arriving. He continually watched the skies and waited. Everyone else on Midway was doing the same. "Could that be the alien?" someone said and pointed. Lee watched as a strange winged animal descended. The flight abruptly ended as the creature landed in the ocean eighty yards from shore. "I guess not. Whatever that was has drowned by now," he said. The crowd refocused their attention on the skies.

The silence was pierced by a deep booming voice. "Do not approach and stand clear. Failure to follow these instructions will result in physical harm." The residents of Midway were surprised as the small creature folded its wings and walked out of the surf and headed toward the cemetery. The alien had wings like those of a bat. "It's cute; I think it looks like a cross between a hyena and a flying squirrel," someone said. "The alien is here to assist and is extremely intelligent. Everyone clear out and follow his instructions. We need to stay out of his way," Lee said.

Lee watched from afar as the diminutive alien approached the coffin. The creature produced the smallest data pad he'd ever seen. After thirty minutes of analyzing the coffin with his device, the alien approached. "You are either a brave or stupid human for remaining so close to me. Regardless, come help me lift the top off the coffin. My name is Welnarm," the alien demanded loudly. Lee thought he was well hidden. "Are you talking to me?" he asked. "You're the only one here. Come help me and follow my instructions exactly. Once we get the lid off, you must leave. Get as far away from here as possible and tell everyone else to do the same. We will lift it straight up and set it on the ground. Lift now!" Welnarm commanded. The lid came off easily and Lee peered inside. The coffin held a rectangular glass box containing electronics and seven glass tubes filled with liquids of varying colors and viscosity. "What are those?" he asked. "You need to leave. If I require further assistance, I'll come find you."

Mars bustled with activity. The Alliance was well prepared and began terraforming quickly. Dalton listened as Teb provided an update. "What about Earth? When will this stalemate end?" he asked. "I don't know. The updates don't show any sign of progress yet, but I'm sure the military leaders are doing everything within their power to successfully end the stalemate," Teb replied. "What if the Annunaki on Earth are victorious? The Alliance has thousands of people on Mars. Massive resources are being spent on terraforming the planet. What happens if we lose Earth?" Dalton asked.

"The Alliance will lose Earth if the Annunaki detonate the biological weapons. Every lifeform on the planet will die and your race will be brought to near extinction. The Alliance would attack their vessels immediately. Our military leaders estimate the Annunaki will be easily defeated once an actual battle takes place. Unless the Annunaki Empress magically appears with more firepower, the Sol System is safely in the hands of the Alliance. The terraforming of Mars will continue uninterrupted," Teb explained.

"If there is anything we can do to help, please let me know. How is the terraforming progressing?" Dalton asked. "Were you not listening when I told you a few minutes ago?" Teb was clearly irritated. "I guess my thoughts were focused on Earth. Can you please repeat the report?" Dalton asked. "Atmospheric pressure has begun to increase, and the magnetic shield is providing protection from the sun. Massive amounts of methane and other hydrocarbons are constantly being added to the atmosphere. Oxygen levels continue to rise and water is beginning to accumulate in specific regions. All terraforming projects are on schedule and proceeding as planned." "Thank you for the information. It sounds like Mars will become a paradise for humans and Martians in the future, but what of the child? What have the Alliance experts learned about Zabu?" Dalton probed. "The child is still young and developing. The tests and reports are preliminary; however, initial tests indicate the child is highly intelligent, physically healthy and likely has strong telepathic abilities. These traits are highly sought after by the Alliance. Martian refugees from Vandi will arrive shortly and additional refugees will be sent to Earth when the planet is liberated. Procreation is encouraged and recommended between Martians and humans. For obvious reasons, the Alliance would like to get as many Martians and humans together as possible. Tests will remain ongoing with Zabu."

Dalton arrived to visit with Patrick and Alixias and was surprised to find a guard at the door. "What business do you have here?" the guard asked. "I'm a friend. My name is Dalton. Please let Alixias and Patrick know I'm here."

"Goddamn it Dalton, this is exactly what we wanted to avoid when we decided to have a child," Patrick grumbled as Dalton entered the room. The Alliance placed cameras and recording devices throughout the home. "Where are Alixias and Zabu?" Dalton asked, ignoring Patrick's irritation. "They are in the bedroom, but I wouldn't go in in there if I were you." Dalton ignored the warning and entered the bedroom. He found three medical experts conferring and observing Alixias and Zabu. "You'd better take care of this now. I'm not normally a violent person, but we value our privacy and won't tolerate this any longer!" Alixias fumed.

"By orders of Teb, all Alliance personnel and equipment is to be removed immediately. Pack up your equipment and report to Teb," Dalton ordered. "We've received no such orders," one of the experts said. "I don't care. Get out of here. If you have a problem, take it up with Teb." Dalton watched the Alliance personnel gather their equipment and leave. "Thank you, Dalton. I wasn't aware you spoke with Teb on our behalf," Alixias said. "I didn't speak with Teb regarding this exact situation, but your family is entitled to privacy. I'm sure Teb will summon me when he finds out about this. I'll negotiate an agreement with him. Please agree to allow the Alliance to interview you and your family once a week. It's likely the best I'll be able to do. Teb probably won't be too happy about it, but I think it's fair," Dalton said in an attempt to appease the family.

Lee pointed the unloaded rifle at Welnarm. He was as far away as possible while remaining in sight of the small alien. He watched through the scope as Welnarm scurried around the coffin. After many hours the small alien approached. "I've submitted my report. The Alliance will act soon. I require food."

Commander Evir reviewed Welnarm's report that contained the exact dimensions of the device and the biological material contained within. Some of the material was unique and not native to Earth. Commander Evir ordered a scan of Earth. "Scan for the listed biological materials not native to this planet. We should be able to find all the devices. Tell the fleet to standby," he ordered.

It didn't take long before the scan results were disclosed. "All forty-two devices have been located and their locations recorded," the planetary analyst reported. "Send the data to the Tactical Council on Rabanah and update the fleet on the most recent developments," Commander Evir ordered.

"Why aren't we returning to Earth?" Isabella asked. "We've been ordered to stand by and assist as necessary. I'm sure we'll receive new orders soon. The Alliance believes the intelligence we've provided will make a difference. We will remain in geosynchronous orbit above Earth and wait for now," Vincent replied.

The Santa Maria had been orbiting for eight days when a new message arrived. "Captain, we've been ordered to the moon to pick up a small team of personnel to study the ships in Montana," Isabella reported. "How are we supposed to get a team to Montana? The Annunaki threatened to blow up the devices if any ships approached the surface," he asked.

"All the details have been worked out already. The team will parachute down from high altitude," Isabella replied. The Santa Maria quickly returned to the moon and picked up the personnel.

"We've reached the required altitude and the team is ready to jump," Julia reported. "Good luck! Jump when ready and stay safe!" Vincent ordered. "They're on their way down, Captain," Julia reported. Vincent hoped the team would be useful at the base. He studied Andy and wished he had the same patience as the Rabanahian. "If it were my home world, I'd be impatient also," Andy said. "Can you read my thoughts?" Vincent asked. "No, I'm just very perceptive."

"Captain, we have an incoming message from Commander Evir," Isabella interjected. "Hopefully he has something new for us to do. Put him on the viewscreen please," Vincent ordered. "Greetings Captain. I appreciate the effort you've put forth in coordinating with the ground forces. I expect a final mission plan from the Alliance within the next few days. It's likely the Tactical Council will have found a way to destroy the Annunaki weapons on the planet. With that in mind, I have devised a mission for the Santa Maria and the vessels in Montana. Are you prepared to assist in the forthcoming battle?"

"We are more than ready, sir. What is our mission?" Vincent asked. "All Annunaki vessels are in orbit protecting the flagship and their leader Buxare. Your mission is to eliminate any remaining Annunaki and Kracian forces on the planet. You are to destroy their bases of operation. It's important to remember that our enemy will fight to the death. Do not engage in any combat on the ground until all their bases have been eliminated. Your orders are to destroy the enemy from the air. Once you eradicate their bases of operation, your orders are to land and liberate any humans in the area. Capture any unarmed or injured enemies. Defend yourself at all costs, but do not slaughter defenseless enemies," Commander Evir ordered.

"What are we to do with prisoners of war?" Vincent asked. "Any captured Annunaki or Kracians are to be temporarily imprisoned until they can be relocated. The Alliance has studied ways of increasing their moral comprehension. In time, it may be possible for our enemies to join the Alliance. Leadership believes peace might be possible in the future, therefore we will not kill helpless sentient lifeforms. Please coordinate with the team in Montana and prepare for your mission. A message to the entire fleet will be transmitted once I receive orders from the Tactical Council." Commander Evir ended the transmission.

"I don't like our mission. It feels like we've been left out of the battle to simply slaughter the remaining forces on the ground," Monique said. "The ground forces likely killed millions of people and they won't hesitate to kill more if they think it will serve their Empress," Isabella replied. "Commander Evir is using his resources wisely. He now has more vessels available to attack the Annunaki. The Santa Maria and the vessels from Montana conducting ground operations will free up more resources," Andy clarified. "We must trust the Commander and have faith in his training and experience. We don't have the knowledge or experience to question the decisions of the Alliance or Commander Evir," Vincent said.

"Thank God the Alliance sent down some specialists. I don't know how much more I could've taken," Enzo said. "He's your friend," President Louis replied. "I know, but I can't keep up with him. Randy is passionate about his work and he is the resident expert on Earth as far as spacefaring vessels are concerned. I'm simply relieved he has someone to talk to who might understand what he's saying. I can only nod my head in agreement so many times," Enzo replied. Randy got little rest after the team from the Alliance arrived. He followed the team from ship to ship learning as much as possible and asking any question that came to mind.

"We've received our orders from the Alliance. Do we have capable crews for all the ships?" Enzo asked. "We've been training people around the clock. These are untested ships with virgin crews. The Alliance team has been assisting and will also board the ships once the battle starts. We're moving forward as fast as possible," President Louis replied. "Are you prepared to follow the Alliance directive regarding prisoners of war?" Enzo asked.

"I'm not used to obeying orders; I'm used to giving them. It's been a long time since I've been given orders to obey, but I know my role in this new reality. It's against my military judgment, but I will abide the order. All personnel have been ordered to detain enemy combatants when possible. I've told them that failure to do so will result in court martial and a dishonorable discharge from the service," President Louis replied. "What sense does that make? The government has been destroyed and they are the last remaining members of the military."

"They are still committed members of the United States military. All of them took an oath and are trained soldiers with an obligation to duty. It still means something to them and it means something to me. If this is the last action of our military, we will do it right to honor all those who gave their lives for this country and this planet in the past. We may not have done everything right, but the United States tried to protect freedom," President Louis solemnly replied.

"Mister President, we have an incoming message from Commander Evir. The message will be broadcast to all Alliance vessels in the fleet," the communications officer reported. "Make sure all the ships here receive the message as well" President Louis replied.

Enzo and the President listened as Commander Evir's message was broadcast: "The biological devices placed on the planet by our enemy can be defeated from orbit with high energy weaponry. There will be a two second window after we fire on the devices in unison. Buxare will have two seconds to issue the order to detonate before our weapons destroy the bombs. Eighty-four ships will fire upon the forty-two devices to ensure redundancy and the destruction of these horrible weapons. Orders have now been sent to every vessel. Should the Annunaki detonate the devices within the two second window, Earth will be destroyed. The attack will begin in thirty minutes. Please keep your channels open as I attempt to contact our enemy."

Vincent and the crew of the Santa Maria listened to the message. "Jesus Christ. Everyone on Earth dies if they screw this up?" Monique said. "Two seconds is a very short time. It's unlikely the Annunaki will be able to respond so quickly," Andy mused. "I don't like it. All life on Earth will be extinguished if the Annunaki act quickly. It's one hell of a gamble," Vincent replied nervously.

Commander Evir felt more pressure than ever before. "Once communication with Buxare begins, prepare to fire on my hand signal. Request communication with Buxare now." he ordered. The Annunaki leader appeared on the viewscreen. "I've been authorized to discuss a settlement with your species. We must come to an agreement to resolve this issue," he stated "The Empress will bring this war to an end. She is all powerful and you are wasting my time. We will resolve this issue when all members of the Alliance are dead," Buxare replied. "Your Empress is a bitch, a weakling and guides a species of immoral idiots. You are a fool for following her." Evir held up his hand. "You follow the orders of a very incompetent leader."

Evir stood transfixed as someone attempted to get Buxare's attention. The words he chose distracted and angered her. "My Empress will take all your worlds and you will become her slave!" Buxare screamed at him. "Not today. What is the status of the devices on Earth?" Evir asked. "All devices have been destroyed," the tactical officer reported. "Your weapons on Earth have been disabled. The stalemate is over. Surrender now or die."

He watched as Buxare conferred with her crew. "We will never surrender!" she said defiantly. Commander Evir watched the viewscreen go black as the transmission ended. "Initiate the battle plan and tell all forces to fire at will," he ordered as he watched Alliance vessels converge and fire upon the Annunaki.

"Captain, Commander Evir has issued the order to engage the enemy." Maxis reported. The largest concentration of Annunaki and Kracians on Earth were in Las Vegas. Andy quickly descended and Isabella opened fire. "Make sure you don't fire on any of the hotels we've identified that are housing human slaves," Vincent reminded Isabella as he watched her unleash missiles into the ground floor of nearby hotels. The missiles inflicted complete damage. The Bellagio exploded in a massive fireball and collapsed into a burning pile of rubble. "Good riddance Sin City!" Isabella joyfully screamed. Within minutes there were only two hotels left standing. "Damn, that's a lot of death and destruction," Monique said. "Continue to fire upon the outlying areas and bring us to old downtown," Vincent ordered. The Santa Maria quickly destroyed all known structures housing the enemy. Within seconds the Santa Maria was over the Fremont area and Isabella unleashed the Santa Maria's firepower again. "I think that takes care of Las Vegas. Let's move on to our next target," Vincent commanded.

"Please provide an update on operations," President Louis ordered. "Our vessels are successfully continuing offensive operations in New York, France, Egypt, Russia, Iceland, China, Brazil and Australia. The ship in China is experiencing engine trouble and might need to make an emergency landing," Sargent Mathers reported. "Isn't that the ship Randy is on?" Enzo asked. "Yes, it is. Order the ship to land in a desolated area if an emergency landing is required.

What is the current estimate for the destruction of all targets on the planet?" President Louis asked. "It depends on the status of the ship in China. If the ship needs to make an emergency landing, our schedule will be delayed, but if the vessel remains operational our targets should be destroyed within four hours," Sargent Mathers responded. "I want to speak with the Captain of the ship in China," President Louis ordered. "I've lost contact, Mister President. It appears the ship has either crashed or made an emergency landing. The vessel was unable to travel to a remote location and has landed in the heart of Beijing. The ship was unable to destroy nearby targets before it landed. Our personnel are in enemy territory and in danger," Sargent Mathers reported. "Redirect the Santa Maria and the ship in

Russia to provide support and to rescue the crew," President Louis ordered.

"We have new orders, Captain. We are to assist one of the ships from Montana immediately. It has crash landed in China," Monique reported. "Andy, fastest possible speed to China. Do we have any additional information on the ship that crash landed?" Vincent asked. "Yes, the ship went down in enemy territory and is likely under attack," Monique replied. "Captain, I've contacted the ship. Randy Stedman is standing by," Isabella stated. "Randy, it's Vincent. What is your status." "We are under attack. There are hundreds of Kracians attacking our ship. We keep retreating and are closing bulkheads, but the enemy is onboard and continues to advance on our position!"

"How long until we reach China?" Vincent asked. "Thirty seconds," Andy replied. "Prepare missiles; we must destroy every lifeform near the downed ship," Vincent ordered. "Belay that order. Missiles are the wrong choice. Computer, identify and target all Annunaki and Kracian lifeforms. Prepare the cannons to fire upon all identified targets," Isabella commanded. "Why have you questioned my orders?" Vincent asked. "I'm sorry Captain, but she's taken the correct course of action; missiles could destroy the ship. The cannons are the better choice in this situation," Andy replied.

"Fire!" Isabella commanded. The computer fired and killed all Kracians and Annunaki outside of the vessel. "There are still twelve inside the ship and closing in on the position of the survivors," Monique relayed. "We don't have any options. Bring us down and prepare for combat. Gather your weapons and prepare to fight," Vincent ordered.

The Santa Maria landed and the crew prepared for combat. "Julia, stay on the ship, monitor communications and fire on the enemy if you get the chance. Let's go! The Annunaki will not be expecting reinforcements from the ground. We should be able to take them from behind," Vincent said.

The noise was overwhelming as the Kracians drilled through the last bulkhead on the downed vessel. Vincent and his team entered the ship and quickly made their way to Randy's location. Within a minute they entered a large room with many workstations. He motioned for his team to take cover. Thankfully, the Kracians were still focused on the drilling and hadn't seen them.

"Fire!" He commanded. He watched with satisfaction as Kracian soldiers dropped to the ground. The remaining enemy quickly fired back. "Take cover!" Andy shouted as he threw a stun grenade. Enemy fire stopped. Vincent didn't detect any movement and

171

approached the bulkhead door. "We are from the Alliance, please open the door," he said.

Randy was scared. When the ship crashed into enemy territory he retreated with the rest of the crew, but he knew it was only a matter of time. There were no options left. The drilling paused briefly and he heard weapons fire. It didn't take long before drilling recommenced. The bulkhead was breached and a lone figure appeared. "Jesus Randy, I thought you were our expert. How in the hell did your ship crash?" Vincent asked as he moved into the light. "Goddamnit, you scared the hell out of me. It's good to see you!" Randy smiled in relief and hugged his friend.

Vincent was pleased the mission worked out. He was still full of energy and walked down the street to a local park. He sent a report to Commander Evir updating him on the successful recovery of the crew from the downed vessel. He closed his data pad and quickly turned as he heard someone approaching, but as he turned it was too late. A large Kracian soldier quickly wrapped two hands around his neck. Vincent struggled and felt the short claws of the alien puncture his skin. He tried to scream and couldn't. The last image he saw was the alien's ugly sneering face.

The battle didn't unfold exactly as Evir hoped. Buxare committed her fleet to fight in the most suicidal way possible. He ordered a new course of action hoping to end the battle quickly. All ships would attack simultaneously and overwhelm the enemy fleet. When Alliance vessels opened fire, all Annunaki ships retreated toward the sun. Evir ordered a pursuit course and instructed all Alliance vessels to continue firing on the enemy ships. The Annunaki vessels were on course for a very dangerous encounter with Sol. "Order all ships to a full stop. What course are the Annunaki ships taking?" he asked.

"They are taking a low altitude slingshot course around the star. Only the flagship has taken a higher altitude and slower course. Before the enemy fleet went out of sight they were observed scooping hydrogen from the sun's atmosphere. When the enemy fleet reappears, the vessels will be traveling at tremendous speeds," the tactical officer reported. "And they will have acquired massive amounts of hydrogen aboard all their ships. Order the fleet to formation forty-nine and tell them fire at will when the Annunaki are within range. Instruct the entire fleet to stay as far away from the enemy ships as possible. The enemy vessels are now traveling bombs," Commander Evir ordered. "Shouldn't we retreat to empty space?" the tactical officer asked. "We cannot. Earth and Mars would be left unprotected and the Annunaki now have the ability to destroy both planets."

Death while defending the Empress was the greatest honor an Annunaki could achieve. Buxare bestowed the honor to her entire fleet. Every crewmember in her fleet was dead. All environmental suits were left on Earth. The lone exception were those assigned duty on her flagship. "Give me an update!" she ordered. "The atmosphere inside all ships are now a hydrogen and oxygen mix. All crewmembers are dead due to atmospheric contamination. We have automated control of navigation and weapons on all vessels. We will be in attack range momentarily."

Buxare would destroy as many of the inferior lifeforms as possible. "Very good. Ensure all ships are on collision courses with Alliance vessels and fire at will when the ships are within range. The last thing our enemies will see are the dead bodies of our brave warriors!" Buxare exclaimed.

Tactically, Commander Evir knew he made a mistake; he should have continued to pursue the Annunaki vessels around Sol. "The Annunaki ships have reorganized and are coming in fast. Prepare for attack," the tactical officer transmitted to the fleet. Evir knew the outcome before a weapon was fired. It came down to simple math and the Alliance had more ships than the Annunaki. Success was guaranteed, but it would come with a very high cost.

He quietly watched the viewscreen as Alliance ships stood their ground and fired as quickly as possible. Enemy ships were traveling much too fast. A few Annunaki vessels were destroyed before they reached their targets, but the destruction of the ships made no difference. The wreckage travelled at such high speed it sliced through the targeted Alliance vessels. The resulting explosions were immense, powerful and highly destructive. Very few Alliance vessels managed to maneuver quickly enough to avoid the incoming ships.

"Please provide a full report and begin search and rescue operations. I want details of the damage," Evir ordered. "Thirty-one percent of our fleet remains," the tactical officer reported. Evir failed miserably. The military council only estimated a ten percent loss. "Commander, the enemy flagship still remains. The vessel is near Sol and is undamaged," the tactical officer reported. "Order the ten closest ships to fire on the weapons systems of the flagship. I want Buxare alive."

Chapter 10

Buxare watched as Alliance vessels burned in space; her plan worked better than she anticipated. Upon arrival, the Empress would find a severely weakened opponent. "Enemy ships are approaching and firing," the tactical officer reported. "Return fire," Buxare ordered as multiple explosions rattled her ship. "We are unable to fire. All major weapons systems have been destroyed."

Buxare wouldn't be captured alive. She activated her personal ETS suit and took control of navigation. Sol wasn't far away. Buxare set a collision course with the star and engaged the engines at maximum speed. "What are you doing?" the tactical officer asked. "I'm serving the Empress," she replied and entered an emergency command. Hydrogen was added to the air onboard the ship; however, Buxare hadn't engaged safety protocols and the air quickly caught fire.

Safely inside her ETS suit, she watched as skin burned off the screaming crewmembers in the command center. She was the lone Annunaki remaining in the Sol System. Her ship was ablaze and would be consumed by the star within minutes. Buxare wondered why the Empress hadn't been successful as she turned off her ETS suit. Her scream of anguish was short.

Vincent awoke panicked and tried to reach for the alien hands around his neck. He couldn't move his arms. "Please remain calm. Your injuries have been repaired," a disembodied voice stated. He heard voices and closed his eyes. He didn't know what was going on and was confused. A new voice spoke out. "Vincenzo, I'm glad you followed my advice. If you hadn't associated with such honorable friends, you'd be dead," a familiar voice said. Vincent opened his eyes and saw a face from his childhood. "Uncle Enzo! What happened?" he asked. Monique suddenly appeared. "Luckily, Andy was following you. He killed the Kracian soldier and brought you back to the Santa Maria," she replied and kissed him gently.

The restraints retracted and Vincent stood and found Isabella and Andy in attendance. "Thank you, Andy. You saved my life." "I was just repaying a favor, Captain. You saved my life and I'm whole again."

"I've been told of everything that's happened and I'm proud of you, Vincenzo. You have honored Maria's memory and proven her theories correct," Enzo said as he hugged Vincent. "Thank you, Enzo. I couldn't have done it without your help. It's time to get back to work. What are our orders?"

A new voice rang out. "I've personally received your new orders from Commander Evir." Vincent was surprised as President Louis entered with Randy.

"What are my orders, President Louis?" Vincent asked. "You are to attend the victory celebration tonight. The war is over. Sol has been liberated. I was wrong about you and Enzo. You took a little too long, but I'm glad you brought back new friends." President Louis smiled warmly.

Vincent didn't know how to respond. He'd been waiting for this moment for so long. Tears flowed down his face and he needed to ask the question. "How many people on Earth survived the invasion?" he asked. "Approximately nine hundred million. Most were held as slaves to serve the invaders," President Louis replied. "We shouldn't have ever left. Almost ninety percent of mankind was wiped out. We could have fought the Annunaki," Vincent lamented. "One ship would have made no difference. What you accomplished on Vandi and with the Alliance was of much greater importance. It's time to celebrate!" Enzo exclaimed.

The base in Montana was transformed into a makeshift seat of government for Earth. The base was suddenly sprawling with visitors and Vincent counted members from at least fifteen distinct species mingling with humans at the base. "Isn't that Commander Evir's ship descending?" Monique asked Enzo as she pointed into the sky. "Yes, it is. Your President asked the Commander for a meeting. Let's join him on the tarmac and hear what he has to say. It should be very interesting."

Enzo, Vincent and Monique stood behind President Louis as Commander Evir disembarked and descended the ramp. "Welcome to Earth Commander. I'd like to thank you on behalf of humanity for all you've done. I'm sorry you encountered such heavy losses during battle," President Louis stated. "I was following my orders. The cost was high and we are continuing search and rescue efforts, but some survivors protected by emergency bulkheads have been found alive. Unfortunately, the vast majority of personnel inside the impacted vessels were killed.

Why did you request this meeting?" Commander Evir asked. "As far as I know, I'm the last remaining head of state on Earth. Our planet has been decimated. We have no infrastructure, no leadership and we are unable to self-govern or help the millions who have been displaced and are in need of food or shelter. I'm resigning my position as President and request the Alliance govern this planet for the foreseeable future." Enzo was impressed. It was unlike President Louis to give up total power under any circumstance.

"On behalf of the Alliance, I accept your formal request of assistance. You couldn't self-govern in the past under normal circumstances. Under these conditions it is an impossibility. Governance of your world was anticipated by Alliance leadership. Most of the personnel assigned to the task were killed in the battle; however, a replacement team is being assembled on Rabanah and will arrive within the next few weeks. Until then, I will coordinate with the people of this world and do my best to fulfill any needs that arise," Evir replied.

"Commander, what is currently being done to assist the remaining people of Earth?" Enzo asked. "The vessels not currently assisting with search and rescue operations in space have been redirected to the surface. The needs of the survivors are being assessed. Food, water and communication pads are in the process of being distributed and the remaining survivors will be given the tools to become self-sufficient. Alliance personnel will establish bases of operation where necessary on the surface to assist." Enzo was pleased. "It sounds like Earth is in very capable hands. Please come inside and enjoy some of the refreshments Earth has to offer." President Louis offered.

"It's been too long since we've really been given an opportunity to relax." Monique said as she took a drink of wine. "There's still a lot of work to do and we have a dangerous task ahead. Returning the Nalis could get very complicated," Vincent replied. "We'll be careful, but let's enjoy tonight. Most of our friends are here and we will be free of the Annunaki for the rest of our lives. There are no longer any gates for the Annunaki to travel through." Monique was joyful as she refilled her glass.

Vincent knew he wouldn't be able to completely relax until the Nalis was safely returned. He glanced around the room and saw Andy enjoying the company of fellow Rabanahians. Evir and President Louis appeared to be bonding and Isabella and Enzo were deep in conversation. "Enzo and Isabella have been talking for a long time. I wonder what they could possibly be discussing?" Vincent asked. "Isabella is probably just regaling him with all of our adventures. There are a lot of details he doesn't know about."

Enzo's discussion with Isabella left him pleased. Other than a few minor hiccups, the crew of the Santa Maria represented Earth quite well. He joined Commander Evir and President Louis. "What's going to happen now?" he asked Evir. "The child on Mars is demonstrating advanced intelligence and moral fortitude. The time has come for humans and Martians to join. Martian refugees from Vandi will be relocated to Earth and Mars based on their personal preference. Any humans on Earth who wish to be relocated to Mars will be allowed to do so. Mars will be terraformed as quickly as possible. Humans and Martians will soon be able to live together and reproduce on either planet. The Sol System has been secured and the Alliance will become stronger with your addition. Unless Zabu is an aberration, the hybrid species of Martian and human will rate highest on the morality scale."

"I don't understand. What is the morality scale?" President Louis asked. "All governments and societies can pass laws and punish injustice; however, such laws are only required because individuals within their societies lack a high sense of morality. A society rating high on the morality scale will require few, if any laws due to their ability to restrain from committing atrocities," Commander Evir explained.

"Are you telling us that humanity acts in a morally responsible manner?" Enzo asked incredulously. Commander Evir emitted a loud noise. Enzo guessed the alien was laughing. "Humanity has no morality. Your species can't make peace internally, let alone coexist peacefully with alien races. If it weren't for Martians, your species likely would never have been granted membership into the Alliance."

"Humans have the ability to identify immoral weaknesses in other species. If I hadn't recruited new allies, the Sol System would still be under control of the Annunaki. Sometimes moral sacrifices are necessary for the greater good," Vincent countered. "But at what cost?" Commander Evir stated and looked at Vincent knowingly. Somehow Evir knew about the Nalis and the Cardonians. "What do you know?" Vincent asked.

"I'm a military leader and receive regular intelligence reports. You'd be surprised how much I know. You are factually correct and yes, we gained new allies, but in the past these species were refused admission to the Alliance and refused our advances. I fear there will be a heavy price to pay for their assistance."

"The Alliance preaches morality. There are times when morality must be shown and demonstrated to an immoral species. You are correct, mankind on a whole is not very moral, but there are still passionate humans willing to risk their own destruction to prove we should be given a chance. The new allies of the Alliance assisted in saving Earth. Without humanity, this battle would have been lost," Vincent argued. "Do what you must to appease our new allies. Should they turn on the Alliance, there will be many questions. For now, we will bring humans and Martians together," Commander Evir replied.

The morning sunrise was beautiful. Vincent and Monique approached the Santa Maria and prepared for their mission to return the Nalis. "Welcome aboard Captain," Andy said as they entered the ship. "Thank you, Andy. You're up early today. Monique and I will be returning to Rabanah by ourselves. You are dismissed," Vincent ordered as he noticed Julia at the navigation console. "I don't think so, Vincenzo. You will complete this mission with the guidance and assistance of your friends. Besides, I'd like to see this beautiful planet Rabanah everyone speaks so highly of," Enzo said as he and Isabella stepped out from the shadows.

"I made a mistake and we must do this on our own. I won't endanger anymore lives. Please remain on Earth." Vincent said. "What you did was not a mistake and without the help of the Cardonians Earth and Mars might have been lost. The Alliance would never sanction what you did, but it was the right thing to do under the circumstances. Sometimes the ends justify the means. At any rate, we're not getting off this damn ship," Enzo stated forcefully.

"Very well, do so at your own risk. You've been warned. Andy, please set course for Rabanah. Let's get this over as quickly as possible. I'd like to get back to Mars, visit Dalton and see how the terraforming is progressing. Why isn't Randy here?" Vincent asked. "He's staying on Earth. The Alliance is going to station military vessels in the Sol System as the threat from the Annunaki remains. It will only take them a century or two to make it back. Military spacecraft will be built on both Earth and Mars, splitting the Alliance's fighting forces between Sol and Rabanah," Enzo explained. "We are on course for Rabanah. The Alliance is always preparing in one way or another for the Annunaki. The species is relentless," Andy interjected.

A red, dry world appeared and grew larger outside the window as the ship approached. "Is that it father?" Zanther asked. "Yes, this is the fourth planet from the star I showed you on the device. It's also our new home. We are now safe from the Annunaki and will live free for the rest of our lives." Maxis smiled down at his son. "What if we get thirsty? I don't see any water," Zanther asked. Maxis and Tissa both laughed. "Don't worry. We'll make sure you always have something to drink," Tissa replied.

The celebration on Mars lasted for days. Alixias always thought survival was unlikely and was amazed Mars was completely spared from the Annunaki. It was now time for a new celebration. "The population on Mars is about to quadruple. I would imagine you'll be happy to see other Martians again. When will they be here?" Patrick asked. "The ships have landed outside the pyramid, so the refugees from Vandi will be here any minute," Alixias replied.

Most everyone on Mars gathered in the underground courtyard. Conversations suddenly stopped and the room grew quiet as footsteps echoed down the corridor and the first Martian from Vandi appeared. Alixias smiled. Maxis was the first to enter, followed by Tissa and Zanther then hundreds more entered the chamber. Maxis approached a dais at the center of the courtyard after the last of the Martians entered. Alixias was informed protocol dictated Maxis was to be the first to speak. She decided to change it up a little and joined him.

"Ladies and gentlemen; I give you Maxis, the Ambassador for Mars. He's been representing the interests of our planet in the Alliance Council and he is also my friend," she said and hugged Maxis as everyone in the courtyard burst into applause.

"Thank you for welcoming us! This is the most historical day in the history of both Mars and Earth. It is an awakening for both of our species. We have learned that we can be greater together. The transformation has already begun and is destined to continue. This is the first step into our bold new future. Martians and humans have always been family. It is now time to unite and follow our destiny. To all my fellow Martians, welcome home!" Maxis said as he held out his arms. The courtyard once again erupted into applause.

"There you are. I was having trouble finding you in this crowd. It was a good idea to find a babysitter for Zabu. If the child were here, it would be a complete circus," Dalton said as he approached Patrick. "We didn't want to subject Zabu to so much attention. Do we have the resources to support so many Martians? I didn't think there'd by this many," Patrick asked. Dalton smiled at him. "The people from the Alliance have been working day and night and the transit system has been fully repaired. There are still unexplored underground portions of the planet. Total sections were completely blocked off and we didn't even know they existed until the Alliance arrived. Mars could support thousands of additional refugees. This is only the first group and many more will follow. Human volunteers from Earth will also be relocated. I've been told the terraforming abilities of the Alliance are astounding. In very short order, we will be able to breath the air and occupy the surface of the planet where food will be abundant."

"What about animal life? Mars must have more lifeforms than humans and Martians." "The Alliance was prepared. Remember the underwater pyramids at Lake Vida in the Antarctic and the one on Europa?" Dalton asked. "I remember; Vincent mentioned something about it. Why are they important?" Patrick asked. "The pyramids are biological warehouses for lifeforms. Any lifeform stored can be reproduced. All life indigenous to Mars will be reintroduced. Insects, bacteria, fish, birds, reptiles, mammals and many more I can't think of. The Alliance is reintroducing species that can produce oxygen first; it will speed up the terraforming effort. The first twenty-two species were reintroduced today." Dalton was visibly pleased with the Alliance's recent accomplishments.

The information was astounding. Mars would soon become a paradise. Patrick was about to ask another question when he glanced up at the dais. Alixias was surrounded by Martian women and the group was growing. The mother of his child appeared distressed. "Come with me. I need to get her out of here," Patrick instructed Dalton. "Excuse me please, it's time we returned to our child. We appreciate your questions and support," Patrick said as he reached Alixias. "Come on, let's go home." An authoritative voice intervened. "I'm Laxi and I'm here with my team to study Zabu. May I accompany you home?" she asked. Patrick was about to reply when Dalton intervened. "It's been a long day. Alixias and Patrick will return home to their child now. Your question will be addressed in the morning. I'm sure you can understand how such an emotional day must be put in the past before we can move forward," he said. "I understand and don't wish to be intrusive. We will speak tomorrow. Sleep well," Laxi replied.

"I'll escort you home in case anyone else tries to trouble you tonight. You were surrounded quickly; what were the Martians asking?" Dalton asked. Alixias breathed in deeply. "The questions centered around Patrick. With the birth of Zabu and our continuing cohabitation, the Martian females were curious. They wanted to know what it was like to have a human as a mate," Alixias said. "What did you tell them?" Patrick asked. "I told them the truth. Every relationship requires dedication, understanding, compassion and hard work. They were surprised when I told them human males were capable of being adequate mates." "Well, I'm glad adequate is good enough. Did they ask you anything else?" Patrick asked. Alixias hesitated before responding. "The rest of their questions were of a more personal nature."

The arrival of Martians was a relief for Patrick. He always felt guilty Alixias lived among aliens. Now she could interact with her own kind. A familiar aroma he hadn't smelled for months filled the air. "I missed you, old friend," he said out loud and took a drink of coffee. His enjoyment was interrupted by a chirp from his data pad. It was likely Dalton with his morning community update.

Patrick was taken aback by the surprising message. "I wish you would have taken me to the celebration." Zabu's message instantly made him feel guilty and question his parenting skills. He didn't want to respond without sharing the message with Alixias. He woke her up and showed her the message. "We will go to her now," Alixias replied.

"Zabu, we didn't want you to be overwhelmed by so many curious people," Alixias said gently. "You won't be able to protect me forever. There will be situations for me to learn from, but I understand your concern and am ready to meet with Laxi. Thank you for attempting to protect me." "You're welcome. How to you know of Laxi?" Patrick asked. "I know of him," Zabu simply replied.

Circumstances made Dalton the de facto leader of Mars. It was a position he didn't ask for or want. He did the best he could and the burden was now gone. Zabu's continuing education was no longer his responsibility either. Historical experts from the Alliance would quickly finish decoding the golden walls, so he decided to get back to what he enjoyed the most. Carefully, he swept dirt off the top of the object and gently dug along the edges. The solitude and work were welcome; it was what he liked and what he became accustomed to when he was on Earth.

"It looks like you've found something interesting." A voice from behind interrupted his solitude and Dalton stood and turned. A female Martian appeared out of nowhere. "I enjoy solitude and discovering history," he replied testily. "We are all on a quest for knowledge. I too enjoy uncovering the histories of ancient civilizations. My name is Spaxon. May I join you?" The choice was difficult; Dalton needed to decide between being selfish or diplomatic.

"Please join me. Perhaps the Alliance has techniques I'm unaware of. Did you seek me out specifically or did you come out to conduct your own research?" he asked. "On our way to Mars, I studied what was known about the personnel here. You have personally uncovered the work of a Martian genius, successfully delivered a hybrid child, decoded the golden walls and managed to keep this community from falling apart. You are a fascinating human."

"I'm flattered and impressed with your research, but I'm getting old and wish to be left alone. The future is important and you should find someone to have a future with," Dalton replied. "As far as Martian women go, I'm fairly old myself. You'd be surprised what the Alliance can do to extend life expectancy. Perhaps it's time you open your mind to new possibilities," Spaxon replied. The day suddenly become much more complicated. "Fine then. If you're really interested in helping, get down here and help me identify and remove this artifact."

Enzo wished he left Earth when the Santa Maria first departed. Space was beautiful and Rabanah was amazing. The Santa Maria docked and Enzo found a lone person waiting. There were no words. Beaming with pride, Enzo kissed and hugged Dominic. "I'm so proud of you. You have surpassed my expectations."

"It's good to see you, papa. Welcome to Rabanah."
Enzo spent the next four days exploring the planet and
catching up with his son. "It's now possible for us to
visit more often. Continue your work here for the
people of Earth and I will visit when I can. In time,
someone will be found to replace you and you'll be able
to come home. For now, I love you and will see you
soon." Enzo kissed his son and departed.

"What's your plan?" Enzo asked when he arrived
in the command center of the Santa Maria. "There are
two books. Each faction wishes to have both. If the
status quo is to be maintained, I must return one book
to each faction," Vincent replied. "You may have thrust
the Alliance into a new war. Neither faction will rest
until both books are in their hands. It's only a matter of
time before the Alliance finds out and must act. Your
involvement as an officer of the Alliance gives the
Cardonians a reason to declare war against us," Andy
stated.

"I no longer possess the books and have sent
them back to Cardonia in a small probe. While Tony
was on the planet he identified a group which isn't
beholden to the teachings of the Nalis. The books have
been sent to Salk, a rebel leader on Cardonia. We will
inform the Cardonian leaders of my actions. It's time to
go to Cardonia," Vincent ordered. "You're either bold

or reckless; I'm not sure which. Course has been set and we're on our way," Andy replied.

One of the centers of government on Earth was in Lincoln, Nebraska. Alliance leadership decided the area was well suited due to abundant agricultural resources. In addition, most buildings remained upright and undamaged after the Annunaki occupation. Alliance vessels descended from orbit in Lincoln. President Michael Louis and Randy watched as one of the vessels descended. "Jesus, those ships are majestic." Randy was in awe as the ships landed and passengers began to disembark. "I never would have thought something like this was possible. So those are Martians? I'm not so convinced about this supposed grand plan of the Alliance. Where is the evidence showing it's in the best interest for humans and Martians to interbreed? What if it's really a grand plan to conquer humanity?" President Louis asked. "Let it go Michael. It's time for some trust and faith. We've been liberated," Randy replied. "Since when do you call me Michael? I'm the President." Randy thought about the question for a few seconds. "What exactly are you the President of? You were the last and it's over." he replied. "I guess you have a point. Michael will be fine from now on. Maybe I'll research the grand plan and see how I can help, but for now it's time for me to find a new purpose. Let's go meet these

Martians." And with that, the final and former President of the United States set forth to meet the new inhabitants of Earth.

Randy and Michael arrived at the welcoming ceremony and patiently waited as Commander Evir finished his speech. "What happens now?" Randy asked. "The Martians will integrate into society. Housing has been prepared and they will be assigned jobs suitable to their individual skills. In the short term, our focus will be to grow enough food for everyone and ship some of it to Mars. We currently have seven transports traveling between Earth and Mars daily. The number will likely increase as both worlds adapt and grow. Martians are hard workers and will be an asset on this planet, obviously as slaves on Vandi their knowledge was very limited. Here education will be a big part of their daily lives," Commander Evir replied.

"Socially, how is this supposed to work? Is everyone just supposed to suddenly find a mate somehow?" Michael asked. "It's not that simple. For some, the process might go quickly; for others it will take years, decades, or it may never happen. There will be no forced relationships. Your two species will begin to interact socially and the inevitable biological outcome will take place. Alliance specialists will be available to assist with any initial concerns or problems."

"Randy has a task to assist with shipbuilding. I would like to study the history of humans and Martians to comprehend the grand plan. Can you help with this request?" Michael asked. "Certainly, you will be assigned an advisor and given the resources to conduct your studies," Evir replied. The burden of command was gone and it was a welcome relief. Learning why the two species from Sol were meant to unite would hopefully give him the peace to relinquish his authority over humanity.

"Captain we are being approached by twenty-five heavily armed Cardonian ships," Isabella reported as the Santa Maria entered orbit around Cardonia. "Please make contact with Olube and Ekraq," Vincent commanded. "Are we going to survive this?" Enzo asked. "They think I'm here to return the Nalis. We'd be destroyed the moment the books are returned. I threatened them and told them Tony would come back and steal them again. Once they get the books back security will be increased tenfold and Tony won't have a chance. This is our only option," Vincent replied as Olube and Ekraq appeared on the viewscreen.

"Human, we upheld our part in the arrangement. Thousands of lives were lost when we liberated your planet. Return the sacred texts now," Olube demanded. "On behalf of the people of Earth, I thank all

Cardonians and their families for sacrificing so many in this cause. I sincerely appreciate what you've done to free the people of Sol. The Nalis has already been returned to your people and I've upheld my end of our arrangement. I believe our business is concluded."

"What are you talking about? I have not received anything! Did you return both books to Olube?" Ekraq angrily replied. "I have not received anything either! Where are the sacred texts?" Olube demanded. Vincent was amused and enjoyed watching his adversaries become angry and confused.

"Remember when you captured me and attempted retribution? Your disrespect was noted and I've decided a new course of action is required. There is a segment of your population that does not believe in the Nalis. I returned the books to one of the local leaders. You and Ekraq are only united on one issue: killing in the name of religion. It is morally repugnant and disgusting. It's time for you to listen to a different voice from a member of your own species. You are now free to resume your internal war without interference. Keep in mind, however, that I'm the only one who knows exactly where the Nalis was sent. If you are unable to find the ancient texts within a year, I will come back and give you a location to search. For now, I suggest you begin negotiating with local rebel leaders. We will be leaving now." Vincent said.

"Give us a moment to discuss this new development." Ekraq was clearly indignant as the viewscreen went blank. "So, they're deciding on whether or not to kill us I guess," Monique said. "Vincenzo's gamble was a good one. I'm confident we'll survive. They won't kill the only person who has knowledge of where the Nalis was sent," Enzo replied as Olube reappeared on the viewscreen.

"You are to surrender at once. Your ship will be boarded and you will be tortured until you reveal the location of the sacred texts." Ekraq demanded. "I will take a few minutes to discuss your offer my crew." Vincent was incensed. "Isabella end transmission! Fuck! That's not what was supposed to happen! What are we going to do now?" he asked. "You must call their bluff. Do what must be done," Enzo replied sternly.

Everyone aboard the Santa Maria looked at him expectantly. A difficult decision needed to be made. Vincent took a breath and momentarily closed his eyes. "Resume communication with Olube," he ordered. "We will begin the boarding process shortly, human. Your internal discussions have no bearing on our actions." the alien said. "Very well. I hope you enjoy the vessel. We will not be captured alive. All airlocks in this ship will open in ninety seconds. There are no records regarding the whereabouts of the Nalis aboard this vessel or with any of my crewmembers. I retain the only knowledge of where the Nalis was sent. You need to understand that we will not be tortured or die at your hands. You will not recover the information under any circumstances," Vincent replied passionately.

"Do you not value self-preservation? Once we have the information you will be released," Olube replied. "You and Ekraq are depraved and cannot be trusted. Our airlocks open in twenty-three seconds." The Cardonian leader quickly conferred with someone offscreen. "We will allow you to leave. Do not open your airlocks. You are to return in one year if the Nalis hasn't been found," Olube said.

"Do not pursue us. If this vessel is attacked, I will open all airlocks immediately. Pause countdown and set a return course to Rabanah. Get us the hell out of here as fast as possible!" Vincent ordered. "Countdown has been paused and we are on course for Rabanah," Andy replied.

The Santa Maria was in empty space and there were no Cardonian ships in pursuit. "Captain, I have an incoming message from Olube," Isabella relayed. "Put it on the viewscreen." he said. "All Cardonian diplomats have been recalled from Rabanah. Any Alliance vessel approaching Cardonia will be destroyed in the future. The Captain of the Santa Maria will be hunted down, tortured and killed once the Nalis has been recovered. The leaders of Cardonia will no longer negotiate with the Alliance. This is the only warning the Alliance will receive." Olube ended the transmission.

"Jesus, that was close. Would you really have opened the airlocks?" Monique asked. "I would have ordered the computer to open the airlocks if it really came down to it, but I'm not even sure if the computer would do it. It's probably against safety protocol," Vincent replied as Andy spoke up.

"I was prepared to open the airlocks when the countdown ended. The navigator is responsible for opening airlocks should the command be issued. The order is active and the countdown is paused at seven seconds. Would you like to cancel the countdown?" "Yes Andy, please cancel the order at once." Vincent quickly replied. "Jesus Christ. I think we need to work on our communication. I'm going to get a drink," Julia said and was out the door before anyone could reply.

The flagship was unbelievably massive. Empress Zovad ensured her personal ship was opulent and intimidating. It took considerable time for Tony to explore all the nooks and crannies of the large vessel. He now knew where to study the enemy and where the scientists conducted their work. What the Empress wanted to accomplish appeared to be impossible. The Annunaki possessed technology mankind could only dream about, but they did not have the knowledge of the bygone ancient species who created the gates. The scientists came up with dead end after dead end and Tony studied the data himself and could find no solution.

One group of scientists was tasked with trying random combinations and variables using dark matter and other exotic substances. So far, the guesswork didn't produce any tangible results. Tony watched as another test failed. The Empress made good on her word and killed many of the scientists who failed her. The tests were getting more desperate and looked as if they'd go on forever. A workable solution appeared to be beyond the Annunaki scientists.

Tony continued to study how the shields protected the Empress. He wasn't even sure why she needed shields as her people worshipped and adored her. The solution to the shield problem was his last obstacle. He had a plan in place to kill the daughter of the Empress and learned where the new emergency rearing facility was located.

When he learned of the tactical situation, he knew it was time to exercise patience. After discovering how to access the communication records on the ship, he learned there was no longer an active threat to the Sol System. He cried tears of joy when he learned Earth and Mars were completely liberated. Knowing his friends likely survived the invasion was a great relief.

The consciousness that briefly touched his mind hadn't returned, but he wished it would. The mind was friendly and he was lonely. Reaching out with his mind didn't produce any results and it was possible contact would never be made again. Tony now had more time than he would ever need. He made progress on the shielding problem and believed he understood all the details. He could take as much time as he needed, but soon there wouldn't be anything new to learn.

Chapter 11

Dominic was at the space dock and was angry. The Cardonian diplomats departed suddenly and the Alliance was told in no uncertain terms not to approach the planet or attempt communication. The secret that was being withheld cost the Alliance a very valuable ally. He didn't wait for the crew of the Santa Maria to exit and boarded the ship as soon as it landed.

"What the hell is going on? We've lost an important military ally," he asked when he arrived in the command center. Vincent sighed heavily. "Have you told anyone else we might be involved with the Cardonians?" he asked. "No, I haven't shared the very little that I know. Enough with this business of you trying to protect me. I need to know what's going on!" "When you resign your position as Ambassador, I will share every detail with you. For now, the information cannot be shared," Vincent replied. "That is no longer good enough. You do realize as an Ambassador I outrank you and can review the records of this vessel?" Dominic stated testily.

"Son, you will not do that. Listen to Vincenzo. He is correct. You have matured greatly and taken on a massive responsibility since you left Earth, but you must have faith and trust in my judgment and that of Vincenzo. Tonight, let's forget about the Cardonians and enjoy the company of family and friends. Tomorrow we're leaving for Mars and I'd like to spend some time with you." Dominic sighed and rolled his eyes. "You're all a pain in my ass. Come on then, let's go get something to eat."

The lost city was fascinating. Dalton recently uncovered the remains of the oldest Martian specimen to date. Upon initial inspection, he found the skeletal remains to be smaller and slightly different from modern Martians. "Very interesting. Is this the first time you've found any physical variations?" Spaxon inquired. Dalton was warming up to the Martian female. She shared his interests and he found her to be a kindred intellectual. "Yes, it is. I think it's now safe to bring the remains back for further study. Let's pack up and return to the pyramid," he replied. "We've accomplished much today and I'm ready for some rest. It's beautiful isn't it?" Spaxon said.

Dalton didn't know what she was talking about until he glanced up and saw she was looking at the horizon. In the distance, he saw small patches of green dotting the landscape. "What is it?" he asked. "It's algae and it's part of the terraforming process. This planet will soon be vibrant and colorful."

It wasn't easy for Patrick to convince Alixias to allow Laxi and her team access and time to study Zabu.

The newly arrived experts from the Alliance finished spending another three hours with the child and Alixias grew frustrated. "What is the purpose of all this testing? I will not allow my child to become an ongoing experiment to entertain the Alliance," she gruffly informed Laxi. "When we arrived, one of our team members made telepathic contact with Zabu, but since the initial contact Zabu has been unwilling or unable to use her ability. From what I've been told, Zabu is likely a very strong telepath, perhaps stronger than anyone we've ever encountered. We are trying to uncover the problem."

"I insist you spend no more than one hour a day with Zabu from this point forward. Family life and normalcy is required," Alixias demanded. "Your request will be followed. We are no longer receiving any new data from our most recent tests, so my team will enter a phase where we only observe. In time, we will have new subjects to study as well," Laxi replied.

Alixias was confused. "What do you mean?" she asked. "You should follow the daily updates," Laxi said as she departed. When Alixias arrived home with Zabu she found Patrick sleeping. "Wake up. Have you checked any of the daily updates lately?" "No, I haven't checked. I'll do it now," Patrick groggily replied. Alixias waited impatiently for the latest information. "Oh my God. We've missed quite a bit in the last few days. There are two new pregnancies reported on Mars and seven more on Earth! Zabu will soon have company."

"I can't believe it. It took us so long to conceive Zabu. I guess it's easier than we thought," Alixias said. "There are a lot more people trying now, so I'm sure the numbers will increase daily. There is one more item of interest. Terraforming is proceeding as expected and is slightly ahead of schedule. It has been calculated that water will begin flowing shortly. Shallow seas will soon form and rivers will begin to flow," Patrick shared. "That was expected, so I don't understand why it was included in the update." "Well, the nearby river is expected to bring the remains of Ambassador Mox into the sea in approximately five days," Patrick replied. "We will honor her and be present when the waters arrive," Alixias said determinedly.

The recovered bones of the ancient Martian were safely stored and Dalton returned to his quarters. He thought about asking Spaxon to share a meal, but he was too tired. More pregnancies were reported in the daily update as he listened to the report and prepared for bed. Martians and humans were successfully procreating. If he wasn't so tired, the information would have kept him awake half the night, but he fell asleep without a second thought on the matter.

The pounding on the door slowly woke him up. He looked at the clock and found he'd only been asleep for two hours. "Goddamn it, hold on! I'll be right there. This better be damn important!" When he opened the door, he found Patrick standing with a goofy smile on his face. "It's late. What do you want?" "An Alliance ship is about to land," Patrick said. "Alliance ships come and go all the time now. Why are you waking me up for this one?" Dalton asked. "It's the Santa Maria. Our friends have returned."

The planet was very different. Small patches of blue and green stood out amongst the orange and red. "The last time we were here our ship crash landed. Let's hope for a different outcome this time," Vincent said. "We've been given permission to land inside the pyramid whenever you're ready, Captain," Isabella reported. "Take us down Andy," Vincent ordered. As the Santa Maria descended toward Cydonia, Vincent watched as the side of the pyramid opened. "That's amazing. I didn't have the chance to appreciate it when we left." Andy carefully maneuvered the Santa Maria into the entrance and landed the ship where it was originally found.

The door opened and a smiling face greeted Vincent. "It's good to see you're still alive. I've missed you, Dalton." "It took you long enough to come back!

Did you think our trip to Old Snowy Mountain would ever lead to this?" Dalton replied. "Never in my wildest dreams. I think it's safe to say we proved all of Maria's theories correct. Tell me what's going on around here." Vincent grabbed Dalton and pulled him in for a bear hug. "I think we should all go somewhere and relax. There's a lot to cover."

For the next few hours, Dalton shared all the discoveries including the terraforming progress and the information about Zabu. "What's happened here is amazing, but if you hadn't uncovered the research of Salkex, the Alliance would have lost the war. The experts are certain Zabu is telepathic?" Vincent asked. "Yes, they are very certain. It's probable all hybrid children will share the ability. I've spent some time with the girl; she is very advanced for a child."

"The new hybrid species is supposed to be an improvement over humans and Martians?" Enzo asked. "I'm not sure if improvement is exactly the right word. It's expected the new species will be different in many ways. Zabu has shown to be highly intelligent for her age. The hybrid species will hopefully combine the best of both species. Intelligence, morality, mental discipline and physical strength are all expected to improve, but I think the best attribute humanity is contributing is our ability to act when necessary. Martian history has shown that the Martians were often too timid and took morality to an extreme when threatened. We'll learn a hell of a lot more in the coming years. We all better get some sleep. The ceremony for Ambassador Mox is set to take place in fifteen hours," Dalton replied and succumbed to a huge yawn.

Vincent was exhausted, but didn't want to go to sleep yet. He was curious and spent the next few hours exploring as much as possible. It was surprising how much was accomplished by the small group of humans despite their lack of resources and technology. There was one last place he needed to visit before he went to bed. It took him twenty minutes to get there and when he entered the chamber he placed his hands on the golden walls. "Is there something I can help you with Captain?" a nearby voice startled him. He interrupted an Alliance historian working on the wall. "No, I just wanted to come back and take a look. So much work and time went into documenting the early history of Mars; it's good to know all the work wasn't done in vain," Vincent shared. "Dalton often speaks of you and I envy you both. To find such an amazing piece of history is a once in a lifetime achievement," the historian replied. "Dalton deserves all the credit. He came back to Mars and made a real difference. I look forward to reviewing the remaining history you are uncovering. Have a good night," Vincent replied as he left.

Alixias woke up and was content. The ceremony for Ambassador Mox would finally conclude properly in the ancient tradition. "How do we know the water will arrive at the time we've been given?" she asked. "The engineers have erected a small dam so the water can be released according to schedule," Patrick replied. "Very well. This will be a good life lesson for Zabu. She will see that every beginning eventually has an ending."

Vincent activated his ETS suit after he was properly dressed. "Pretty soon we won't need the suits on this planet. Terraforming is ahead of schedule," Monique said. "And in time we will be obsolete. The hybrids will become the dominant species on both planets. It's a difficult concept and I'm having trouble wrapping my mind around the thought of it."

"It's destiny. The creation of the hybrids was predetermined. You're just afraid of change," Monique responded. "I think you're right, but what if there are others who feel the same way? We shouldn't be forced into this." "The Alliance seems to be a very accommodating organization. I would imagine that groups of humans and Martians who wish to remain independent will be allowed to do so. I'm sure suitable planets exist where such colonies could be established. For now, how about we go pay our respects to Ambassador Mox?" Monique asked.

The shores of the empty river bed were occupied by thousands of Martians and humans. Alixias previously presided over the ceremony for Ambassador Mox. There wasn't any protocol for a situation like this. She decided a few more words would be appropriate to honor Mox. The Alliance provided a platform and a loud speaker to transmit her words. "The dedication of Ambassador Mox is one of the reasons we are free. If it wasn't for her lifetime of work, determination and dedication, the hybrids wouldn't exist. The rebirth of Mars has begun. She will continue the cycle of life."

A small trickle of water began flowing down the riverbed. The volume of water quickly increased and pushed up against the block of ice encasing Ambassador Mox. It took a few minutes before the water rose high enough to move the ice. The tomb gently rose from the surface and made the short journey to the new sea.

"It was a good service. A proper sendoff for someone who accomplished so much," Enzo said after returning to the Santa Maria. "She was an amazing woman and it's a shame only a few of us had the honor of meeting her. She persevered through the hardest of times for her people," Vincent shared as Dalton boarded the ship. "A celebration is taking place in the courtyard for Ambassador Mox," Dalton said. "She lived a life worth celebrating," Julia added.

Dalton couldn't remember the last time he was surrounded by so many friends. He sat at a table with Vincent and the crew of the Santa Maria. Patrick, Alixias and Zabu were also present. He raised his glass. "A toast to Alixias. She honored Ambassador Mox in Martian custom." Everyone raised a glass and complimented Alixias. The conversation grew more relaxed and turned to the terraforming of Mars. "Oxygen levels are increasing at an exponential rate and the atmosphere will soon be breathable for everyone, including the hybrid children," Dalton replied to a question.

"I don't like being called a hybrid," a small voice rang out. Everyone looked at Zabu, who had been sitting quietly. "I am a child of Sol. My species will be known as Solian," she stated. The room quickly went silent. "As you wish, Zabu. Your species will be called Solian from this day forward. We didn't mean to offend you," Alixias softly responded. "Thanks Mom," Zabu replied with a confident smile.

Bedlam erupted in the village. Salk was trying to keep order, but it was proving nearly impossible. An alien device fell from the sky and created hysteria within the community. He held up the clear box containing the Nalis for all to see and a sense of dread and fear spread throughout the village. After hours of pleading, he managed to convince everyone to stay. "We will be slaughtered! Ekraq and Olube will torture and kill everyone to recover the Nalis," a young villager wailed. "We have their most prized possession and I will hold it ransom. Prepare the fire pit for a massive fire. If they kill us, we'll take the Nalis into the afterlife," Salk vowed.

Ekraq and Olube stopped working and cooperating after their latest encounter with Vincent. Each wanted to recover both ancient texts required to make the Nalis whole. Ekraq was surprised by how many villages of non-believers there were. He ordered his soldiers to torture villagers until they revealed the location of the Nalis. Once it was determined the villagers had no knowledge of the Nalis, they were executed as non-believers. So far, the results were discouraging. If Olube succeeded and he failed, the results would be catastrophic; all his followers would join with Olube. He ordered more soldiers to search.

Salk hadn't been able to sleep. He'd spent the night and early morning trying to decide what to do. By sunrise he decided upon a plan and met with the villagers at breakfast. "Everyone is to pack and prepare for evacuation. You should go to the mountain caves and prepare to defend yourselves. The situation is graver than I initially thought and it's only going to get worse. I'm responsible for what's happened. Tony had the Nalis when he was here. He knew we are rebels and returned the Nalis to me. I will remain behind and deal with Ekraq or Olube. I require ten volunteers to assist me with a task for the next hour, then all volunteers will leave when the task is complete."

Fifteen people volunteered and Salk selected the ten strongest. "We will prepare the fire pit for the largest fire we've ever had. Gather as much dry wood as possible. At the bottom of the pit we will place a tub containing vehicle fuel. I want to have a hot explosive fire available at a moment's notice. Put some flat pieces on top so I'll be able stand over the pit," he ordered.

After the pit was prepared, the last of the villagers retreated to the mountains. Salk climbed the large pile of wood and waited. After waiting most of the day, he dozed off at sunset. Sleep wasn't easy on the solid surface. He suddenly jolted upright. Was it a real sound or something he dreamt which woke him? Salk wasn't sure as he took in his surroundings. As his eyes adjusted to the pale moonlight, he could see soldiers quietly searching the empty homes of the villagers.

Calando would be a hero if she could recover the Nalis. For days she searched the countryside in vain with no success. The empty village caught her by surprise. She hadn't encountered any empty villages during her previous searches. All signs indicated this village was occupied only hours ago. A sudden shout from a soldier brought her out of the home she was searching.

All her soldiers were looking in the same direction and she followed their gaze. A lone figure stood high in the darkness holding a flaming torch. A voice suddenly rang out. "I have the Nalis. The leader of your group is to approach. Everyone else is to retreat. Failure to follow my instructions will result in the destruction of the sacred books."

The solitary figure raised something into the air. Calando zoomed in and analyzed the object with her visor. The analysis indicated there were ancient texts inside the container. She activated the live feed to Ekraq and ordered her soldiers back. "You have a very simple choice: hand over the Nalis or be killed. Come down from there and give me what you have."

Salk expected such a response. His demands were very simple. "I will hand over the Nalis once I share my message with everyone on Cardonia. Once my message has been shared, I will give you the ancient books. Failure to meet my demands will result in the destruction of the Nalis."

Ekraq watched the scene unfold in the small village. At long last, the Nalis would finally be his. He would soon achieve victory and Cardonia would become united under his reign. A speech from a non-believer would have no lasting impact once he had the

Nalis. He sent instructions to Calando to broadcast the lone villager's message planet wide.

Every screen on Cardonia displayed the same message. "Ekraq has found the Nalis. Prepare for unification and stand by for a blasphemous speech from a non-believer." Calando was instructed to broadcast immediately and recover and return the Nalis as quickly as possible. "Your demands have been met. We are now broadcasting live across all of Cardonia," she said.

Salk didn't know if the leader spoke the truth. In the end, it didn't matter. He would follow through with his plan. He removed the Nalis from the protective case. "Ekraq and Olube have you killing each other over ownership of these ancient texts. Those before them did the same. Countless lives have been lost over generations, but it ends today. I first decided I would hold these books hostage to spread my message and guarantee the safety of my friends, but I've decided the unification of Cardonia is more important. It's time to quit fighting amongst ourselves. I ask you all to hold our religious leaders responsible if they fail our species," Salk said as he dropped to his knees and held out the Nalis.

The inconsequential speech from the villager meant nothing in the grand scheme. Ekraq was ecstatic and watched as Calando climbed up to retrieve the

Nalis. He would soon be the most powerful person on Cardonia. Finally, ultimate power was within his grasp.

Salk watched the soldier slowly ascend the pit to accept the Nalis. He raised the torch high into the night sky. He jumped off the small platform and fell halfway through the broken logs and landed hard. The torch burned bright and he ignited the dry wood nearby. Fire slowly began to build. He looked up as the soldier reached the pinnacle. "Give me the Nalis," the soldier hissed and reached down. "Go get it!" Salk yelled and let out a primordial scream. A look of horror appeared on the soldier's face as the torch and the Nalis landed in the tub of fuel. Salk smiled for the last time.

Ekraq was celebrating when the triumphant broadcast was suddenly interrupted by an explosion. "What happened?" he screamed. He watched in horror as the events replayed. "This is what we must do. We tell everyone it was hoax. It was only a copy of the Nalis. The original texts are still out there!" Silence filled the room as his guards approached. "There will be chaos, but you are to protect me at all costs. Transmit my message!" he ordered in sheer panic. His most trusted guard told everyone to leave. As Ekraq began to speak, the guard pulled out a blade and he knew what was to come. He was thankful his guard would make it quick. He failed his followers and they would have tortured him if given the chance. He stood motionless as the blade swung through the air.

Enzo never liked to admit he was overweight, so it made sense that his favorite feature of Mars was the lower gravity. He could really feel a difference and was enjoying the strange and unique environment. As he walked toward the Santa Maria he tried to understand why Isabella recalled the crew. He was the last to arrive in the command center.

Isabella didn't waste any time. "We've received an encrypted communication from Dominic." Vincent knew Ambassadors could speak privately with those they represented. "I think this is the first time Dominic has sent an encrypted message. I wonder what he doesn't want the Alliance to see?" Vincent asked. "Let's quit wondering and play the damn message," Enzo said.

Dominic appeared on the viewscreen. "The attached video was recorded by a stealth surveillance satellite in orbit around Cardonia. Ekraq and Olube are dead and the planet is in chaos. I'm not sure if this was part of your plan or not, but I think you'll find the video quite interesting."

The crew of the Santa Maria watched the recorded news broadcast from Cardonia. Vincent was disappointed at the headline. "So, Ekraq recovered both books. I was hoping they would be kept separate," he said. "Sshhh!! Let's see what happens," Monique interjected. The explosion caught everyone by surprise. "Holy shit! I can't believe it. The Nalis has been destroyed," Vincent said. "Yes it has, and your enemies are dead. With chaos reigning on Cardonia, your actions will not be remembered. Blame has been squarely placed on the religious leaders of the planet," Monique stated.

"I'm not so sure about that. There were others on Cardonia who were aware of what I did. What will happen on the planet now?" Vincent asked. "The enlightenment of the people will take a leap forward. Based on the history of other planets, the people of Cardonia will become more spiritual. They will become less focused on who's version of worship is better. The remaining religious leaders will either be killed or become outcasts. After centuries of fighting, the Cardonians will unite. Your plan wasn't endorsed by the Alliance, but it benefitted the people of Cardonia enormously," Andy said.

Vincent rolled his eyes and glanced at Enzo. "Yes, it worked out exactly as planned," he deadpanned. "May luck favor the brave and the foolish," Enzo said and let out a hearty laugh.

Vincent left the Santa Maria quickly. He needed someone to talk to, but didn't want to confide in any of his crew. He found Dalton and shared the story of the Nalis and Cardonia. "I didn't even know what I was doing. The Alliance wouldn't have ever done something so crazy. I was only trying to help liberate Earth and Mars. I really just wanted to stay out of trouble."

Dalton couldn't remember the last time he'd seen Vincent so unnerved. "I would agree that your primary concern was to help Earth and Mars. Protecting yourself is natural and self-preservation is an obvious necessity for any species. You approved the mission to capture the Nalis. Once the war was over, you could have reestablished the status quo and divided the Nalis. It would have been the easiest of solutions, yet either consciously or unconsciously, you chose the high ground. And as a result, the Cardonians might finally find peace now. They are hopefully done fighting amongst themselves and can now focus on a peaceful and unified future. In the heat of the moment, what you did was right."

Vincent appreciated Dalton's support and his perspective. He always believed he was trying to stay one step ahead of trouble and perhaps the Cardonians would benefit from what happened. "Thank you. As always, your counsel and advice are welcome. I'll think about what you've said.

What's the latest with Zabu?" he asked. "She's walking now and suddenly quite inquisitive. I think she understands she's the first of her kind and wants to learn as much as possible," Dalton replied.

It was an unseasonably warm day on Vandi and the water was refreshing. Gly was happy for his people. All the invaders were gone and the planet was no longer occupied. His species didn't have any great aspirations. Living in peace and having ample food was enough. A storm appeared on the horizon and it was approaching quickly. He looked more closely and realized it wasn't a storm. Sunlight suddenly disappeared as a massive flock of Strithu eclipsed the sky. Gly hadn't ever seen so many of the birds in one place. He thought he knew all the leaders, but he didn't recognize the one leading the massive formation.

The lead Strithu was the largest and oldest he'd ever seen. It was unusual for a bird to have so many grey hairs. When the giant creature landed, Gly noticed something in her pouch. A mammal tumbled out onto the ground. "It has been protected. Care for it and teach it. We will be watching," the old bird communicated as it quickly flew away and regrouped with the formation.

Gly couldn't remember ever observing a Strithu acting in such a manner. He looked at the mammal; it was unlike any other he'd seen before. He learned the languages of both humans and Martians, but the mammal didn't respond to either language even though it resembled both species. With no other choice, he opened his mind.

A half day later, Gly regained consciousness. The mammal's mind was stronger than anything he'd ever encountered and it rendered him unconscious. The attempt at contact was forcibly denied and overwhelmed his brain. The creature huddled in the corner of the ice cave shaking. Gly tried to clear his head. "Build a fire. Our new friend is cold," he ordered to those who gathered. Gly wouldn't underestimate the mammal again and hoped communication could still be possible. The mental power of the creature was frightening.

The fire warmed the cave and the unusual mammal stopped shaking. Food and water were provided and many Volmer came to observe the creature who still hadn't moved or eaten. "Everyone out. Let's give him some privacy. Go back to your normal activities and stay away from the cave. I will summon you if I require assistance," he ordered.

Gly decided to observe the mammal from a distance and waited for him to exit the cave. After a few hours, the strange creature peered out of the cave and cautiously took in his surroundings. After making sure nobody was nearby, Gly watched the animal remove branches from nearby trees and bring them inside the cave. As it grew dark, an orange glow emanated from the cave. Gly was about to go to sleep when the intruder reemerged with a spear. The creature ran towards the ocean and jumped in. Seconds later he clambered back ashore with a large fish on the end of the spear. The mammal was physically fit and resourceful. Gly estimated it to be a young adult.

For the next ten days, Gly continued to observe the intruder in plain sight. Each day he ventured a little closer and on the eleventh day, Gly joined the mammal gathering wood and followed him back inside the cave. He made sure the translation unit was active. "Can you understand me? What's your name?" Gly asked as he sat on the floor. The creature stared intently into the fire. "I understand. My name is Keeras."

"You are safe here. We do not mean you any harm. Are there others like you? Where did you come from?" Gly asked. "There are no others. When I escaped, the Strithu brought me to an isolated location. On the southern coast, I built an underground shelter near the ocean," Keeras replied. "How did you escape and who are your parents?" Gly asked.

Keeras continued to stare into the fire and gathered his thoughts before responding. "It's difficult for me to talk about. My father was a Martian and my mother a human. The Annunaki brought in humans and Martians from the camps and conducted many experiments. There were more of my kind before me.

Empress Zovad visited and immediately ordered the death of all hybrid offspring. Nobody really knew why and I was very young. An old Kracian female called Xara brought me to her home."

"What happened after that?" Gly asked. "There were no more children and Xara never let me leave the home. She showed me videos of my parents and I was allowed to watch some of the experiments. I planned to bide my time and rescue them when given the chance. One day Xara told me the Empress would be visiting for a special occasion.

I watched in person when Empress Zovad decreed that humans and Martians were no longer allowed to interact. She then commanded all remaining test subjects be brought before her. All were restrained and their eyes were removed. She personally killed everyone including both of my parents. That same night I climbed to the roof. My life was no longer worth living. As I prepared to jump, a Strithu landed. I'm not sure what happened next, but I woke up on the beach. The ocean was beautiful and I was finally free. I reevaluated my situation and chose to live."

"I am sorry about your parents. Their deaths must have been horrible to watch. The Annunaki and Krace have been removed from this planet. There is a reason the remaining offspring, humans and Martians were killed. You have a very powerful mind and it's a threat to the Empress. When I tried to contact your mind, I was very nearly killed," Gly said. "My reaction was instinctive and quite harsh. I apologize," Keeras stated. "I understand. You have not been taught mental discipline. It's something you need and require. With your permission, I would like to help you." "For what benefit?" Keeras asked. "You need to understand your gift and how to use it. I have a friend who could use your assistance as well," Gly responded. "I have no desire to interact with others. Why would I help this friend of yours?" Keeras asked skeptically. "My friend is attempting to kill Empress Zovad. Would you like to begin your training?" A sly smile emerged on the face of Keeras. "Yes, as soon as possible!"

Chapter 12

Empress Zovad consulted historical records after her most recent encounter with the mind of The Shadow. She learned her mental discipline would grow stronger if she contacted a greater range of alien minds. Controlling her own devoted followers was never an issue. The surprising new threat required her to increase her mental power. Underestimating an opponent would prove fatal if proper precautions weren't taken. The prisons on her flagship contained a vast assortment of alien species. She began visiting the prisons and assaulting the minds of the inmates. Most of the alien minds were easy to enter. She probed their thoughts and learned details of the crimes they committed against her. Each prisoner felt fear and terror when she invaded their minds.

A few of the alien species were more difficult. She found if she injured the ones with stronger minds she could more easily enter their thoughts. There was one alien she was unable to make a connection with. She was a reptilian found on a trade ship and came from a very distant solar system known as Krotalli. Empress Zovad tried for days and nearly killed the reptilian in anger. She finally was forced to give up. Killing the reptilian was an option she considered, but in the end she decided she might try again once her mind grew stronger.

The Empress returned to the testing laboratory and was informed one of the new scientists might be on the verge of a breakthrough. She ordered assistants for the scientist and sent instructions that his team was to work day and night, under heavy guard, and in isolation. If the Overlord was near, she couldn't have him learning of her plans.

The following morning, Empress Zovad visited the scientist. "Why do you think you're making progress when everyone before you has failed?" she asked. "Greetings Empress, I'm humbled by your visit. My name is Axadro. I've introduced new variables into the equations and inserted mirror matter and quark matter. The results are encouraging thus far and I believe we are making progress." Axadro replied. "Your life belongs to me. I don't care what your name is. If you wish to be remembered, you will succeed very soon. Don't forget what happened to those who came before you. I want results, not what you see as progress. Do I make myself clear?" "Yes Empress, very much so. We will continue our work until the task is accomplished," Axadro cautiously replied. The Empress decided to analyze his efforts. She quickly entered her encrypted password to access the royal database and reviewed his work.

With extreme caution, Tony entered the room. He needed to know if the Annunaki scientists were making headway. The Empress appeared annoyed as she discussed the lack of progress with the experts. He inched closer as the Empress approached and accessed a data screen. With his advanced vision, he noted how she accessed the royal database and committed it to memory. With her access information, he would be able to control anything on the ship, knowledge that could prove very useful in the future.

It took several days before Keeras started to feel comfortable around Gly and other Volmer. The hybrid didn't have any formal education and was unaware of the history of humans and Martians. Keeras said little and appeared introspective. As best he could, Gly attempted to explain the history of Sol to the juvenile. "Does Tony really need my help?" Keeras asked. "Your mind is much stronger than his. The Annunaki are an immoral and barbaric species. Peaceful species everywhere are at risk of annihilation if the Empress remains in power," Gly replied. "Do what you can to prepare me to help Tony. I'll do whatever is necessary."

Teaching the young hybrid wouldn't be easy. Gly requested all Volmer stay away in order to teach in solitude without interruption. "Where are we going?" Keeras asked. "For now, don't ask any questions and follow my instructions." The duo walked the short distance to the ocean. "Sit down and close your eyes. Take deep breaths and feel the energy surrounding you. Switch off the noise of the birds and the ocean. Focus your thoughts inward. Communicate only with yourself and in your own mind. Continue in this state until I tell you to stop," Gly said as he sat down silently behind Keeras.

As dusk approached Keeras hadn't moved. Gly was about to tell him to stop when he felt an overpowering presence. It wasn't directed at him specifically. The mind was exploring lifeforms in all directions. The raw power was unnerving; it frightened Gly. "That is enough for now, you may stop," Gly said, but the presence remained. Gly repeated himself louder without result. Keeras was breathing even more deeply. Gly stood up and gently shook him. The young Solian was briefly startled. "That is enough for now. Tell me what you felt."

"At first, I couldn't do anything; however, as I got deeper I managed to make contact with the lifeforms surrounding me. I was about to focus on your mind when you interrupted me," Keeras stated. "I'm glad I interrupted you when I did. Such immediate success bodes well for a slow progression. When you reach out to a mind, it must be done gently, respectfully and with empathy. The only exception is with an enemy. Your mind is strong, and you must learn total control if you are to achieve proper equilibrium.

"I don't feel like a have a strong mind. How do you know this?" Keeras asked. "I have communicated with many minds and yours is undisciplined but powerful and must be restrained. Even dreaming could prove dangerous until you learn proper control. All higher-level lifeforms have the ability in a portion of their brain, but not all have learned to use it. The use comes naturally for your species. Your training must be completed as quickly as possible if you are to be useful in defeating the Annunaki," Gly explained.

Mysteries annoyed Tony. Axadro and his team's separation from the rest of the scientists was vexing. The isolation room was guarded and locked securely. Empress Zovad had a secret she desperately wanted to keep hidden. Tony followed Axadro when he left the isolation room. The scientist didn't speak about his project with anyone. Following the other team members hadn't helped either. Nobody was talking about the project and all the information was locked in the isolation room.

After days of contemplation, Tony couldn't come up with a solution that would give him access to the information. He resumed his work on the shielding issue which protected the Empress. In short order he solved the shielding problem and only needed to make minor programming changes to implement his plan.

He was working on the programming when a familiar consciousness entered his mind. After being alone for so long, the contact from Gly was welcome. What Gly shared was astonishing. Tony hadn't planned to leave until after the Empress was dead. Defeating the Annunaki was all that mattered, and he knew the strange new hybrid would be a valuable asset. A new ally and someone to talk to would be welcome.

Leaving without first discovering the secret the Empress was hiding gave Tony a moment of hesitation. He didn't think it possible the Annunaki could threaten the Alliance immediately, but just to be safe he'd make the trip as short as possible. The new problem would be finding a way to hide Keeras when they returned. He made his way to the hanger and found a ship. On the way to Vandi, he would contemplate how Keeras could help him kill Empress Zovad.

"Zabu is unconscious, has been heavily sedated and is stable for the moment," Laxi said. "What the hell is going on? What happened to her?" Patrick asked. "We're in the process of trying to find out. For the moment, it's best she remains unconscious. I need to know when she first showed any changes and what's been happening. Alixias, will you please tell me what has been going on with your child?" Laxi asked.

"About twenty days ago she began whimpering in her sleep. It continued nightly for the next twelve days and then she began sporadically having other symptoms. She was fidgety and began trembling. If I asked her a question she wouldn't answer, or she would snap at me. This morning she appeared dizzy and was losing her balance. Later in the day, she simply began screaming and wouldn't stop. That's when I summoned you."

"Why did you wait so long before reporting these issues?" Laxi asked. "Zabu is the lone member of a new species. I'm a new mother. As far as I knew, her symptoms were simply part of the growth process. If I knew there was any real danger, I would have contacted you immediately. I made a mistake and feel horrible about it. What is your prognosis and what do you plan on doing for my child?" Alixias asked. "Our first task is to make sure her vital signs remain stable. I cannot give you a reliable prognosis without more information. Once we've determined her vital signs are stable, the telepath will attempt to make contact with her. We will do everything possible for Zabu. For now, there are no definitive answers," Laxi replied gently.

Simple things were often the most enjoyable. Vincent was playing pinochle with Enzo, Monique and Isabella. Andy was watching and Julia was explaining how to play. "That's the game. Isabella and I have kicked your ass again," Enzo said. "You two must be cheating," Vincent replied. "I didn't detect any acts of chicanery," Andy smiled and everyone laughed. "Well, I guess wisdom comes with being old. I'll give you that Uncle," Vincent said.

"I don't like to lose and winning is a great formula for success. What's the latest with Zabu?" Enzo asked. "Nobody seems to know. The Alliance has their best experts trying to figure out what's wrong," Isabella said. "We might have to accept the fact that this species may not be genetically able to survive. I don't see how this supposed ancient alien race that constructed this grand plan foresaw all possible variables," Monique replied. "Current evidence suggests otherwise. I've studied what has occurred on other worlds. The plan of the ancient race has been questioned time and time again. Their methods are rarely understood, but one way or another, the results are always beneficial to the Alliance," Andy said.

"I don't see how the death of a hybrid species will benefit the Alliance," Monique replied. "The child still lives and I have confidence the Alliance will find an answer. If not, the child will have died for a reason,"

Andy answered. "This grand plan seems overly complicated, so I hope you're right," Vincent said.

Alixias and Patrick watched for five hours. The telepath was still trying to make contact with Zabu when Laxi arrived and asked for an update. "I cannot make contact. I think it might be the sedatives. You must reduce the dosage," the telepath instructed. "Turn off all medications. She will become more lucid with each passing minute. Keep trying," Laxi ordered.

Three hours later, the telepath ordered all medications to be resumed. She reported her findings to Laxi. "The minds of the Solians are stronger than any I've ever encountered. I was briefly able to explore Zabu's troubled mind and understand her pain. The child has not been taught how to block out telepathic noise. All developing minds of unborn Solian children on Mars and on Earth are assaulting her. It would be like one hundred people speaking gibberish to you at the same time constantly. Her body shut down because her mind was overloaded," the telepath reported. "Were you able to show her how to block out the noise?" Laxi asked. "I was barely able to diagnose the problem. Two-way communication could prove dangerous. Zabu would need to be brought to a higher level of consciousness." Laxi was concerned for the young girl. "It must be done. Zabu must learn how to do this and to teach those yet to be born. We have no choice." "After I rest, the attempt will be made," the exhausted telepath replied.

Patrick was holding Zabu's hand when the telepath returned. "I need everyone to leave the room. We must not be interrupted for any reason." Patrick and Alixias left the room and joined their friends in the waiting area. "The best possible care will be provided. The Alliance is quite resourceful. Have confidence; all will be fine," Andy said. "I hope so. Does anyone know how long this will take?" Alixias asked. "I asked Laxi that exact question, but she was vague. Her best guess is between thirty minutes or as long as a day," Dalton replied. "I'm hoping it's closer to thirty minutes. This stress is taking a toll," Patrick said as he sat down.

The dreadful noise in her head grew louder once again. It was never-ending and unstoppable. Zabu tried to get up, but her legs wouldn't move. She tried to open her eyes and couldn't. The noise became deafening and she began to scream. For a moment, she thought she heard someone call out her name through the cacophony. She stopped screaming and tried to focus. Hearing her name again, Zabu tentatively reached out. "I'm here. Please end this," she pleaded. "If you follow my instructions you will be fine. Focus deeply on me. Ignore all else. I'm here to help," the telepath replied. Zabu focused her thoughts only on the new voice and the noise suddenly stopped. "Much better. You must use your ability and focus. If you fail to focus, the thoughts of outsiders will consume you. Stop focusing on me and let the voices return. I must be certain you can block out the noise. When the noise returns, focus on me again."

Zabu was not going to let the noise return. She found an island of sanity and refused to let it go. The telepath broke the link and the noise returned. She instinctively reached out to the telepath and made contact. "Good. For now, I will be here for you and I'll teach you other techniques to block out the voices," the telepath informed Zabu.

Alixias and Patrick had to be physically restrained when Zabu began screaming. "She might be dying!" Patrick yelled. Five hours later, the door to the medical room finally opened. The telepath and Zabu walked out together. "I'm fine now." Zabu stated as Alixias and Patrick hugged her. "Are you sure she'll be alright?" Alixias asked. "She will be fine and is out of danger, but the experience was very exhausting. It took me a long time to break through the noise and it wore me out. I must get some rest. Zabu will require some alone time and additional sleep for the next few days. She's gone through a very traumatic event."

Many cycles passed since he'd been awake in the middle of the night. The timing of the human couldn't have been worse. Gly watched as Tony exited the Annunaki vessel. "You woke me up. I don't appreciate it. Come with me," Gly stated abruptly. "I'm here to retrieve Keeras and must return at once," Tony responded. "You will not return until we meet with Keeras together. If you wish to be successful, you'll listen to my advice. Come with me and meet someone almost as unique as yourself."

Tony complied and followed his friend into a large cave. Someone was snoring loudly near a fire. "Is that Keeras?" he asked. "Yes, it is. You must understand something, human, if the Empress finds out about him she will use every resource she has to kill Keeras. You must protect him at all costs. I've trained him the best way I know. There are likely others within the Alliance who could train him more thoroughly. His desire to see the Empress dead is as great as yours and his mind is the most powerful I've ever come across. What's your plan?" Gly asked.

Tony formulated his plan on the way to Vandi. I will hide Keeras on Olanion. The natives that remain are helpful and the planet is poisonous to the Annunaki. I spent time there before I went to Tanas. Our friend will be well hidden until I've determined the time has come to kill the Empress, then Keeras will be retrieved. He will destroy her mind and I will destroy her body. We will accomplish the task together," Tony

236

replied. "Very well. Keep in mind you must protect him. Keeras has a desire equal to yours to see the Annunaki defeated," Gly said.

"Do I have no say in how we will proceed? Empress Zovad killed my parents," a voice suddenly interjected. Keeras stood up and confronted Gly and Tony. "Greetings Keeras, my name is Tony and it's a pleasure to meet you. All opinions are welcome as we all have the same common goal. There will be extreme danger in what we attempt to do," Tony stated. "I know who you are and I'm aware of the danger," Keeras said. "Do you have anything else you'd like to say? It sounded like you wanted to add something to our conversation." Gly asked. "Not really. I like what I've heard and the plan sounds good. I just didn't want to be ignored. Can we go now?" Keeras asked. Tony laughed. "I think we're going to get along just fine. I'm ready when you are."

As the spacecraft rose into the sky, Gly hoped he would finally be left alone. He didn't have any desire to counsel or train anymore humans, Martians, or hybrids. The old Strithu that brought Keeras to him gracefully followed the ship into the atmosphere. Gly was amazed by the majestic bird's loyalty. The Strithu would miss Keeras. He was happy everyone was finally gone and he could go back to sleep.

On the way to Olanion, Tony was trying to make a decision. It was likely Keeras had the mental power to extract the isolated information the Empress was hiding. Gly stated the Alliance could have likely trained Keeras more thoroughly. If Keeras opened his mind to extract the information, the Empress would learn of his existence. It was a risk he was unwilling to take. Keeras possessed a powerful mind but was young and inexperienced. Tony set course for Olanion. He would continue to try and uncover the secret on his own.

Returning to the planet was painful. Tony didn't plan on coming back to Olanion until the Annunaki were defeated. He brought Keeras to his old home on the hillside. Tulari ran into his arms as they crested the hill. "I've missed you! I'm glad you're here. Why did you return before your mission was accomplished?" she asked. "I've made a new friend and he needs to be hidden from the Empress. Will you take care of him until I return? When the time comes, I will need his help. His name is Keeras. I must return now," Tony said. "I will see to his needs and we will discuss how he can help you. You can survive your encounter with the Empress and come back to me. I will wait. You will become the first Overlord to accomplish the mission and you will live," Tulari beamed. "I will survive and come back to you. You've given me a reason to continue this life." Tony kissed Tulari passionately.

"Thank you. I will share our knowledge with Keeras; it could prove useful. You should remember that everyone on Olanion and in the Alliance is counting on you," Tulari said as Tony embraced her. "Thanks, more pressure. That's exactly what I needed."

Randy was most comfortable when he was in charge. The Alliance deemed him worthy of a mere apprenticeship. He wouldn't be in charge of anything but himself. It had been a long time since he studied so much, but a continuing education was something he always preached at Leviathan. He would need to follow his own advice. The workforce was growing and there was a lot of competition. Martians didn't seem to be very competitive and they didn't need to be. They were intelligent and hard workers; he was just hoping to keep up.

Randy looked out his window at the beauty and majesty of Earth. The Alliance decided to conduct most shipbuilding on the moon where a massive base had been recently constructed in the Mare Imbrium Crater. Low gravity made the work much easier and the ships could be tested more safely. The recent battle with the Annunaki took a toll on the fleet and vessels were being constructed as quickly as possible. There were ten currently under construction.

In his youth, he could work and study nearly non-stop, but the current schedule was wearing him out. With the arrival of the Alliance, his skillset was no longer useful. Before their arrival he was an innovator and a leader in the space industry, but now he was just another worker. He decided it was time for a vacation. His friends were on Mars and he missed their companionship. The terraforming process was something he was curious about, so Randy requested a leave of absence and reserved a seat on the next interplanetary ship to Mars.

"I've consulted with the telepath and Zabu will no longer hear the voices. In time, she will play a crucial role in the development of the Solians. She will train the new Solians who hear the voices. Her help will be necessary both here and on Earth. Once other young Solians have been trained, they will be able to assist and train others themselves," Laxi stated. "Why can't the telepath train the others?" Alixias asked. "The telepath was barely able to train Zabu. Her mental recovery is ongoing and it's possible she's suffered permanent mental damage. There isn't a telepath within the Alliance with a mind as strong as Zabu's. Not to mention, she's not a Solian and what she accomplished was difficult and dangerous. As a native Solian, it will be very simple for Zabu. There will be no risk and it won't take long at all. She will only need to train a few. After that, there will be many more to assist," Laxi replied. "Obviously, she is needed. I understand and Zabu will do what must be done. After that, she must return to a normal life," Alixias stated. "I'm glad you agree. It's in the best interests of the Solians."

The pass was horrible. Enzo couldn't believe it. "Are you helping him at all?" he asked. "No, he must learn on his own," Julia replied. "I guess that's it then. We're down the river and have lost," Enzo said in defeat. "You need to relax; it's only a card game," a voice said as someone new entered the room. "Son of a bitch! You actually left your shipbuilding and graced us with a visit?" Enzo said as he gave Randy a hug. "I'm not a very important person anymore. The Alliance has plenty of resources. My contributions are fairly redundant," Randy replied.

"That might be true, but if it weren't for you, none of us would be here. You started it all, got us into space and fulfilled your destiny," Enzo said. "I'm happy most of us survived. Viewing Mars from space is amazing. The blue and green patches are growing by the day," Randy shared. "Terraforming is on schedule and oxygen levels and pressure are increasing daily. Animal and plant life are beginning to take a foothold. In short order, the surface will be habitable for us as well," Dalton stated. "The technological ability of the

Alliance is unbelievable. I never thought it could be done so quickly," Randy said.

Tony returned to the enemy flagship and resumed his task of completing the necessary programming. Within just a few hours, the task was complete. The reprogrammed shields protecting the Empress would now change on his command. He controlled all aspects of the redesigned shielding and ensured the shields would work in his favor. The ship suddenly vibrated ever so slightly; it was nearly imperceptible. He felt the vibrations caused by the ongoing tests. The scientists were still trying to unravel the mystery of the gate.

His effort to discover the isolated information proved fruitless once again. It couldn't be accessed and nobody was talking. Even with Empress Zovad's access to the database Tony couldn't find anything. He was seriously reconsidering using Keeras to extract the information from Empress Zovad. When he brought up her tracking information he was surprised to find she'd been visiting prisoners lately. She was spending an inordinate amount of time with one of the captives in particular. Tony decided it was time to visit the Annunaki prison system.

It was sad to see so many unique lifeforms held under such deplorable conditions. Tony vowed to free them all. He found the cell he was looking for. "Hello. I need to speak with you." The sleeping prisoner didn't respond. He assertively repeated the message again and again, but there was no response from the snoring inmate. Intelligence was needed. Tony didn't have any choice but to open his mind and attempt contact. He was met with stony silence and sat down to take a closer look at the battered prisoner. The alien suffered major damage to most parts of his body. Open wounds and bruises covered the strange creature. Tony needed to understand what happened and decided to wait.

"Why did Empress Zovad spend so much time with you?" Tony asked when the prisoner finally awoke. "Who are you and what do you want?" the prisoner grumbled. "My name is Tony. I'm here to kill the Empress and if I'm successful, you and everyone else imprisoned here will be free," Tony replied. "I am called Tuzard. The Empress is under the impression that I have strong telepathic abilities. She has spent many hours trying to contact me." Tony was intrigued. "How did you manage to block her mind?" "My species is strong and proud. We thrived until the Annunaki arrived, but we have no telepathic abilities. We communicate with ordinary words. I didn't do anything to block her mind."

The information took Tony by surprise. In his brief experience he'd never been completely blocked by a mind. "You appear to be intelligent. Your species either has a very different brain structure, or you have a natural ability to block all telepathic communication," he replied. "Whatever, I really don't want to be bothered anymore." Tuzard turned away from Tony. "I will leave you now, but in the future I might ask for your assistance. If you wish to be free, you must be prepared to help."

The planet would have been gorgeous if it weren't for the recent devastation. Keeras assumed he'd spend most of his time on Olanion waiting for Tony to return, but Tulari put him to work studying and asking him questions. "You may not be an Overlord, but you are highly intelligent and have been given a tremendous gift. Study and discussion will keep your mind sharp," she advised him. "I don't understand how Tony thinks he'll succeed. None before him did," Keeras said. "He's been patient and has been planning for quite some time. None of the previous Overlords were as strong mentally or physically according to our records and your powerful mind will help take the Empress by surprise." Tulari responded.

"How do I fit into his plan?" Keeras asked. "I don't know; I'm not even sure if Tony does yet. You must try and do one thing if it's possible and doesn't endanger the mission." Tulari said. "What's that?"

Keeras asked. "Make sure Tony lives. He's prepared to die if necessary, but please bring him back to me," she pled. "I will do everything within my power to protect him."

Leaving Olanion without Keeras was a tactical decision which might prove problematic. If Empress Zovad decided to leave, he would be separated from the unique hybrid. Retrieving Keeras and trying to catch up with the Empress would prove problematic at best. After contemplating the problem for a few days, Tony found a solution. There were hundreds of cargo containers in the storage bay; they weren't huge, but they were big enough. Tony prepared one in the back of the bay so Keeras would have a place to sleep, a bathroom and access to the Annunaki database. Tony locked up the container so only he could access it and left for the hangar bay. It was time to bring back a friend and it was time to kill the Empress.

"The Alliance has summarized an update about recent events on Cardonia," Isabella shared. "Jesus, what now? Am I the most wanted man in the universe?" Vincent replied. "Wow, your ego is truly massive, but I'm afraid it's not something so grandiose. The destruction of the Nalis has brought about extraordinary change and the remaining religious leaders are trying to hold on to their power. The people on Cardonia are angry; their religion and belief system are under attack. The Alliance believes for the first time in known history, a non-religious leader will soon emerge from the chaos. Members of the species might stop killing each other. Your name was never mentioned by the way," Isabella reported sarcastically.

"You've saved thousands of lives, Vincenzo. A real man does what's smart. There are times when you must keep a secret to do what's right. Those who might have died on Cardonia can change the destiny of their species. People who seek change for the better are often the most heavily persecuted," Enzo said. "Even if the Chief Administrator were to find out now, you'd likely only receive a minor reprimand. In this instance, the Alliance would likely choose to look the other way and accept the positive result. The Cardonians might very well be allies again in the near future. Honestly, I'm still trying to decide if you're lucky or good," Andy added.

"I'm just happy to stay out of jail. What's the latest with Zabu?" Vincent asked. "She's been more withdrawn than usual, but Laxi says it's normal after what she went through. At the same time, she's been happier and smiling a lot. She knows the other Solians will need her help and she has a purpose. Laxi thinks she's looking forward to her upcoming tasks. The outlook for the Solians is good now that the problem with Zabu has been taken care of," Julia replied. "That's good. What I wouldn't give to live another couple hundred years to see how it all turns out," Vincent mused. "You'll get to see more than me. Be grateful for what you have, Vincenzo," Enzo said.

A message was sent to Keeras instructing him to board the ship when he landed. Tony sent a message to Tulari. He didn't want to see her again until he knew they would be safe. Seeing her again would distract him from what was to come. The hybrid was nowhere in sight. Tony sent a message to Tulari and didn't receive a response. He ran to his old house thinking something might be wrong. When he entered he found Tulari and Keeras waiting for him.

"We are fine, but you will not be leaving quite yet," Tulari stated. "We need to get back. What if the Empress suddenly decides to leave?" he asked. "If she leaves, you will follow her, but for now, I think it's a good idea for us to hear your plan. We will take the time necessary to criticize and alter your plan as necessary," Tulari responded. Tony could tell that Tulari was determined. "I'm always open to constructive criticism and willing to change if it's for the better. We will stay for a brief time and once we agree on the plan it will be time to act," Tony replied.

"Tell us how you will eliminate the Empress," Tulari demanded. "I've studied her routine extensively and learned she is constantly protected by a forcefield, but her servants and guards can breach the forcefield with an access device. Empress Zovad personally controls and distributes the devices. The forcefield deactivates any unauthorized technology," Vincent explained as Keeras interrupted. "So, you're going to steal one of the devices to get through the shielding?" he asked.

"No, I'm not. My part of the plan is flawless. I'm not going to go into technical details, but I will be able to confront the Empress without having to worry about Annunaki reinforcements. Before I confront the Empress, I will kill her daughter. Her successor must be eliminated first."

"What about the emergency rearing facility?" Tulari asked. "Assuming I survive my encounter with Empress Zovad, it will be destroyed. After the Empress is killed, we will have a very short time to destroy all Annunaki vessels and military installations. The resources and technology allowing them to wage war must be decimated."

"How do I fit into your plan?" Keeras asked. "I don't know what will happen when my mind makes contact with Empress Zovad. I believe I'll be able to overpower her. In the event it's more difficult and she has grown stronger, I'll need your assistance. Previous Overlords believed their minds were stronger than hers, but history has shown they were wrong. Either the Empress was withholding power, or she strengthened her mind after learning of their existence," Tony replied.

"What makes you think my mind will be of any use?" Keeras asked. "Gly is very confident in your abilities and the power of your mind. Are you satisfied with the plan?" Tony asked. "It's dangerous, but there's no other way. Be mindful of the unexpected. Something minor could derail the whole thing," Tulari cautioned. "I guess it's time to go. Thank you for your hospitality," Keeras said. "It was a pleasure, remember what we spoke about," Tulari whispered to him. "Your teachings have expanded my understanding of the Annunaki in ways I couldn't have imagined. We will not fail in our task," Keeras replied. "He has learned much. You must believe in yourself as I believe in you. I'll see you soon." Tulari said as she embraced Tony.

The flight back was spent in silence. Tony reviewed everything and couldn't think of a way to improve upon the actions he was about to take. The biggest unknown was the mental strength of Empress Zovad. There was no way of knowing her true power. "We've arrived. Your new accommodations will not be luxurious. An automated cargo bot will drop you off at the container I've prepared. Get into the storage container, the bot will be here shortly and I'll be there to greet you when you arrive." Tony instructed.

Keeras was not impressed. "How long am I supposed to live here?" he asked. "As long as necessary. We have a mission to accomplish. Creature comforts will have to take a back seat for now," Tony said. "You said your plan was ready. Let's get this over with as soon as possible," Keeras replied. "It will only be for a few days. I just have a couple of more issues to work on."

After accessing the Annunaki database, Tony learned the Empress hadn't visited the prison while he was gone. There was still no data about the isolated experiments and the isolated room was still heavily guarded. There was only one way to retrieve the information.

Keeras was trying to figure out how to work the data pad when Tony entered. "This doesn't make sense to me. Can you please help?" he asked. "Forget about it. Tomorrow is the day. There's nothing left to be done. Prepare yourself and get some rest. I'm going to retrieve my bullak." "What is a bullak?" Keeras asked. "It's the weapon that will end the life of Empress Zovad," Tony said confidently.

Sleep was proving difficult; Keeras wanted to act. His mind raced as he prepared to confront the alien who murdered his parents. He was eager to do his duty and when he finally fell asleep, he dreamt. The reoccurring nightmare returned. Again, he watched, as Empress Zovad killed his mother and father. Once more he failed to save them. Instinctively, he opened his mind and screamed.

Chapter 13

Empress Zovad reviewed the latest information from Axadro. The scientist appeared to be making real progress. Suddenly, she felt immense pain throughout her entire body. Her guards watched as she began having a seizure and passed out. As she lost consciousness, she realized her mind was being assaulted. When she woke, her guards stared at her with a confused look in their eyes. Empress Zovad briefly shared minds with the intruder and deciphered his location. The mental power he possessed was beyond anything she'd ever experienced. She must learn his secret and master it herself. "Flood the storage bay with gas immediately. There is an intruder. Bring him to the medical bay and keep him heavily sedated. If he dies, you will all die as well. Am I understood?" "Yes, Empress!" her guards responded in unison.

Tony was at peace and sleeping deeply. Suddenly it felt like his mind exploded. Mental power far stronger than his cried out in anger and sadness. When he awoke, he didn't immediately understand what happened and didn't know how long he'd been out. The mind wasn't that of the Empress, rather it was Keeras. He rushed to the storage bay, but it was too late to do anything. Keeras was unconscious and armed guards were dragging him out of his hiding spot.

Empress Zovad was present to oversee their actions. "The prisoner is to be kept unconscious constantly. Prepare him for testing!" she ordered.

Tony watched as his new ally was hauled away. His contingency plan was gone, but it wasn't time for any rash actions. Tony made his way to the top of the ship, stared into space and considered his options. It would be too dangerous to try and free Keeras. If he were killed or captured trying to rescue his new friend, Empress Zovad would live a full life and remain a threat to the Alliance. Tony knew he must confront the Empress on his own. However, he had one last card to play. He made his way to the prison.

Tuzard was still recovering from his injuries. "Your day of freedom will arrive soon. I'm going to release you and everyone else who is confined," Tony said. "Why do we suddenly deserve such an honor?" the reptilian responded. "Because I need your help and the assistance of the other prisoners. You're the only ones who have a chance of freeing my friend." "I wish to be free and don't give a damn about your friend," Tuzard sneered. "Your freedom and the future of your species will be determined by what happens in the next few days and I need my friend to defeat the Empress," Tony replied.

"What do you want us to do?" the reptilian asked cautiously. Tony proceeded to explain how the prisoners could free Keeras. "If you follow my advice, we can accomplish this. This is a pivotal moment for everyone. Success means your freedom and you will not have to fear the Annunaki in the future. Spread word of our plan to all the other prisoners. Carefully explain to them what is at stake. We're in this together and we will fight side by side."

"You don't have to try and convince me anymore. I understand and will do it. Many species in the prison do not like each other, so realize they might start fighting amongst themselves as soon as they're free." "If they do that, we'll all die. Explain it to them. They must put their petty differences aside for now. I'll be back to check on your progress. When the time comes to release all prisoners, you must be able to coordinate and fight as a unit. Find those with military and combat experience." Tony quietly left the prison bay.

He wasn't sure if it was an operating room or a torture chamber. It was likely both. He could see Keeras was in a clear, rectangular medical container. It reminded Tony of a coffin. The medical device administered a drug of some kind into his system and Tony watched as liquid flowed through the tube. It wouldn't do much good to free Keeras if he was going to be comatose for days or weeks.

It took several hours, but Tony finally thought he found the drug the Annunaki were using on Keeras.

The color and the consistency were the same as the liquid in the tube. The chemical make-up of the drug would keep someone unconscious if it didn't kill them first. The difficult part was trying to find a way to counteract the drug and bring Keeras around quickly. Usually the Annunaki database held the answers to any questions Tony could ask, but for the first time there was not an answer to his question. There wasn't a database in the universe that could answer his question. How do you prescribe a stimulant to a Martian and human hybrid? Tony located the medical file the Annunaki were keeping on Keeras. All his vital signs were recorded since the moment he was captured and thankfully he was stable. His primary organs were all in relatively normal locations. Tony reviewed all the data and decided to prepare a safe but somewhat mild stimulant, hoping it would be enough. The attack on the Empress could wait until Keeras was fully conscious.

"How did it go with the other prisoners?" Tony asked. "Some of them didn't want to participate or vowed to enact vengeance on their enemies when they were freed. I gently persuaded them to reconsider their position." "And how'd you do that?" Vincent asked. "I told them they wouldn't receive any weaponry and I'd kill them myself without hesitation," Tuzard replied. "That's a very compelling argument. Nice work. In addition to freeing Keeras, I have one additional task for you."

"You're already asking an awful lot. What now?" "My friend is unconscious and I need you to remove him from the medical container and administer a shot to wake him," Tony explained. "I'm a prisoner, not a doctor. Why don't you do it yourself?" Tuzard sniped. "It's too risky. My priorities must be with the Empress." "So, we have to do all the fighting while you sit back and watch?" Tuzard argued. "Would you like to do the planning and fight the Empress yourself? Once you accomplish your mission, I'll accomplish mine. Prepare everyone. The next time I come, it will be to free all of you. I'll bring the weapons and the medication you must administer to Keeras. Prepare to savagely kill your enemy in order to restore peace and a return of morality."

Mars was changing for the better. Everyone was determined and felt a sense of purpose. The planet was reborn and thriving. Before long, new Solians would inhabit the world. Unprecedented changes were occurring and Enzo felt out of place. "There's not much of a purpose for me here, Vincenzo; I think it's time for me to return to Earth. A retirement of sorts is in order. It's time for me to enjoy my golden years." "There's plenty for you to do here. Your advice is invaluable and everyone can benefit from your wisdom." Vincent said hopefully. "My voice is redundant. The Alliance has arrived and is doing quite well. They have all the real answers moving forward. I'm ready for the open air and a return to nature on Earth," Enzo replied, clearly tired.

Vincent didn't want his Uncle to go. Enzo was family and Vincent learned to count on him as an advisor. "Where will you go and what will you do?" he asked. "Your Grandmother and I used to vacation at a deep lake in Washington State; I will go there.

Someone must document the events that have transpired since you first left Earth, so perhaps I'll try my hand at writing," Enzo replied. "How will you survive?" Vincent asked. "I'm not without skills. I'll fish and draw water from the lake if need be. I'm sure the infrastructure on Earth is being rebuilt. I'll figure out a way to make pizza and have some beer and wine. I plan on enjoying my retirement. It's time to leave the work and drama to the young. I've worked hard my entire life and want some peace and relaxation, Vincenzo. A day will arrive when you feel the same." "I understand. You will be missed, especially by me. I've come to count on your advice. I'll see if anyone else would like to return with you."

After checking with the crew, the only other person who wanted to return was Randy. He was passionate about continuing his work on the moon. Vincent asked Dalton out of common courtesy, but he knew his friend was dedicated to his research on Mars. He found Enzo to finalize travel arrangements. "You and Randy are the only ones who want to return right now. Is it alright with you if we leave in a week or so?" Vincent asked. "That will be fine. It will give me time to say goodbye to the new friends I've made here. I'll come back and visit. I'd like to actually walk on the surface and breathe real air when it's possible," Enzo said. "I'll come get you anytime you'd like to come. Maybe you'll like it so much you'll decide to stay," Vincent replied with a smile.

Axadro was running out of time and he knew it. The Empress was not known for her patience. He was getting closer. Each test ruled out a wrong answer and he was hopeful eventually he'd stumble upon the correct formula. He reviewed the data on the devices the Alliance used to shut down the gate to the Rabanah System and altered his formula again. Two hours later, he conducted another test without success. The door opened, and he knew without a doubt whom was entering. "I hope you have some concrete results to show me, Axadro. If not, it's time to give someone else the opportunity. You confidently claimed you could produce a gate and you've failed miserably over and over," Empress Zovad stated. "I respectfully ask for just one more chance. If I fail, you can take my life," Axadro pled. "There's no question I will take your life, but I'm feeling generous and will give you one last opportunity to prove you're different than the rest. When your missiles fail again, you will be on the next missile into space. I will return shortly to watch your final failure."

Surrendering his life to the Empress was to be expected. She was wise and her decisions were in the best interests of her subjects. Those who failed to serve properly were disposed of, but Axadro knew he would be successful if he were given more time. He prepared his last formula and watched as the missiles were launched. It took only seconds before the weapons reached the coordinates and exploded, yet space remained unchanged. "Your life is now surrendered," Empress Zovad said. "I apologize for my failure. Please make sure the next scientist reviews my notes." Axadro dropped his head in defeat.

Unexpectedly, a bright light illuminated the room from outside the viewport. Everyone turned and watched. It lasted only a few seconds and blinked out. The fabric of space remained distorted for a brief moment. It was the first result which changed the consistency of space. "You may resume your work; however, I expect you to immediately improve upon this result," Empress Zovad stated. "Thank you,

Empress. Once I fine tune this formula, you will have the result you asked for. We will be successful."

Empress Zovad was finally feeling optimistic. She issued orders to arm and ready all ships for departure. The Alliance believed she was defeated, but they would soon feel her full wrath. Once probes determined the level of danger, she would quickly decide on a course of battle. She rarely visited her daughter. It was improper for an Empress to visit the Princess, but on this occasion she made an exception. "We will soon defeat all of our enemies and when I'm gone it will be your responsibility to destroy any threats to our new kingdom. You will have absolute power over your realm. Do not fail me and those who came before. Are you prepared to lead with absolute authority when it's your time?" she asked. "Yes, Mother. Thank you for all you've done. I will continue your work and eliminate any species that dares challenge our authority." Empress Zovad nodded. "For now, you will continue to study and learn. I plan to live a long life. You will rule this empire, but not anytime soon."

Only Enzo and Randy were leaving, but Vincent talked all his friends into going for a ride. A short stay on Earth was planned and everyone was curious about what was taking place there. "This ship is truly amazing," Dalton remarked. "This is nothing. At some point you need to take a break from Mars and do some traveling. Rabanah is a beautiful planet. There are wonders you couldn't possibly imagine," Monique added. "Someday. For now, I prefer to uncover the secrets of the past. Mars has many unsolved mysteries," Dalton replied.

"I enjoy spaceflight. Perhaps it's my old age. Computer, cease artificial gravity," Enzo requested. Nobody was belted in and everyone began floating around as the computer complied. "That's nice. I just lost two hundred and twenty pounds. Let's not rush to Earth. Take your time, Vincenzo!" Enzo said as he flew across the command center. "And people say I'm weird," Dalton commented.

It took longer than expected to find the ingredients necessary to make the antidote to hopefully awaken Keeras. Accessing restricted areas was tricky, but Tony was becoming proficient in hacking the security system without alerting anyone. He was trying to figure out how to retrieve weaponry when an alert flashed onto the screen. "Hostilities will resume shortly. Prepare to fight for your Empress."

Tony didn't understand. There weren't any enemies to fight as far as he knew. Did it have something to do with Axadro's work? He searched the database and found nothing new. He replayed the video feeds from the most recent test results. The external view from the ship was the only source of information available. All previous tests were unsuccessful. The most recent one was different than the rest. "Oh shit!" he said out loud.

"When you provide me a functioning gate, how do you know the location of the other side?" Empress Zovad asked. "A complete understanding of the laws of equational logic is necessary to explain it to you. Would you like me to go into more detail?" Axadro responded. "If you are successful, an explanation will not be necessary. If you fail, I'll want a detailed account of your calculations. Fire the missiles and prepare the probes," Empress Zovad responded. The missiles launched and exploded brilliantly moments later. Empress Zovad waited with Axadro and his team. She reacted too early during the last test and held her tongue this time. The entirety of nearby space lit up in a blinding white light. As the light slowly dimmed, a shimmering oval remained. "This gate better lead to Sol. Send in the probes! I need to know if the gate is stable and will remain," Empress Zovad ordered. "Readings from the gate are the same as the others we've encountered. There's no reason to believe this gate will close," Axadro replied confidently.

The Annunaki decided the Hawking Space Telescope wasn't a valuable target. It was still performing its preprogrammed mission. The telescope was currently tasked with taking images of any changes to the outer Kuiper Belt. A change was found and recorded. The telescope transmitted the image and sent the data back to Earth. The NASA team on Earth tasked with reviewing information from the telescope were killed when the Annunaki destroyed all NASA facilities during the invasion. Nobody on Earth received the image of a dim gate at the outer edge of the solar system.

"The probes have returned and we're receiving data," a technician reported. "Let's have it as quickly as possible," Empress Zovad demanded. "There are no nearby vessels on the other side. The other side of the gate is in the Sol System. Data from Mars and Earth indicate fifty-seven Alliance vessels are capable of engaging in combat," the technician responded. Under normal circumstances Empress Zovad would have conducted a simulated battle plan, but she didn't need to this time. The number of Alliance ships was insignificant. "Send all vessels through the gate immediately. We will be the first. Set a course for the gate immediately," she ordered.

"You have done well, Axadro. If this gate remains stable, you will receive the honor of becoming one of my personal servants." "It's my duty to serve as you command. I can now open a gate back to the Rabanah System if you wish," Axadro replied. "I will provide the vision of our future and you will follow my instructions. Never think otherwise. When I decide to open a gate to Rabanah, you will do your duty," Empress Zovad replied.

The Annunaki flagship moved closer to the gate and it loomed larger on the horizon. Her vision didn't work out as planned, but she would be successful none the less. The rippling fabric of space approached and her ship passed through. Immediately, an image of the fourth planet appeared. It was time to address all those who served her. She instructed the technician to open all communication devices in order to address her species. "The Alliance has been busy terraforming our home world. We will use our technology to make Mars habitable for our species. First, we will kill every human and Martian on Earth before returning to Mars. These people from Sol are proving to be an annoyance. Prepare to fight and destroy every sentient being in this solar system. Notify me immediately of any tactical changes. At long last we will completely defeat the Alliance. We are home."

It was a barely perceptible change, but Tony felt it. The flagship hadn't moved in months and it was suddenly traveling again. The change woke him and made him nervous. It was likely the ship was moving closer to Tanas to take on more supplies. Tony stood up and looked out the viewport. The approaching gate shook him to his core. The ship passed through the gate moments later. It took him a few minutes to travel to the closest terminal. Tony accessed the database and read the latest message from the Empress.

After reviewing the data and the battle plan, Tony knew Earth and Mars were doomed. The Annunaki fleet flowing through the gate was massive. The gate needed to be shut down immediately. He tried to open a communications channel to warn the Alliance. "Please enter authorization code," the screen prompted. Empress Zovad knew he was near and recently changed security protocol. There were no longer any options. It was now or never.

The guard stood stoically in front of the door like some sort of statue. Even during bathroom breaks the guard was replaced. Tony needed the weaponry in the room beyond for the prisoners. He would have to be quick and waited for a shift change. A new guard arrived. He was staring into his data pad when Tony thrust the bullack into his chest. Blood spilled onto the floor and Tony entered the weapons room. At best he might have a few minutes before the guard's body would be discovered. After recently researching Annunaki weaponry he selected the most effective weapons as quickly as possible. He placed the selections in the largest container he could carry and quickly ran toward the prison.

Small mistakes could ruin his plan. Tony set down the container of weaponry and peered around the corner to the entrance of the prison. The locked entrance was suddenly guarded by seven guards when there were none on his previous visits. Empress Zovad continued to change security protocols; she was not taking any chances. Tony decided to review her changes and hid the weaponry.

Commander Evir was tired of administrative work. The Alliance still hadn't sent a replacement to oversee governance of Earth. He was much more comfortable in space commanding his fleet. He was in the process of redistributing nutritional resources across the planet when he was interrupted. "Sir, celestial cartography has reported a recent anomaly. There appears to be a new dim gate at the edge of the solar system," his aide reported.

Evir laughed. "There haven't been any new gates in millennia. What do the science vessels report?" he asked. "There are currently no science vessels in the system. They all returned to Rabanah. We do not have any advanced imagery," his aide replied. "Send the closest ship to check it out. I'm sure it's a mistake of some kind."

It was finally quiet on the Santa Maria. Vincent didn't understand what Enzo was up to; his uncle spent most of the night drinking and playing loud music. "I just don't get it. He's too old to have a midlife crisis," he said to Monique. "Enzo built an empire on Earth. He was powerful and well respected. The world he created for himself is gone now, so give him his space and let him do what he wants."

As he contemplated Monique's suggestion, Isabella interrupted his thoughts. "We've received orders from the Alliance. They want us to research an anomaly in the Kuiper Belt," she said. "We're on vacation and heading to Earth. Can't they ask another ship?" Vincent asked. "We are the closest ship and are expected to alter course immediately," Isabella replied. "I guess we're back on duty. Head for the anomaly," Vincent ordered.

"Why have we changed course?" Enzo asked after waking up. "There's some anomaly the Alliance wants us to check out; I'm sure it's nothing," Isabella replied. "How close are we?" Vincent asked. "We can now take detailed imagery of the area," Andy replied.

"Please proceed. Let's get this over with so we can return to Earth. Put the images on the viewscreen," Vincent ordered.

"Oh………. Fuck!" Vincent slowly exclaimed. It couldn't be possible. New gates were beyond current Alliance technology. This new gate was distinct as were the enormous number of Annunaki ships traversing it. More passed through as he watched. The sheer number of enemy vessels were beyond anything he could have imagined. "Oh my God. How did they do it?" Monique asked Vincent. "Broadcast this on every Alliance channel immediately. Let's get the hell out of here as fast as possible!"

"Sir, you need to see this immediately," the communications officer reported. "What is it?" Commander Evir asked. "It's a feed of the anomaly from the Santa Maria. There really is a new gate. What are we going to do?" his panicked communications officer asked.

"This can't be happening; it's beyond the bounds of known science. Transmit the video to Rabanah immediately and get me a tactical analysis," Commander Evir ordered as he continued to watch the feed from the retreating Santa Maria.

"What are we going to do? Can we evacuate everyone from Earth and Mars to Rabanah and then blow up that gate?" Isabella asked. "I've been studying the tactical situation. From their current position, the Annunaki would be able to intercept any vessels before they reached the gate to the Rabanah System. Evacuating to Rabanah is not a viable option," Andy replied. "You are familiar with Alliance tactical procedures. What other options do we have?" Enzo asked.

Andy was given no choice but to reveal the brutal truth. "It's likely there are no survivable options. The size of the Annunaki fleet is unexpectedly large. Initially, the Alliance will destroy the gate connecting the Rabanah System and the Sol System to buy the Chief Administrator and the Ambassadors some time. Then the Alliance will mount a defense when the Annunaki construct a new gate to Rabanah, but it's unknown how much time destroying the gate will buy the Alliance. The Annunaki could create a new gate within hours or it might take years since nobody knows how it's done. Everyone on Mars and Earth will be left to fend for themselves and will be completely abandoned."

"So, what in the hell is everyone on Earth and Mars supposed to do?" Monique asked angrily. "Fight or flight are the only choices. Fighting probably offers the best chance at survival. A very small percentage of the inhabitants of Mars and Earth could attempt to relocate to the closest habitable exoplanet. There aren't enough Alliance ships to evacuate more than a few thousand inhabitants, but the Annunaki will follow and eventually hunt everyone down," Andy replied grimly. "What do you think the odds of success are in battle?" Dalton asked. Andy referenced his data pad. "It's less than one percent. Barring some tactical miracle, we will lose."

Dominic quickly reviewed the information that brought about the emergency session in the Great Chamber. He couldn't remember the last time he was so pissed off. Chief Administrator Kizak stood at the raised podium. "You have all been given the information and the recommendation from our military leaders. Unless there are any objections, the voting will begin now." Dominic stood up. "I object and would like to be heard," he said.

"The Ambassador from Earth has the floor," Kizak responded. The stress and pressure was overwhelming and Dominic wasn't given time to prepare. "How long are we going to run from the Annunaki? You all consider yourself moral beings, yet you allow entire races to become extinct due to your unwillingness to confront the enemy. The time for running is over. It's time to rid this evil race from the universe once and for all. We must look at other options as well. New allies are vital and we must attempt to recruit the support of the Cardonians and the Osarians again. We should enlist the support of any species willing to assist whether they are members of the Alliance or not. It's time to show bravery and courage, but more importantly we must all do what is right and morally correct."

Tissa objected on behalf of Mars and made a similar passionate argument. "Voting begins now on this emergency," Kizak informed all the ambassadors. Dominic hoped his speech and Tissa's passionate words would change some votes. Maybe there was a chance. He spoke better than he thought possible and was still learning the ways of diplomacy. Preaching to the Alliance's moral virtues made sense and could change the tide of the vote.

Five minutes later, Kizak announced the results of the emergency vote. "The motion has passed and the gate leading to the Sol System will be destroyed as soon as any Annunaki vessels approach. Commander Evir has been instructed to fight the Annunaki when they arrive. The battle plan will be updated as conditions change. Failure in the Sol System is expected. Additional information from the Sol System will be provided as we receive it. Construction of military ships will be our highest priority. We will retreat until our military has built a force capable of engaging the Annunaki successfully. This session is now closed."

His speech didn't matter at all and was a waste of time and energy. Dominic reviewed the results. Only he and the Martian Ambassador voted against the motion. Frustration and anger consumed him. He wanted to curse and beat the shit out of someone. Instead, he sat in defeat as the other Ambassadors filed out of the chamber. Footsteps approached from behind. "It was a good speech and I contacted any potential allies before the session. However, the Cardonians and Osarians refuse to participate. There are no other species that will help, but feel free to try yourself. If you can find new allies, I'll order a new emergency session. The Alliance must survive. If we all die, there is no morality to be taught. The requirements of our society supersede the demands of the doomed," Kizak stated. "I don't give a damn right now about your society! Everyone I love is about to die and I can't do anything about it," Dominic replied irately.

Changes to security were not as extensive as Tony anticipated. The only major change was more guards posted around Keeras and the prison. Empress Zovad ordered the Annunaki fleet to travel as fast as possible and it was now within the orbit of Neptune. Tony gathered his stolen weaponry and went to the prison. It was still heavily guarded, so Tony threw an explosive down the corridor. After the detonation, none of the guards moved. He quickly entered the command that unlocked every cell door in the prison. Tuzard appeared moments later. "Time is short. Here are your weapons. Follow the plan. I will wait until Keeras has been freed and is fully awake to kill the Empress. Revive my friend as quickly as possible."

Tony quietly entered the chamber of the Princess. Once Keeras was free and conscious, it would be time to kill her quickly and find the Empress. He stood over her bed and prepared himself for what needed to be done. She slept peacefully. Tony was repulsed by what she hoped to become. Since he was waiting on Keeras, he set the bullack down and prepared to rest. All his energy would be required for what was to come. The ship continued to vibrate imperceptibly. Tony was used to it and was startled by a sudden noise.

Empress Zovad issued orders. She knew The Shadow managed to free the prisoners. Many of the escapees were traveling toward the engine room. "They are attempting to stop or blow up the ship. Send everyone available to kill them!" "There is a small group near the nutritional center," the communications officer reported. "Ignore them for now. We will deal with them later. Focus on the prisoners travelling toward the engine room." Empress Zovad replied.

In the heat of battle, time passed slowly. Tuzard felt he'd been in the nutritional center for far too long. "It's time. Let's get to the medical center!" he ordered. His small group of selected, specialized prisoners followed. There were only three Annunaki soldiers guarding the facility and Tuzard and his elite team dispatched them without hesitation. He quickly removed Keeras from the medical container and administered the medication, but the strange alien did not respond.

It was a dumb mistake. Tony placed the bullack on its end and it fell to the ground due to minor vibrations from the ship. He picked up the weapon and stood. The Princess was awake and looking around the room. She couldn't see him, but she saw the weapon and screamed for her guards. Tony panicked and quickly swung the blade through her neck. The Princess briefly struggled for air as her blood sprayed across the room. He waited to make sure the Princess wouldn't be discovered by her guards and revived. Thankfully her guards hadn't heard the scream and the Princess wouldn't be revived. There was no other choice; it was time to find and kill Empress Zovad.

Tradition dictated mental communication between an Empress and her child was not to take place unless there was a dire emergency. Empress Zovad only communicated with her daughter telepathically on one previous occasion. At the time, the Princess was an infant simply reaching out. But now her daughter's mind suddenly reached out and was silenced. She knew her daughter was dead and the Overlord would be coming for her.

Tuzard didn't know what else to do; Keeras was not waking up. The communication device chirped and he opened it. "The schedule has been moved up. I'm on my way to the Empress now. What's going on with Keeras?" Tony asked. "I gave him the medication, but it's not working." "You must get him conscious. We're running out of time!"

Tuzard shook and slapped Keeras in vain. He ordered the prisoners traveling toward the engine room to double back so he could meet them at the prearranged location. Tuzard picked up Keeras and ran to the location with his men.

Chaos reigned on both Mars and Earth. In an instant, there was nowhere to run or withdraw to. "We should have gone with Vincent. The only thing left for us is to wait for is death," Alixias said in despair. "You thought we were going to die the last time too and we managed to survive. Have faith in destiny," Patrick replied. "The Alliance has made it very clear they are not coming this time. The destruction of these worlds has been preordained," Alixias dejectedly countered. "All is not lost," Zabu said with an imperceptible grin. "See, our child agrees with me," Patrick stated. "The delusional opinion of an extreme optimist and the ramblings of a young child won't change my mind."

Chapter 14

The Annunaki fleet would arrive in less than half a day. Commander Evir impatiently waited for instructions and guidance from the Alliance. The Tactical Council and the military experts were taking their time. It was likely they couldn't come up with a plan worth sharing as none would work. There simply wasn't enough firepower to repel the Annunaki.

"Commander, we've received the plan from the Alliance," the communications officer reported. "Put it up on the screen." After quick examination it was just as Evir thought. The Tactical Council sent an uninspired plan that smacked of desperation. The military leaders wanted him to order all Alliance ships to depart and travel outward far away from each other. The Captain of each ship was then expected to defeat three or four Annunaki vessels on his own. Commander Evir hated the plan. Each ship would be put into a dogfight with horrible odds of success.

"We're not doing this. It's suicide without purpose. Put my plan up on the screen. This is what we are going to do. The Annunaki are so cocky they've put their flagship out front. It's likely the Empress is on this vessel. We will focus all available firepower on her ship. If we can destroy the flagship, we destroy their leadership. Once the flagship is destroyed, I'll implement the plan from our military leaders and we'll spread out to fight the remainder of the vessels. If the Empress is killed, our enemy will likely become disorganized and we might really have a chance," Commander Evir said optimistically.

"Captain, we've received the battle plan from Commander Evir," Isabella stated. Vincent reviewed the plan. "I'll drop you all off on Earth and I'll engage the enemy on my own. There's no need for all of you to be here for this fight." "Bullshit, we're not going back to Earth. We're no safer there than we are here! Besides, you need all the help you can get. If anyone doesn't agree with me, please speak up," Monique replied as silence followed.

"If that's how you all feel. What's the status of the Annunaki fleet and when will they arrive?" Vincent asked. "There is no change from the last update. The entire fleet is on course for Earth and will arrive in three hours. Provided they don't change course, we will engage them near the orbit of the moon," Andy replied.

Empress Zovad seethed in pain and fury. The assassination of a Princess hadn't happened in over a thousand years. Her daughter was dead and there was no longer anyone in succession to the throne. A new successor must emerge immediately and a message to her people was in order.

"Your Princess has been assassinated by the Overlord known as The Shadow. The seventeen youngest females onboard are to report to the emergency rearing facility at once. All rearing facility personnel are to begin preparation of the royal jelly. I will oversee initial operations in the rearing facility before I kill the Overlord personally. Any remaining escaped prisoners are to be killed on sight." Her guards quickly followed as she set out to oversee rearing operations.

Tony stopped traveling toward the royal chamber after hearing the announcement from the Empress. The plan was going to have to be altered again. He didn't expect the Empress to leave her chamber after the death of the Princess. Her absence would buy Tuzard more time to revive Keeras. "What's the status with Keeras? Is he awake?" Tony barked into the communicator. "There's no change. He's still unconscious. I don't know how to wake him!" "There's been a delay; I need all of you to hide in the emergency locations we discussed. That order also applies to the team retreating from the engine room," Tony said. "How long of a delay will there be?" Tuzard asked. "I don't know yet. Be ready to leave in an instant."

The servants nervously scurried around the rearing center. "All chosen females report to your assigned location. You may now indulge in the royal jelly. I expect the new Princess to complete this task quickly. Be worthy of your new title and dispatch your enemies without mercy," Empress Zovad directed. The young females were eager and anxious. The opportunity to eventually become leader was at stake and it was extremely rare for leadership to change bloodlines. Empress Zovad watched as the combatants began consuming and bathing in the royal jelly. One of the females would eventually become her successor. All were covered in royal jelly and began sizing up their adversaries.

Once she killed the Overlord, she would preside and revel in the rare occurrence. The victorious female would need training and guidance. One of the most important lessons would be how to defeat an Overlord. She returned to her chamber and prepared for her own battle.

"Is there any chance this plan might work? Have there been any changes to the battle plan?" Vincent asked as the Annunaki fleet approached. "We've received no operational changes from Commander Evir and have received no new reinforcements. The odds remain the same," Julia reported.

The image of the enemy fleet on the view screen was intimidating. "Computer, please enhance and enlarge the image." Vincent ordered. Looking at the armada up close was unnerving. "How many ships in total and what type of formation is that?" he asked. "There is a total of one hundred and forty-nine ships. Ninety-two are Annunaki vessels and the other fifty-seven are Kracian vessels. The massive flagship is leading the Armada. It's possible the flagship alone could defeat all our vessels. It's heavily armed and all Kracian ships have taken up a position in the rear," Andy replied.

"Why aren't they protecting the flagship? It seems like a bizarre formation," Randy asked. "It's a unique formation the Annunaki haven't used in the past. They are returning to their home solar system. The Empress is demonstrating to her people she is brave and should be feared. In addition, they don't see us as a threat. When the fleet gets closer, the flagship will be protected from attack. The Annunaki fleet will then attempt to destroy all Alliance vessels. Kracian ships won't be used unless it's absolutely necessary. The Krace are considered less intelligent, untrustworthy and subordinate to the Annunaki. Once the battle is complete, the flagship will take its proper place in front of the formation and travel to Earth or Mars," Andy informed the crew.

"She sure is an arrogant bitch. Somebody needs to knock her on her ass!" Isabella hissed. "When will the enemy fleet arrive?" Vincent asked. "We're down to eighty-nine minutes and counting," Isabella replied. "If anyone has any new ideas, now would be a wonderful time to share."

There was no point in looking for the Overlord. With the Princess dead, Empress Zovad knew he would be coming. She ordered more guards to her chamber, even though it was unlikely they would be useful. The Overlord managed to bypass her security on multiple occasions. She planned on killing the Overlord herself anyway. The loss of her daughter hurt more than she expected. Her anger built to a flashpoint and it was time to seek out her enemy and unleash her fury. She focused all her hatred and passion, opened her mind, and sought out the Overlord.

Tony was preparing to order all the prisoners to the rendezvous point when he felt the presence of the Empress. She was attempting to enter his mind. Her mind had grown more powerful and she was angry. It took all his training and will power to keep her out. After a couple of minutes, she gave up. The improved mental power of the Empress was concerning and Tony was no longer confident he could defeat her by himself.

He opened his communicator. "What's the status with Keeras?" he asked. "He's still unconscious and I'm not sure if he'll ever wake up," Tuzard replied. "We're out of time. We could all be found any minute. Proceed as planned and get Keeras conscious!" he ordered as he picked up his bullack and went to confront the Empress.

After accessing the database, Tony sprinted down the corridors. Empress Zovad was returning to her chamber. He thought about his friends and ran faster. When he encountered Annunaki in the corridors, he cut them down without stopping. His adrenaline was pumping as he reached the chamber of Empress Zovad. She returned and was protected by her guards and the shields. Tony found the closest terminal and entered the command. The shields were now under his command. Only a few guards were left inside the new shields protecting the Empress.

He surprised the three guards when he entered the royal chamber. Their screams echoed throughout the chamber as Tony expertly sliced his bullack through the air into their bodies. Annunaki blood dripped off the shiny blades. Tony turned and faced the throne.

He was alone with the Empress. She had her back to him and slowly turned. "It's satisfying to know I'll be killing a worthy adversary," she said. "You're the weakest Empress in the history of the Annunaki. History will record that you were the first to be defeated by an Overlord. I hope you put up more of a fight than your daughter did," Tony replied and opened his mind.

Through the eyes of the Overlord, Empress Zovad watched her daughter die. There was surprise and pain in the eyes of the Princess as she took her last breath. Blinding anger resurfaced; she searched the mind of the Overlord and learned everything he knew, including his plan. He rescued the disgusting hybrid and was trying to harness the unprecedented power of the rare creature. She would finish the Overlord quickly and then kill Keeras. The hybrid possessed the most powerful mind she ever encountered and couldn't be allowed to live.

The mind of Empress Zovad was stronger than Tony thought possible. Somehow she grew more powerful. He searched her consciousness and found nothing helpful. The Annunaki were planning total domination and Empress Zovad was certain she would be victorious against him and would destroy the Alliance.

Annunaki guards arrived outside the shielding and were trying unsuccessfully to enter the chamber. Tony took a step toward the Empress. "That was a good trick with the shielding, but I've got one of my own," Empress Zovad said. Liquid began falling from the ceiling reminding Tony of a primitive fire system in an old building on Earth. The liquid was bright red and slightly sticky. He raised his right hand and looked at it; it was easily visible. The liquid continued to fall erasing his camouflage.

Empress Zovad slowly unsheathed two long blades and brandished one in each hand. "I don't need any tricks to defeat you," Tony said as he raised his bullack and charged. He took a chance and swung at her head, but she was quick and easily parried his attempt. "Is that the best you can do?" she laughed as she swung her blades toward the Overlord. Tony quickly moved aside and blocked her attempt.

"For an Empress you're pretty slow and weak." Tony responded confidently. He was physically superior to the Empress and knew it was only a matter of time before he would deliver a fatal blow. He initiated another attack when Empress Zovad assaulted his mind. The bullack swung through the air. This would be the end. Tony knew he was faster, yet somehow the Empress evaded his blade. Tony retreated.

"We will never be defeated. Your pathetic Alliance will soon serve the Annunaki!" Empress Zovad screamed. Tony quickly took a deep breath and tried to focus. His last attack was far too slow. He attempted to refocus his mind and shutout the Empress, but she was still there.

"I'm stronger than you. You will be dead momentarily," Empress Zovad said. Tony took a quick glance outside the shielding. The Annunaki guards were all dead. Tuzard and the prisoners arrived and slaughtered them all. Keeras was still unconscious and being held upright by two of the prisoners. "It looks like your plan has failed. It was a good try. I will torture everyone you've ever cared about when I'm done with you," Empress Zovad sneered as she advanced.

The Empress was quick and her mental abilities began overpowering his mind. Tony barely managed to block her next attack. She invaded his mind as he swung his weapon. His attempt failed miserably and the bullack struck the floor loudly. The Empress was on him quickly. She stuck a blade into his right arm and another into his left leg. The pain was excruciating. Empress Zovad backed away and reveled in her victory. "Is there anything you'd like to say before I end your life?" she asked.

After killing the guards, Tuzard watched the battle from outside the shield with the rest of the prisoners. Empress Zovad gained the upper hand and Tony was struggling. He needed to do something.

Tuzard took Keeras's nose into his mouth and bit down hard.

Tony didn't know how much blood he was losing as his blood mixed with the red liquid from the ceiling. He stood up and bravely raised his weapon. "Bitch, we're not quite done yet," he said. "Your bravery is to be admired. I'm much faster, you're injured and have a weak mind. It's no wonder all other Overlords failed. You shall join them in the afterlife and share your unique tale of failure," Empress Zovad raised her weapons. The fight with the Overlord was challenging, but she never doubted her ability to defeat him. Her empire was safe and she would rule until she died of old age.

As she raised both blades to finish off the Overlord, her mind was brutally assaulted. She watched through the eyes of a child as his parents were slaughtered. The child lived alone and craved companionship, but most importantly the child sought vengeance. Empress Zovad instantly knew it was the mind of the hybrid Solian. It was still too late for the Overlord. She would strike him down quickly and the freakish hybrid would be next to die.

Tony knew he was losing. He was bleeding heavily and despite his best efforts he was going to fail. A familiar mind suddenly intruded as Empress Zovad swung both blades toward his chest. Tony rolled to his left and stood up. "You're a cocky bitch. You never should have fucked with the people of Sol!" he said and opened his mind.

Tony was reenergized and ready to continue. Adrenaline and confidence graced his severely injured body. The bullack sliced through the air majestically and Empress Zovad was too slow. The combined attack on her mind was having an effect and Tony watched with satisfaction as his weapon severed her left leg. The Empress weakly swung her weapons in his direction. Tony now had the upper hand and knew it. "You will not have Mars! It is ours and always will be. Once you're dead the Alliance will destroy your ability to wage war. Your species will never rise again!" Tony said as he plunged the bullack through her shoulder.

Empress Zovad never felt such mental and physical pain. Her only option was to try and buy more time. "Don't kill me. We can find peace! I'm ready to negotiate," she begged. "I've fulfilled my purpose and defeated you. My friend is due personal vengeance and your life is now in his hands," Tony replied and deactivated the shielding. The bullack proved to be a valuable weapon and Tony handed the blade to his friend. "Thank you," Keeras said.

With her body and mind growing weak, Empress Zovad watched helplessly as the hybrid stood over her.

Keeras projected the image of his parents into her mind, swung the weapon high and sliced open her belly. Empress Zovad screamed in agony as her entrails spilled onto the floor. Her torso was split from breast to genitals and the last thing she saw was a smile on the face of the Solian.

"It's finally over!" Keeras said. "Not quite yet," Tony replied as he took the bullack. Tony used all his strength to slice the blade through the skull of the Empress. "Nobody can rush her to a medical center for revival now," he said. "Let's get to the command center. I need to communicate with the rest of the Annunaki," Tony said. "You're severely wounded. We need to get you medical attention," Keeras said. "I'll be fine; my wounds are already healing. Move out!"

It was nearly time to begin his new duty of serving the Empress. Axadro was preparing himself when the consciousness of the Empress abruptly went silent. He became dizzy and his heart began beating faster. The room spun, so he sat on the floor and began to sweat and was struggling to breathe. Axadro needed the Empress as much as he needed air.

Patrick was trying his best to console Alixias as she'd been sobbing and crying for hours. "It's just not fair!" she yelled. "Take a deep breath and try to relax.

We're still alive right now. What's that noise? I think it's coming from Zabu's room."

Patrick and Alixias stood at the doorway and looked at Zabu. Their child was laughing hysterically. She was laughing so hard tears were running down her face. "What the hell? What's so funny Zabu?" Alixias asked. There was no answer; Zabu was laughing and giggling so much she was unable to respond.

"Commander Evir, there is a minor change in the formation of the Annunaki Armada. One of the ships appeared to be making a minor course correction, but the correction was never completed and the vessel is about to collide with another Annunaki ship," his advisor reported. "I'm sure they'll make the correction and avoid the collision," he replied as he watched the ship drift on the viewscreen. Thirty seconds later the ships collided. It was only a glancing blow and neither ship was severely damaged, but both were now spinning out of control and traveling aimlessly away from the rest of the armada. "What the hell is going on?" Commander Evir asked.

Flarzul wasn't receiving any information from the Annunaki flagship or any other Annunaki vessels. As the leader of all Kracian ships, he knew it was unusual for communication to suddenly go silent. It was as if they all suddenly disappeared. "Commander, I've finally established communication with one of the Annunaki ships," his assistant reported. "Begin communication. What the hell is going on? Whey aren't any of you responding?" he asked. There was a long pause before he finally received a response. "Empress Zovad is missing."

Flarzul knew it was unprecedented for the Annunaki to be out of contact with their Empress. Something drastic must have happened and the upcoming battle was only minutes away. He made a quick decision. "Open a channel to all Annunaki vessels. This is Commander Flarzul of the Krace. I'm taking control of the fleet and you will take orders from me. Prepare to engage the enemy and execute the battle as planned. You will all do your duty and serve the Empress. It's time to finally defeat the Alliance and liberate your ancestral home world."

Tony, Keeras and the prisoners raced through the corridors unopposed. The Annunaki they encountered were listless and unresponsive. On the way to the command center, Tony briefly stopped at the emergency rearing center. The females inside were far from listless. Tony counted four dead and thirteen remaining. It was a scene of frenzied madness. The combatants were covered in jelly and blood. A female with a piece of flesh in her mouth glared at him with a look of pure hatred. "Damn, she reminds me of my ex-wife. Let's get the hell out of here. I'll deal with these bitches later," he said.

The command center on the flagship was enormous and Tony found fifteen Annunaki present when he arrived with his team. "Kill them all. We need total control here," he ordered. The prisoners found little resistance as they slaughtered the Annunaki in the command center. Vincent found the closest terminal and entered the access code he took from the mind of Empress Zovad. Total control of the ship was now his. "What are you going to do?" Keeras asked. "I'm going to end this goddamn war."

Every bulkhead on the flagship suddenly closed. Many Annunaki were crushed by the massive doors as they dropped from the ceiling. "They're all trapped and have no way of getting in here," Tony said. "I hope you're right. If they ever come to their senses we're way outnumbered," Tuzard replied. "I'm opening a channel to every ship in the armada and every Annunaki on this ship. Get ready; I have a feeling they're about to wake up. Attention Annunaki everywhere. Empress Zovad is dead. I'm an Overlord and for the first time in your history an Overlord has killed your leader. Earlier today I killed her daughter. Both your Empress and Princess are dead. I repeat, your Empress and Princess are dead.

None of you will feel their presence in your mind. I took immense pleasure in taking their lives and I'm now in control of the flagship and will kill the next Empress when she assumes power. I advise you to surrender," he said confidently. "Yeah, that might just get their attention," Tuzard said.

"Captain, some of the Annunaki ships are breaking formation. Combat is imminent," Isabella reported. Vincent watched the viewscreen as the armada began to separate. "I'm not a military expert, but that looks pretty random." Many of the vessels began traveling toward the flagship. A missile suddenly flashed out from one of the ships. "They're firing!" Monique yelled. The missile struck the Annunaki flagship near the engines. "What the hell? What's going on?" Vincent asked.

The flagship responded quickly. Multiple weapons decimated the ship that initiated the attack. More Annunaki ships began attacking the flagship. "I have no clue what's going on, but I like it. Outer space is strange," Enzo commented. "We've received orders from Commander Evir to stand by for further instructions," Isabella stated. "He's likely as confused as we are. This is very strange," Vincent responded.

Commander Evir couldn't think of an explanation for what was going on. The Annunaki weren't attacking any Alliance vessels and he wouldn't commit his forces to battle until they were under fire. "Commander, three more Annunaki ships have been destroyed," the tactical officer reported. "What are the Kracian ships doing?" Evir asked. "They are maintaining their position and formation. At the moment, they aren't doing anything. A channel from the Annunaki flagship just opened on all our frequencies. Expect a message at any moment," the tactical officer reported.

Everyone aboard the Santa Maria gasped. "Oh my God. How is it even possible?" Vincent asked. Tony was on the viewscreen. He was covered in some red substance, but it was definitely Tony. "Greetings. My name is Tony Stephens. I'm onboard the Annunaki flagship. Within the last hour, we've killed both the Empress and her daughter the Princess. Needless to say, the Annunaki are a bit pissed and disoriented right now. We wouldn't have been able to kill the Empress if it weren't for this Solian standing next to me. His name is Keeras. He was in hiding on Vandi since he was very young. Empress Zovad murdered his parents and his existence wasn't known until after the planet was evacuated by the Alliance.

I believe I know the reason the ancient race wished for humans and Martians to breed. Solians are the only species which has the mental power necessary to defeat an Annunaki Empress. If it wasn't for this Solian, we'd all be dead by now.

When we win this war, the Alliance must go through the gate to Tanas. Download all information from their central database and once that is complete, every piece of Annunaki weaponry and technology must be destroyed. A new Empress will eventually be anointed. There's already an emergency rearing facility aboard this vessel. When I destroy the one on this vessel, the Annunaki will begin the process again. If you find a rearing facility, kill all the females. Now is the time to decimate the Annunaki, but there is only a short window of time to accomplish the task. Perhaps five or six weeks at most.

I'll take out as many ships as possible. Hopefully we'll survive. If we don't, I wanted you to have all the information possible. I won't be able to help you with the Kracian vessels. I'd recommend you get some additional firepower in the area. I must go now. As you can see I'm quite busy."

"I can't believe he did it! Tony killed the Empress. I thought it was a hopeless fool's errand." Vincent was extremely hopeful. "I've learned never to underestimate Tony. He's a remarkable creature," Maxis said. "We have a real chance now. Shouldn't we be doing something?" Monique asked. "Yes, we should. Isabella, I want to speak with Commander Evir right now," Vincent stated. "Yes, Captain, I'm requesting contact."

A clearly agitated Commander Evir appeared on the screen. "I'm quite busy, Captain. What do you need?" he asked. "Shouldn't we join the attack? Tony needs all the help he can get if he's to survive." "Absolutely not! We're outnumbered, and I won't endanger more lives unnecessarily. The longer we wait, the better our chances of survival. We are working on a new plan to fight the Krace. If that is all, I must return to my duties now," Evir replied testily.

"Just one more thing, Commander. Allow my ship to join the fight. Surely, you can spare one ship?" Vincent asked. "The answer is no. Every ship is needed to fight the Krace and any remaining Annunaki vessels. I know of your propensity to bend the rules and if your ship moves without my express command, I will override your computer and have you removed as Captain. Have I made myself clear?" Evir asked. "Yes, Commander. I will obey your orders," Vincent replied as the transmission ended. "It looks like you've earned yourself quite the reputation, Vincenzo," Enzo said.

Every Annunaki ship ignored his orders. Over and over, Flarzul ordered the Annunaki ships to cease fire and retreat. He watched helplessly as vessel after vessel was destroyed. The massive Annunaki flagship was well armed and defended. "Give me a current update!" Flarzul ordered. "Twenty-one Annunaki vessels remain. The flagship has received heavy damage and the engines have been destroyed. Seventy-six percent of the weapons have been disabled," his second in command stated.

"The Annunaki are trying to prevent the flagship from fleeing or fighting, but really all that matters to them is the death of the Overlord," Flarzul said as he watched the flagship destroy another Annunaki vessel. "Inform all Kracian ships to continue standing by. We will commandeer any surviving Annunaki ships when the flagship is no longer operational."

Tony didn't have much to do. The computer on the flagship was designed to return fire on any ship that attacked. He glanced at the onboard monitors and watched as the Annunaki onboard the flagship went berserk. They were clawing and throwing themselves at the bulkhead doors and those who were trapped in the armory managed to breach four bulkhead doors so far. Seven doors remained before they would reach the command center, but they wouldn't make it in time.

His plan worked well with one exception. He didn't expect the Alliance to have so few vessels protecting Earth and Mars. Help hadn't arrived and he knew it wouldn't be coming. With the engines gone, there was only one likely outcome.

An alert on his data pad woke Dominic. He cancelled the alarm and went back to sleep. Fifteen seconds later he received another alert. When he received the devastating news of the upcoming loss of Earth and Mars he starting drinking at night. He was in no mood to talk to anyone and wanted more sleep. There was nothing that could be done to save his friends. "What do you want?" he answered. "Watch the video I sent you. It's important," his aide replied.

Dominic decided to placate his aide, so he could go back to sleep. He knew he wouldn't be left alone until he watched the video. As he was about to play the footage, he received an alert notifying him of an emergency session in the Great Chamber in thirty minutes. After watching the video from Earth, he poured himself some coffee and prepared to fight for his friends again.

Everyone was talking loudly when Dominic arrived. The video from Earth was an unexpected shock for all. Chief Administrator Kizak demanded silence. "By now, I'm sure you've all seen the astonishing video from Earth. Our analysts believe everything Tony said to be true. The bizarre actions of the Annunaki have reinforced this conclusion. The Tactical Council will provide their recommendation within the next half day. I will now open the topic for discussion."

Dominic stood up. "Chief Administrator, your analysts have verified the truth regarding what is happening in the Sol System. Empress Zovad is dead as is the Princess. A power vacuum currently exists in the Annunaki hierarchy and there will never be a better time to completely and utterly defeat them. A recommendation from the Tactical Council is unnecessary in this instance, so I call for a vote to send all our military vessels to the Sol System immediately. It's foolish to enter war without the ambition to win it."

"I think our best course of action is to wait for the recommendation from the Tactical Council. Is there an Ambassador who wishes to second the motion from the Earth Ambassador?" Kizak asked. Multiple ambassadors affirmed they would. "Voting will begin in ten minutes. Review all the relevant information you've been provided before you cast your vote," Kizak instructed. Dominic reviewed the information provided by the Alliance and found very little new data; he cast his vote in favor of the motion.

Ten minutes later, Kizak provided the results. "Against my recommendation, the motion has passed with seventy-eight percent voting in favor. The order has been given and Alliance vessels will begin traveling to Sol within the hour. The Tactical Council's recommendation will be provided to you when its available. Should the recommendation be against invasion, I will recall all ships and we will debate the topic again if necessary," Kizak stated.

Dominic breathed a sigh of relief. Once again, he felt the urge to return to Earth. "Your words were excellent and I'm not sure if the vote would have been favorable without them," his aide cheerfully said. "Right now, I wish I could do more than just talk. I want to take action and help us win," Dominic replied. "You just did."

Zabu was still laughing when Patrick and Alixias viewed the broadcast from Tony. "There was a Solian hiding on Vandi all along. It's almost inconceivable. You're no longer alone," Alixias said. "I know," Zabu replied with a smile. "Somehow she knew the exact moment the Empress was killed. It's the only thing that explains her crazy laughter. Once again, you gave up pretty quick," Patrick said. Alixias mustered a weak smile. "There's no guarantee we'll get through this. There are still many enemy ships out there preparing to invade. Hopefully I'll be wrong again and I'm sorry I get so emotional. For the sake of our child, I'll try to be more positive."

"No wonder the Annunaki wouldn't allow humans and Martians to breed on Vandi. They must have learned about the mental powers of the Solians. It's why they killed any hybrids and kept the two species separated," Patrick said. Alixias put her head in her hands. "Yes, and it also makes our child, and any other Solians, the most dangerous threat to the Annunaki; they will be targeted by the Annunaki forever." "When this is over, we must find a way to protect Zabu and her species. It would be a good idea to spread them out and send them to live on other planets within the Alliance," Patrick suggested.

A loud cheer erupted in the command center. Commander Evir smiled. "Reinforcements are coming!" the communications officer reported as the information from Rabanah appeared on the viewscreen. "It's about damn time! I hope the ships arrive before it's too late. Send an update to all vessels and tell them a new battle plan will be provided shortly," Commander Evir ordered.

Chapter 15

Five Annunaki ships remained. The last of the weapons on the flagship were either disabled or destroyed. "This isn't looking very good," Keeras stated as the impact of another missile rocked the ship. "No shit? We don't have any options left." Tony watched as four of the remaining ships landed in the hanger bay. "What are they doing?" Keeras asked. "I think they want to kill me personally. Let's make them think they have a chance," Tony said as he opened the bulkhead door leading out of the hanger bay. Tony and Keeras watched as Annunaki from the newly arrived ships disembarked and raced through the entrance. Once all the Annunaki were through, Tony closed the bulkhead door.

"Like rats caught in a maze," Tony chuckled. "We need to get off this ship. There are now four ships in the hanger bay, but how can we get there?" Keeras asked. "I've been thinking about that, but haven't come up with anything. We're in the very center of this vessel. The command center was placed here so it would hold out as long as possible during battle, but there are thousands of bloodthirsty Annunaki waiting for us in the corridors. If anyone here has any ideas, I'd like to hear them," Tony said. The last remaining Annunaki ship in space neared the hanger. Tony believed it would enter the hanger and land. Instead, the vessel hovered outside the ship and fired missiles into the hanger. All four ships which landed previously exploded brilliantly. "And then there's also that to consider," Tony deadpanned.

"Commander, we've located additional Alliance vessels." The information was the last thing Flarzul wanted to hear. "How many and where are they?" he asked. "We've located five.... make that six ships coming in through the gate from the Rabanah System," the intelligence officer reported. "So, the Alliance has decided to send help after all. Direct all vessels to break formation; the attack will begin in sixty seconds. It will be too late for Earth by the time they get here!"

The Annunaki flagship was heavily damaged. Vincent and the crew of the Santa Maria watched as momentum continued to carry the ship toward Earth. "Goddammit, someone has to do something!" "Captain, we have an incoming message from the Commander," Isabella reported as the image of the flagship was replaced by Commander Evir. "All Kracian ships are breaking formation, so it's likely they've detected the new ships coming in from Rabanah. Prepare to engage the enemy," he said.

Without warning, the Santa Maria accelerated and traveled toward the Kracian vessels. "I don't like this. Giving the computer total control makes me feel helpless," Vincent warned. "Extensive testing has been conducted and this method provides the greatest chance for success. In every recorded battle, the Annunaki and Krace have activated an EMP device to disable the computer. You will be in control shortly," Andy reported. "I still don't like it. Andy, you'll oversee navigation and Randy you'll be on weapons. Be prepared to take control when the EMP hits," Vincent ordered.

"I like the battle plan. Attacking the fastest ships first makes sense," Enzo said. "The larger ships will be ignored in the beginning while Alliance vessels attack the most maneuverable Kracian ships. It will be a two on one attack until the Krace adjust. Without an Empress directing the battle, I expect the Krace will reorganize and try to defeat us on their own," Andy said.

The Santa Maria closed on a target and fired missiles while a second Alliance ship fired as well. The lights suddenly dimmed and the displays went red. "That was the EMP. The computer is offline and we are on manual control," Isabella said as a missile struck the enemy ship. "Weapons and propulsion on the enemy ship have been destroyed, but it still has minimal life support," Monique reported. "Good enough; let's move on to the next target," Vincent ordered.

Andy deftly piloted the Santa Maria toward another Kracian ship. "Fire when ready!" Vincent ordered. Randy practiced in simulators and was surprised as he targeted the enemy ship. He couldn't have asked for a better target profile. He fired the powerful Alliance weapons and four missiles struck the enemy ship simultaneously. The Kracian ship exploded fiercely. "Good job Randy! Let's go find a new target!" Vincent exclaimed. "Captain, enemy ships are in pursuit. They've just fired," Monique reported. "Evasive action, Andy!" Vincent ordered. "Brace for impact!" Monique screamed as Randy fired missiles at the ship in pursuit.

An explosion shook the Santa Maria sending it off course. The ship's atmosphere began venting into space and the computer automatically closed bulkhead doors as wind whipped through the command center. "Give me a report!" Vincent screamed. "Our weapons have been destroyed. Propulsion is undamaged," Monique replied. "Get us out of here. Retreat to Earth!" Vincent ordered. Andy piloted the Santa Maria out of battle as Randy monitored his display. The last missile he fired struck the Kracian vessel he targeted and a bright explosion lit up the screen.

"What are we going to do?" Keeras asked. "There is very little we can do," Tony replied as he watched the battle unfold on the viewscreen. The ship began vibrating. "What's that?" Keeras asked. "It's Earth's atmosphere," Tony replied as he opened the communication channel. "This is Tony Stephens onboard the Annunaki flagship. We are declaring an emergency. Our engines have been destroyed and we don't have the ability to enter into orbit. Please send assistance." "What do you think they'll do?" Keeras asked. "I think they're otherwise occupied," Tony replied as he watched an Alliance ship explode on the viewscreen.

The Santa Maria managed to retreat safely. Isabella reviewed the most recent commands. "We've been ordered to the moon for immediate repairs." "Andy, get us to the moon as quickly as possible," Vincent ordered. Isabella scanned through the messages when a low priority communication caught her attention. "Captain, I think there's something you'd like to see. I'm putting it on the viewscreen now."

The crew of the Santa Maria watched Tony's emergency message. "Set a course for the Annunaki flagship. Get us there as fast as possible!" "We are on our way Captain," Andy replied. "There has to be something we can do. Tony doesn't deserve to die after all he's done for us," Vincent said.

"Captain, Commander Evir is requesting communication," Isabella reported as the Commander appeared on the viewscreen. "Captain, your orders are to return to the moon for repairs. What are you doing?" "I'm going to help my friend. Our computer has been disabled and there's nothing you can do to stop me. If this is my last action as Captain, so be it. What are you doing to save Tony? He killed the Empress and has given us a chance to defeat the enemy. Send assistance and stay out of my way. Close the channel!" Vincent ordered as the Commander was about to respond.

"Holy shit!" Isabella exclaimed as the flagship came into view. The enormous Annunaki flagship was a wreck. The Annunaki fleet inflicted heavy damage. The front of the flagship was hot and began glowing brightly as it entered the atmosphere. Large chunks of debris began ripping off the ship. "How much time before impact and where will it come down?" Vincent asked. "Approximately seven minutes and thirty-nine seconds, but it's too early for an exact location. My best guess right now is north of Barrow, Alaska, somewhere in the Arctic Ocean," Andy replied.

"Put us on a safe parallel course with the ship. We don't want to get hit by any of the debris. Request communication with Tony," Vincent ordered. Tony appeared on the screen a moment later. He was alone at a communications terminal. "What can we do to help?" Vincent asked. "There's nothing you can do. We're trapped in the center of this vessel and surrounded by enraged Annunaki. I was able to slow the ship before the engines were completely destroyed, but I was unable to put us on a course that would take us into orbit."

"There has to be some way to get you out," Vincent replied. "None of us can figure out a way, but if you can figure something out we'd be happy to leave. I'd like to save all my new friends onboard this ship. When victory comes, visit the world of Olanion. It's not far from Tanas. Find my mate Tulari and tell her thank you and I'm sorry I couldn't fulfill my promise," Tony requested.

"Andy, is there any Alliance technology that can help? Can you think of any options to save Tony and those aboard the flagship?" Vincent asked. "The ship is massive and it's now a burning missile. I wish there was a solution; unfortunately, it's simply too late at this point," Andy replied.

Tony was glad he was able to see his friends on the Santa Maria one last time. He loved them all and didn't want them to worry. "Hey guys, I accomplished what I set out to do. I was an old man when this all started. Having you as friends during my last adventure was the gift of a lifetime. If it wasn't for your friendship and support, I would have failed."

"You saved the entire Alliance, Tony. Without you, none of us would be here. We will always have the honor of being your friend. We........" Vincent stopped as the screen suddenly went blank.

"We've lost communication, Captain. I'll try to get it back," Isabella said. "Don't bother; I'm sure the communication equipment onboard the flagship has been incinerated. The crew watched silently as the flagship plunged through the atmosphere. How much time is left?" Vincent asked. "One minute and eighteen seconds until impact," Andy reported. "Continue to follow it down," Vincent solemnly ordered.

"Yes, Captain. I'm going to move a little further away. Larger pieces of the ship are breaking away. It's really falling apart." "When we get to seven hundred feet, stop our descent. Report our position and send a request to Commander Evir for a search and rescue team," Vincent ordered as the Santa Maria leveled off.

Keeras and the prisoners didn't deserve to die and earned their right to freedom. Tony felt guilty and sad, but couldn't think of anything he could have done differently. Time was running short. Perhaps there was one last thing he could do. Tony opened his mind and

shared his inner peace with Keeras. Tony was shocked
to learn of the information Keeras extracted from
Empress Zovad's mind before she'd been killed.

Everyone on the Santa Maria watched helplessly
as the flagship plunged toward Earth. "We love you,
Tony," Isabella quietly sobbed. With tremendous force
the ship slammed into and through the thin layer of ice
covering the Arctic Ocean. For a moment there was a
large hole in the ocean. The sound of the impact reached
them moments later as pieces of debris rained down
and a large column of steam rose out of the impact site.

"Son of a bitch. Nothing could survive that,"
Enzo said quietly. The sound of sobbing filled the
command center. Vincent was numb. He wasn't sure
how much time the Santa Maria spent hovering over
the crash site as his numbness turned to anger.

"We have a duty to Tony. We'll make goddamn
sure he didn't die in vain. Set a course for the moon.
We'll get our weapons repaired and find more enemies
to kill. Send a message to Commander Evir. Have him
send out a Tsunami warning to any areas that might be
impacted by the crash. Please provide an update on the
battle," Vincent ordered.

"It could go either way. The battle started out
well for us. The Krace have adjusted their tactics and
recently retreated. Alliance ships have regrouped away

from the Krace. Twenty Alliance vessels are currently fully operational and twenty-four Krace ships are fully operational. An additional six Annunaki ships have passed through the gate coming from Tanas. Analysts have concluded these additional Annunaki ships are old. It's likely the Annunaki brought them out of retirement to hunt down the Overlord. Seventy-nine Alliance ships are inbound from Rabanah and within the next ten hours two newly constructed vessels from the moon will be operational," Andy reported.

"So, there's currently a pause in the battle?" Vincent asked. "Yes, and it's probable both sides are weighing their options and updating their plans," Andy replied. "Let's fix this ship and get back out there!" Vincent said as the Santa Maria arrived at the moon. "Captain, Commander Evir is requesting communication," Isabella reported. "Tell him I'll contact him shortly. I'll have my conversation with him in private after everyone disembarks."

Flarzul didn't like having his orders questioned. "'Why are we still fighting? Even if we win, there won't be enough of us left to take control of the planet. We must retreat and go back through the gate," his second in command said. "Reinforcements have just come through the gate and more will follow. A new Empress will be anointed in the near future. This is our chance to

311

prove we should be treated as equals. If we can complete the plan Empress Zovad gave us, the new Empress will be able to return to her home world immediately. What we do today will define our species for the next thousand years," Flarzul said. "I disagree. Our situation is hopeless and it's time to retreat," his second in command replied. "You're weak and not very brave. How about we quit arguing?" Flarzul said flatly as he took out his sidearm and shot him. "Get the corpse of this weak-minded coward out of here."

Dominic was having dinner with Chief Administrator Kizak when the decision from the Tactical Council arrived. "It appears your gamble paid off. The Council agrees we should send our ships back to Sol," Kizak shared. "You heard what Tony said. There will never be a better time to completely defeat the Annunaki," Dominic replied.

"He accomplished the impossible. After all the endless wars, stalemates, and retreats I never thought an Empress could actually be killed. I know he was a friend of yours and I'm very sorry for your loss. He was a very unique human."

"He was also extremely intelligent and we must follow his advice. The infrastructure of the Annunaki must be totally destroyed. It's imperative for the Alliance to go to Tanas and destroy all Annunaki technology." "If it's possible, it will be done. You should know there will be another emergency session soon," Kizak stated. "Why? The Tactical Council approved the return to Sol," Dominic replied. "That issue won't be debated, rather the debate will be on a new topic." "Well, don't leave me in suspense. What will we be debating?" Dominic asked. "Whether or not the Annunaki should be totally exterminated as a species," Kizak responded.

"I'm relieving you of your command. You're no longer the Captain of the Santa Maria," Commander Evir stated. Vincent expected nothing less. "That would be a mistake." "No, it really wouldn't be. You have little experience as a Captain and you can't follow orders. You're merely a token human who has been allowed to assist in the war effort. I'd like to hear your reasoning as to why it would be a mistake," Commander Evir challenged. "We did well before our weapons were disabled. We spent a very short time attempting to assist Tony on the flagship. You do of course realize we wouldn't be having this conversation if it wasn't for him? The Alliance speaks so highly of righteousness and honor, yet you chose to ignore him completely.

Tony was a great asset to the Alliance, yet you chose not to provide him any assistance. Who knows how he could have helped us in the future? Keeras was the only known adult Solian in existence and we lost his wisdom, abilities and knowledge as well. You made the decision not to assist the doomed flagship. Humanity has been very beneficial to the Alliance lately. It would be unfortunate if your superiors learned that you failed to enlist our ingenuity. I am the damn Captain of the Santa Maria and I always will be. My crew and I will finish what Tony started. It's obvious you are still trying to understand humans; however, it would be wise for you to consider all we've accomplished. In fact, there are accomplishments you are unaware of. It would be smart of you to consider your own future. Think of me as a dangerous animal trapped in a corner. Anything could happen," Vincent said and closed the channel.

It was far too long since he ate. He loaded up a plate and sat down. "How'd it go? Are you still our Captain?" Enzo asked. "I'm not really sure. Commander Evir has something new to think about. For all intents and purposes, I said my peace and hung up on him. Unless he has me physically restrained, I'm going back as Captain. One way or another we will leave soon. If you have any advice for me, I could use it right now,"

"I know very little about warfare in space. From experience, I do know that if you can distract or confuse an enemy it's much easier to defeat them," Enzo suggested. "I'm not sure how to do that." "Distracting your enemy produces frustration and anger. Someone who is angry will lash out and destroy everything around them. The ship will be ready soon, so eat your food, get off your ass and figure it out. We're counting on you."

Vincent didn't know how to distract or confuse the enemy. He boarded the Santa Maria and tried to think of an answer as she underwent repairs. He reviewed battle footage and found an anomaly. There was one ship that was subtly protected and rarely moved. The Commander of the Krace was likely onboard the vessel. Vincent came up with an idea.

"Captain, our ship has been repaired. All crewmembers have been recalled. We will rejoin the fleet shortly," Isabella reported as she boarded the ship. "Very well. I will be sending some unusual messages after we depart. Transmit my messages verbatim," Vincent ordered.

Everyone was onboard and the departure of the Santa Maria was approved. "Apparently Commander Evir still thinks I'm the best choice as Captain. Send the following message on an open channel and make sure it's on a channel the Krace monitor," Vincent ordered. "The condition of Empress Zovad remains unchanged. She is still comatose after being recovered from the wreckage of the Annunaki flagship. The Overlord underestimated her ability to survive. She did not die as he previously stated. We will send additional updates as her condition changes," Vincent said.

The intercepted message was unbelievable. Flarzul didn't know what to do. An advisor told him the ship that sent the message was recorded following the flagship down and present at the crash site. "At all costs, we must save the Empress. Instruct the rest of the fleet to leave the ship which broadcast the message alone. No one is to fire upon it without my prior authorization. Request communication with the ship that transmitted the message."

"A communication request is coming in from the Krace. It's Commander Flarzul," Isabella reported. "Commander, I'm glad you've established contact. We must end this war. I'd like to have you come aboard so we can begin negotiations," Vincent said. "It's my understanding you have the unconscious body of Empress Zovad onboard your vessel," Flarzul replied with caution. "I'm not sure where you heard this rumor. I believe you are misinformed. If Empress Zovad lives, I'm sure you'll hear from her shortly. How about coming onboard to negotiate an end to this war?" Vincent asked. "I will not board your vessel under any circumstance." Flarzul closed the channel.

"Captain, we have another transmission request. This time it's Commander Evir. "What the hell are you doing? You have no authorization to negotiate. What's with this transmission about Empress Zovad being aboard your vessel?" Evir demanded angrily.

"Just try to keep up and assist as necessary. Have all Alliance vessels standing by and ready to attack. The Krace won't dare fire on this ship. If they think there's even the slightest chance Empress Zovad is onboard, they wouldn't dare. If all Alliance ships are in position, I'd like to demonstrate my point. With your permission, I'd like to fire upon the two ships escorting Commander Flarzul's vessel." Evir was clearly frustrated, but he knew Vincent would follow through with his crazy plan. "You're almost more trouble than you're worth. All ships have been advised and are ready for combat. Fire when ready."

"Move in a little closer. Let's see if any of the ships respond. Do not fire on Flarzul's ship. We'll need him to remind the other Krace vessels not to fire on us," Vincent ordered. After we fire, prepare to locate and engage the next closest Kracian ship. Fire on the flanking vessels when ready." "Yes, Captain. Give me a moment or two," Randy replied.

"The Alliance Captain lies. He has the Empress and was attempting to lure me onboard where I'd be killed immediately," Flarzul stated. "What are we going to do, Commander? How are we going to recover the

Empress?" his communication officer asked. Flarzul
was wondering the same thing. It wouldn't be easy.
"We must destroy all the other Alliance ships. Once that
is accomplished, we can take our time with this one and
carefully disable their weapons. Locate a new target,"
he ordered.

As Flarzul sat down in his command chair, the
ships flanking his vessel exploded in bright fireballs.
His first instinct was to fire on the attacking vessel and
he almost issued the order. "Go find a new target
immediately!"

"Nice shooting, Randy. Let's go hunting! Find us
a new customer, Andy. Another Kracian vessel was
quickly targeted and Randy fired again, destroying it. "I
wonder what Commander Evir thinks of my plan
now?" Vincent mused. "He's probably wondering if
he's out of a job. I don't think he's made the best
decisions these last couple of hours. He's ordered all
remaining Alliance vessels to join the fight," Julia
replied as the Krace came under additional fire. Nearby
explosions illuminated the darkness of space.

"Commander Evir has ordered a change in
formation," Isabella reported. "Comply with the order,
Andy," Vincent said. What are the current numbers?"
Vincent asked. "There are twelve Alliance ships

remaining. The Krace are now down to three," Monique replied.

The remaining three Kracian ships were surrounded by Alliance vessels. The crew of the Santa Maria watched as two of the last three were attacked and destroyed. Only Flarzul's ship remained. "Open all Alliance channels," Vincent ordered. "Channels are open, Captain," Isabella reported. "Alliance fleet. Please allow us the honor of taking this last vessel," Vincent requested and motioned for Isabella to close the channel. "Move in as close as safely possible and prepare to fire on my order. Request communication with Flarzul," Vincent ordered.

Flarzul failed himself, his fleet, the Annunaki and most importantly, the Empress. In retrospect, he should have followed the advice of his second in command and fled. "Commander, the Captain of the enemy vessel is requesting communication. Flarzul knew death was imminent, but out of curiosity he commanded his communications officer to open the channel. He glanced at the viewscreen and was surprised. The enemy ship was damn close.

"Why don't you surrender Flarzul? You can still live and save your crew," Vincent asked. "The Annunaki will rise again. With our combined strength, the Alliance will eventually be defeated. You may have won today, but we will return and you will once again become our slaves. Every planet within the Alliance will eventually be ours," Flarzul countered. Vincent looked into the enemy Commander's eyes. "I don't think so. The Annunaki are defeated and you will never retake the Sol System. My friend Tony sends his regards." Vincent pointed to Randy and instantly the Kracian vessel was hit with multiple missiles and exploded gloriously into space.

"Very well done, Vincenzo. Tony would be proud. You've honored him," Enzo said. "It was your idea. I just needed to figure out how to distract the Krace. Your wisdom and experience are still useful in this new era," Vincent replied. "Yeah Dad, listen to Vincent," Isabella interjected.

Everyone in the command center suddenly looked confused. "Wait a minute. Did you just say Dad?" Randy asked. Isabella glanced at Enzo sheepishly. "I needed to have someone out here keeping an eye on all of you. Dominic needed a bit of maturing, so I tasked Isabella to reign in Dominic if he did something crazy." "Well, that explains quite a bit. Why didn't Dominic say something to anyone about Isabella?" Monique asked. "He doesn't know Isabella is his sister. She was raised in Italy. Dominic was left on my doorstep by the wife of one of my enemies when he

320

was an infant. I raised him as my own son. There's a reason I used to spend much of my time in Italy. Isn't that right Bella?" Enzo replied. "Sì Padre."

"Jesus, I think we've had enough surprises for one day. Now we learn you planted a snoop," Vincent said. "She's family and she's intelligent. Her duty was to help protect and advise all of you. She's a smart young lady and I obviously trust her."

"Captain, we've received orders to return to Earth. We are to resupply and have been given some down time before the six Annunaki ships arrive," Isabella reported. "Thank you, spy of Enzo. Why are we going to Earth and not the moon?" Vincent asked. "There's not enough capacity at the moon base for all Alliance vessels, so we've been selected to return to Earth," Isabella replied. "Bring us home, Andy," Vincent ordered.

"I can't believe you didn't even tell me about Isabella. We've been through so much and been friends forever. I should have known something was going on when you recommended her," Randy said. "I've been able to live a long life by playing all the angles. The only thing she lacked was confidence in herself, but I see she now has it. She's been a good employee for you, so what are you complaining about?" "Well, she's definitely her father's daughter. I forgot, you don't like to lose," Randy responded. "Never, and neither does she. Bella values friends and family, but she will not tolerate anyone who treats her with disrespect. She's very strong willed."

His adrenaline was gone and Vincent was exhausted. "Captain, I can't find a place to land," Andy stated. "You've navigated through space during battle and you're having trouble landing?" Vincent questioned irritably. "Take a look down below, Captain," Andy replied. Thousands of humans and Martians cheered the arrival of the Santa Maria. Many held handcrafted signs.

"I didn't expect to be welcomed home like this. Descend slowly, perhaps they will clear out enough for us to land. It's good to know we're appreciated." Vincent smiled wearily. As the Santa Maria slowly descended, the crowd parted, and Andy was able to land. "Why are there so many people here?" Vincent asked. "Watch the news," Isabella replied as she put a broadcast on the viewscreen. The last encounter with Flarzul was rebroadcast over and over. Vincent listened to his own words......."My friend Tony sends his regards."

"I just want some rest. Let's find somewhere to wind down and relax," Vincent said as the ship landed. He led the crew out and found Commander Evir and many more Alliance leaders waiting on the tarmac. "Look, President Louis is here," Monique said. "He goes by Michael now. Let's enjoy this reception; I think it's well deserved," Julia said as she smiled broadly. Vincent wasn't quite so tired anymore as he approached Commander Evir. "Well done, Captain. Your plan was just what we needed. We will discuss your communication skills and your methods at a later time," the Commander said with a slow smile. "I'm just glad it worked." Vincent said.

For the next few hours, the crew of the Santa Maria celebrated. Martians and humans of all ages laughed, danced, drank and ate. Vincent was explaining what happened with an elderly human woman when Commander Evir approached. "You and your crew have earned some time off. The Tactical Council has determined the six new Annunaki ships aren't a threat, so it will not be necessary for the Santa Maria to participate in what will be a quick battle. Enjoy this moment with your crew and your friends," Commander Evir said earnestly. "Thank you, I will inform the crew." A young Martian girl tugged on his jacket. "Thank you, Captain Vincent." she looked up at him with big eyes and a sweet smile.

"The war is over," Patrick said. "What about the new Annunaki ships?" Alixias asked. "They're old, outnumbered and will be easily defeated." "The Alliance must understand how important it is to protect

323

the Solians. It should be their highest priority moving forward," Alixias passionately replied. You're right; it's very important. I will travel to Rabanah and speak with Dominic and Tissa personally. As the representatives for Earth and Mars, they must represent the interests of the Solians.

I have difficulty understanding how Tony was able to succeed. It would be nice to know the details. He was an extraordinary and remarkable human whom I wish I could have spent more time with," Alixias said. "Everything happens for a reason. If it wasn't for Tony, we wouldn't know how important the Solians are. It's too bad Keeras died. He could have shared his unique experiences with Zabu," Patrick added. "He did what was necessary," Zabu interjected.

Chapter 16

The emergency session was called just as Kizak predicted. It was as heated and contentious as any of the previous sessions Dominic attended and the debate showed no signs of ending. "Where is the morality in murdering an entire species? The Annunaki must be given the chance to evolve," the Ambassador from Snilga passionately implored. "It's either us or them. Our long-term survival hangs in the balance. We may never have another opportunity like this," the Ambassador from Hedalion angrily replied.

Even Kizak looked tired and weary. "We will take a recess. Nearly everyone has stated their position on this important matter. When we reconvene, debate will last no longer than two hours. If you have any last thoughts that haven't already been addressed, this will be your time to speak. A vote will take place when the two hours are concluded," Kizak informed the ambassadors.

"Do you know how you're going to vote?" his aide asked. "It's all I've been thinking about. Both sides have compelling arguments, but at the moment, I'm still undecided. Exterminating an entire species seems pretty drastic," Dominic replied.

After a short break, the debate resumed. Dominic studied all the information. He hadn't planned on speaking but changed his mind with only a few minutes left in the debate. "Fellow ambassadors, both positions have merit. Currently, we know very little about the Solians. My friend Tony believed the Solians were created to defeat the Annunaki. In the coming years, we will learn more about the Solian species. It took just one Solian to assist in defeating Empress Zovad. I will vote against the motion to exterminate the Annunaki. It's my belief the Solians will take care of the matter within the next few decades," Dominic argued firmly.

"The time for debate has come to an end. Voting begins now," Kizak ordered. Dominic hoped he made the right decision. If the Annunaki became powerful again, he would regret the decision for the rest of his life. "At least the vote is finally taking place. I wasn't sure if the debate was ever going to end," his aide said. "Maybe it wasn't long enough; I'm still not very confident in how I voted."

After two days of well-earned rest, all Alliance crews in the Sol System were called to a meeting. "What's this all about?" Monique asked. "The results of the vote on Rabanah have been shared and it's been decided the Annunaki will not be eradicated. I would imagine we're here to discuss what happens next," Vincent replied.

An image of Tanas appeared on the viewscreen. Commander Evir pointed to the image. "Tanas is the home world of the Annunaki. A probe was sent through the gate and this image was taken yesterday. We have been tasked with invading the planet and eliminating the ability of the Annunaki to wage war. Right now, we are in the process of extracting all data from the Annunaki's central database. In short, we will destroy everything. The Alliance will ensure that basic shelter and food is provided to the species, but their ability to wage war will be destroyed. All facilities, all ships under construction and their entire infrastructure will be targeted. All transportation networks are to be destroyed as well. The Annunaki will be forced to retreat to rivers and lakes and will farm or hunt their food. Every planet in the Tanas System will be visited and any technology found on other worlds will be eliminated as well.

As I speak, a new Empress is fighting for supremacy and will begin to lead her people in very short order. Our secondary mission will be to find the new rearing facility and to capture or kill the females fighting for leadership of the Annunaki. The facility could be anywhere and additional information will be provided with your orders. We have never been to the Tanas System, so expect surprises and be ready for anything. Do what you can to spare the lives of our enemy and defend yourselves at all costs. Details of the invasion plan will be transmitted to all of you when it has been finalized."

The crew gathered on the Santa Maria. "Does everyone want to continue on to Tanas? If you wish to remain on Earth or go somewhere else, now's the time to let me know," Vincent asked. "I will stay on Earth for now. It's time for me to take a long vacation. I will go to Lake Chelan where Maria and I spent time in our youth. A lifetime of work has taken a toll and some down time is necessary as I grow older. It's time for me to reenergize before I commit to something new. Isabella will step up in my absence," Enzo said. "Take your vacation, Uncle. I'm sure you'll get bored quickly and want a new challenge," Vincent replied with a smile. Everyone else was going to Tanas. It was time to work on the itinerary for the mission. Vincent had an obligation to fulfill.

"I know you're busy; thanks for meeting with me Commander," Vincent said. "Make it quick, I'm very busy. What do you want now?" Evir asked. "Can you please assign the Santa Maria to the world known as Olanion? We will perform the mission as required and track down any Annunaki technology," Vincent asked. "I don't see why not; we have to explore all the worlds, so why Olanion specifically?" Evir asked. "Tony's mate lives on the world. He wanted me to give her a message in person." "The Santa Maria will be assigned to Olanion. Deliver the message to Tony's mate; however, there's another matter we need to talk about. Some of our ships that were damaged in battle have been repaired," Evir continued. "Unfortunately, we lost some very valuable crews. The Santa Maria has excess personnel, so I need to reassign some of your crew to command one of the repaired vessels." "Who did you have in mind?" Evir looked at him squarely. "Monique will be captain of the newly repaired ship and Isabella and Randy will join in her." he said. "I don't like losing valuable crewmembers, but I understand the problem. I'll inform them when I return." Vincent replied diplomatically.

"What do you mean we're being split up?" Monique asked after Vincent shared the orders from Commander Evir. "We make a wonderful team and I don't want to lose any of you, but I couldn't make a logical argument. We're overstaffed and the Alliance is short on personnel, so the three of you are needed to operate one of the invading ships. You'll make a great captain, Monique." Vincent confidently said. "We'll be fine. The mission is simple and there are no longer any Annunaki vessels to oppose us. Our job is to destroy infrastructure," Randy offered. "As long as the ship has weapons, I don't mind. I'm looking forward to the destruction of Tanas," Isabella added. "We have nothing left to discuss. It's almost time to leave and the three of you must report to your new ship. Good luck and stay safe."

"The moment is at hand and Zabu is needed." Laxi told Patrick and Alixias. "What's happened? Why do you need our child?" Patrick asked. "A second Solian child has been born. Alliance medical personnel have decided that mental contact should occur as quickly as possible after the birth of a child. Additional Solians will soon arrive on both Earth and Mars," Laxi responded. "Give us a few moments to prepare Zabu," Alixias replied. "I'm ready now and am aware another has arrived. Preparations are not necessary," Zabu said as she walked out of her room.

The community on Mars celebrated the birth of a new Solian. Humans and Martians gathered to congratulate the new couple. There were many visitors in the medical center. "Everyone except the child must leave this room," Zabu said when she arrived. "You mean everyone except the parents of course," the mother stated. "Everyone but the child must depart. Please don't make this more difficult than it needs to be."

The father placed the infant Solian on a bed and was the last to leave the room. Zabu looked at the helpless infant. "Seek peace and wisdom," she gently said and opened her mind to the child. The mind of the infant was chaotic. Zabu reassured and connected with the new soul. With the connection, the infant now possessed the ability to reach out to Zabu should the need arise. The contact was more emotional than she expected. A living and breathing member of her species arrived and Zabu relished the presence of the newly arrived Solian. She shared basic emotional knowledge and broke the connection.

"All is well, you may return. The connection has been made. He will be at peace and can reach out when needed in the future," Zabu stated confidently. The parents thanked Zabu as she walked toward the exit. "Soon, there will be many more Solian births on both Earth and Mars. Are you prepared to travel and assist the new members of our species?" Laxi asked. "I will always be ready to assist my species. Our existence is essential for ongoing peace."

After Monique, Randy, and Isabella reported to their new ship, the Santa Maria departed for the Annunaki home world. "Captain, we've traversed the gate. Tanas is directly ahead," Andy reported. "Look at all the brown and grey on that world. No wonder the Annunaki are assholes, they don't have anything beautiful on their world," Julia said.

"Have any enemy vessels been located?" Vincent asked. "There are none in the immediate vicinity, but Commander Evir recently reported there are two small Kracian ships on the outskirts of this solar system. They are stationary and the Commander doesn't consider the ships a threat," Julia replied. "Have you located Olanion?" Vincent asked. "Yes, and it won't take us long to get there," Andy said. "When we land on Olanion, I will depart the ship for a few days. Julia will be in charge. I have received permission from Commander Evir to disembark. You will continue the mission as outlined by Commander Evir."

"Fire when ready!" Monique ordered. "How do we know there aren't still Annunaki in the buildings?" Isabella asked. "Commander Evir broadcast a message planetwide and the Annunaki were instructed to leave all structures. If any failed to do so, it is by their own choice. There isn't time to check every building and we are not going to engage in combat on the surface. Let's complete our mission," Monique replied.

"Yes, Captain. Firing missiles now," Isabella responded. Monique observed silently as an Annunaki shipbuilding hangar was decimated. For the next two hours, Isabella fired on her assigned targets. The Annunaki home world was under siege and offered no resistance. Other Alliance ships across the planet inflicted similar damage. At the next target, Isabella suddenly paused. "What's wrong? Why haven't you fired?" Monique asked. "The markings on the building indicate it's a medical facility. The mission briefing provided by Commander Evir stated we shouldn't fire on any identified medical facilities. It's a very unusual structure," Isabella replied. "Please contact Commander Evir and request additional instructions," Monique ordered. "I'll send the message now," Randy said.

The solid ground under his feet was welcome. Vincent spent too much time in space recently and was grateful for the fresh air. Olanion was a beautiful planet and if it wasn't for the recent battle scars inflicted by the Annunaki, the planet could have been mistaken for any other within the Alliance. When the Santa Maria arrived, all local Olanions fled into the countryside. Vincent sat on the ground in the center of the village and waited for someone to return. He didn't want anyone to think he was a threat. After an hour passed, a lone figure approached.

"I'm not going to hurt you. The Annunaki have been defeated. My name is Vincent and I'm looking for someone." "Stay on the ground. I have summoned nearby friends and if you threaten me in any way they will attack. My name is Synimbok. Why are you here?" the Olanion asked. Vincent was pretty sure the alien was alone and nobody else was nearby, but it didn't matter one way or the other. "I told you, I'm looking for someone. Her name is Tulari."

The noise was almost at too high a pitch for him to hear. Vincent put his hands over his ears as Synimbok blew into some kind of horn. Olanions suddenly rushed back into the village. Many were pointing weapons in his direction. "What do you know of Tulari?" Synimbok asked. "She was the mate of a friend of mine. He is now dead and asked that I give her a message."

"Tell me about this friend of yours," Synimbok demanded. "He lived on this world, but I'm not sure for how long. Tulari was close to him. He helped kill Empress Zovad and if it wasn't for him, I wouldn't be here right now," Vincent replied amicably. The weapons pointed in his direction were slowly lowered. "Everyone on this world knows Tulari was assisting an Overlord. Are you a friend of the Overlord she was assisting?" Synimbok asked. "My friend had unique abilities. If Tulari was assisting him, he must have been an Overlord," Vincent responded confidently. "I'm sure Tulari would like to speak to anyone who knew the Overlord. We will escort you to her location at once. Welcome to our world."

"Commander Evir has instructed us to stand by. He is sending additional ships to our location. The Annunaki normally kill the weak or injured, so a medical facility is a rare aberration. Ground forces will clear the building and investigate the situation at this location," Randy reported. "Please advise the Commander I'd like to accompany the ground forces," Monique ordered.

Commander Evir reluctantly agreed to her request and a brief time later Monique left her ship and joined the ground force. "Stay behind. Once we clear the building you will be granted access. You're not a soldier, so obey my orders and don't distract anyone," the team leader ordered. Monique waited as the building was deemed safe for entry. "You may now enter. There is no immediate danger."

The medical facility was empty except for one large room. Monique entered and was surprised to find hundreds of Annunaki children in the massive chamber. "Have you spoken with them?" she asked the team leader. "They aren't a threat and are caged within a forcefield. I brought you here so we could proceed together. I'm not sure if the caged Annunaki children know everyone else evacuated this building."

Monique studied the mission plan extensively when she was promoted to Captain. She didn't want to make any mistakes due to a lack of information and now it was time to try and communicate with the young Annunaki. She knew all Annunaki were loyal to the Empress without fail. "Why do you remain here imprisoned without purpose? Shouldn't you be serving your Empress?" Monique inquired.

One of the older Annunaki children slowly approached. "Empress Zovad does not control us. She's the reason we're here. I hope she dies a long and painful death," the child answered angrily. Monique was taken aback. As far as she knew, Annunaki never questioned their Empress, let alone insulted her. "Why do you betray your leader? What did she do to you?" "We have nothing left to say. Leave all of us alone. We wish to die in peace," the child replied in defeat as she retreated into the corner with the others.

Monique wasn't sure how to proceed. The alien children wouldn't talk and there was no one else around to provide information. "There's a camera in the room. Let's see if we can find the video. Maybe we'll figure out what the hell is going on with these children."

After travelling for two days, Vincent and Synimbok arrived at another village which was decimated by the Annunaki. "You are on your own now. Go to the dwelling on top of the hillside. Tulari should be there." Synimbok pointed to the hill. "Thank you for your help. I will tell the Alliance about what happened here and we will help you rebuild." Synimbok smiled. "If you've truly defeated the Annunaki, you've done enough."

An hour later, Vincent reached the dwelling. It was getting dark and there was no light emanating from the home. He knocked on the ancient door and waited. After trying repeatedly, he sat down. After a few minutes passed, he decided to spend the night in the village below. As he stood up, he heard the creak of a door. "Who are you and what do you want?" a female voice asked. "I was a friend of Tony's. He asked that I find you." The door slowly opened and the alien motioned for him to enter.

A lone candle burned on the floor next to a pillow. Tulari retrieved a second pillow for Vincent. The home was completely silent and Vincent could hear the flickering candle. Vincent sat and silently gazed at the flame with Tulari. He wasn't sure how much time passed before he finally spoke. "Tony saved billions of lives. He saved your world and he saved my world. He accomplished his mission. He asked me to find you and thank you for everything you did for him. He cared for you and he's sorry he broke his promise."

Tulari didn't raise her head and continued to stare at the candle. "I knew he would kill the Empress. He was different than the other overlords. Can you take me back to your world? I would like to see him one last time." she said. "The Annunaki flagship crashed into one of our oceans on Earth. Tony was on it. Search and rescue teams have not yet recovered his body and he's presumed dead." Vincent replied. "How do you know he's dead? The Overlord was unique," Tulari asked. "It was a devastating impact. If Tony were alive he would have found a way to contact me by now. If he wasn't burned alive before the crash, he would have died on impact or drowned. Can you tell me about his time here?" Tulari took a moment to absorb the information before replying. "He spent his time training, studying and planning to complete his task. It was his singular focus. I never expected to become his mate and miss him terribly. I don't believe he is dead."

Vincent and Tulari shared stories for the rest of the night and into the early morning. Dawn arrived and Vincent decided it was time to go. "I better get back to my ship; we have a mission to accomplish." he said. "I'm sure you haven't slept in a very long time. You have honored the Overlord and may rest in his room," Tulari insisted. "I am very tired and will take you up on your generous offer."

The room was lavish and the amenities were welcome. It was designed to provide every possible comfort to an overlord. Vincent couldn't think of anyone who deserved it more than Tony. He was happy his friend found a companion in such hostile territory. The room was adorned with alien artwork and historical documents. One image on the nightstand caught his attention. It was a picture of the crew of the Santa Maria taken in Trundle before they left Earth for the first time. He fell asleep and dreamt of his friend.

The video was disgusting, disturbing and very difficult to watch. It took days to sort through all the footage and Commander Evir arrived to oversee the operation. "Do we have enough data yet to draw any conclusions? Please provide a summary," Evir asked. "There is quite a bit of video to review from many sources. So far we've concluded that approximately five percent of Annunaki children are sentenced to death after being born. Prior to their death, they are fed well and allowed to live and grow. When a certain weight has been reached, the individual is killed. Their remains are either fed to the livestock on the planet or converted into royal jelly." The report was almost as disturbing as the video and Monique wondered when her appetite might return.

"We need more information. Are any of the Annunaki children talking?" Evir asked. "None of them will say a word. We've tried talking to them as a group and have singled out individuals, but no additional information has been given." It was a frustrating situation and Commander Evir decided to try a new approach. "Are there any species within the Alliance who can successfully communicate with the Annunaki telepathically?"

His aide consulted the database and took a moment to reply. "Many species can communicate telepathically, but I've identified only one with the ability to successfully communicate with the Annunaki. The ability of the species is under review and it's unknown if communication could prove harmful," his aide replied. "What is the name of the species?" Evir asked. "They are called Solian."

Vincent wanted to sleep longer, but could no longer ignore what he was smelling. He was hungry and the aroma was very similar to bacon. He rose quickly. "This was Tony's favorite meal. I hope you enjoy it," Tulari said as she handed him a tray. "You've been very gracious. Tony was lucky to have you as a companion." Vincent said. "He will always be a part of me. It's good to know he was lucky enough to have friends like you." "Thank you for the food Tulari, but when I'm done, I must return to my ship. There is still much left to do." Tulari smiled squarely at him. "I look forward to seeing your ship. I'm coming with you."

"Why do you want to return with me?" Vincent asked. "My species needs to know what's really going on and I want to see what Tony accomplished. If the Annunaki have been defeated, I want to see their home world myself." she replied. "As you wish, just be prepared for possible danger. We will meet my ship at the bottom of the hill."

"Please tell me you've overlooked something. The Solians can't be the only species with a mind powerful enough to deal with the Annunaki," Monique said. "There are no others within Alliance member worlds. It's the Solians or nothing," Commander Evir replied. "You do realize the eldest Solian is still a child?" Monique said. "I'm aware of what's going on with the Solians and the database is accurate. I'll forward the information to Rabanah. It will be up to the Tactical Council to make a decision. It won't matter anyway of there aren't any Solians willing to try. The Alliance won't force any species into this kind of danger. I'll send the information to Rabanah right now," Evir replied. "Can you please send it on a secure channel, Commander? I don't want Alixias and the others on Mars and Earth to learn of this new development yet," Alixias requested.

"I'd like to introduce you to Tulari. She was Tony's companion while he was on this world. What is the status of our mission?" Vincent said as he boarded the Santa Maria with Tulari. "Our mission here is over. There was virtually no Annunaki technology or infrastructure on the planet. We located some old Annunaki crash wreckage, but that's all we found here. The Olanions did a hell of a job keeping the Annunaki off their world," Julia reported. "Let's get back to Tanas and see how things are progressing. I'm sure there is more we can do to help," Vincent replied.

"You have a message from Chief Administrator Kizak," Laxi informed Patrick and Alixias. "A message from the Chief Administrator? What the hell could that be about?" Patrick asked. "Maybe it's information regarding the plans from the Alliance to protect the Solians from the Annunaki in the future. Let's find out." Alixias activated the data pad.

Kizak appeared on the screen and began speaking. "There is a situation on Tanas and the Tactical Council believes Zabu is the only individual who can assist. There are no other Solians old enough to make the attempt. Please trust that every safety precaution will be undertaken to ensure your child does not encounter any danger. I've included all details in the attached file."

"Can you believe their audacity? The Alliance is supposed to be safeguarding Zabu, not sending her to the home world of the enemy." Alixias was angry. "I don't understand what's so important that the Alliance needs Zabu's help. We need to review the file and look at the details. The Alliance wouldn't have contacted us if it wasn't important," Patrick replied.

"I don't see what Zabu can do to help the situation on Tanas. The Annunaki are savages and kill without meaning. We are not sending our child to Tanas," Alixias said flatly after reviewing the file. "I understand the position of the Alliance. I think the risk is much greater than the potential reward. We must not endanger our child," Patrick said. "I'm glad we're in agreement. We will send a message to Kizak immediately." Alixias began typing on the data pad in response. "I'm going," Zabu said with finality, her chin raised high as she stood in the doorway.

"How do you even know about this? Our door was shut as was yours. Were you eavesdropping?" Patrick asked. "There was no need. Kizak sent me the message as well." "You are unique Zabu; however, we are your parents and it's our task to protect you and provide guidance and discipline," Alixias said with authority. "Those born with morality and discipline do not require guidance to do what's right. I can help and must go."

The humans were proving to be very useful. Chief Administrator Kizak was enjoying one of their most important contributions as he poured himself a cup of coffee to start his day. A priority alert from Mars was the first issue requiring his attention. The message from Zabu's mother was angry, accusatory, and very personal. Kizak wasn't surprised. The decision to send the message to Zabu herself had been difficult, but in the end he decided the child should make the decision. Zabu was the eldest of her species and tests indicated she was quite intelligent. A group of Annunaki children who despised their Empress needed to be investigated. They were also sentient beings who were sentenced to death. Lives might be saved and a rebellious group of Annunaki could arise. Contacting Zabu was worth the risk.

Vincent was surprised to find Evir landed on the surface of Tanas. He was curious and decided to join Evir instead of sending a message. Monique was talking with Evir when he arrived. He gave Monique a quick kiss. "What's going on here? Why hasn't this facility been destroyed?" Vincent asked. "We've found Annunaki who are not loyal to the Empress. A specialist from the Alliance has been summoned to make contact telepathically as the Annunaki children won't talk," Evir replied. "Who is the specialist?" Vincent asked. "A Solian called Zabu." Evir replied. "Are you talking about Alixias and Patrick's child? Somehow this child is now a specialist?" Vincent asked. "Those are the orders I just received. Monique, I'm ordering you to Mars to retrieve Zabu and her parents." "Yes Commander, we'll leave immediately."

"What are my orders, Commander? Our mission on Olanion has been successfully completed and I've taken care of my personal business on the world," Vincent asked. "You will join the search for the rearing facility. We must find it as quickly as possible to buy more time." Vincent was intrigued. "What should I be looking for?" he asked. "I don't know. We've never done this before, so just use your instincts and cover as much terrain as possible."

"We've been ordered to locate the emergency rearing facility. The Alliance doesn't know what to look for, so I guess we need to look for anything unusual and out of place. A new Empress will soon emerge. We must try and find her," Vincent relayed Evir's orders to his crew.

The emergency rearing facility was always kept in a state of readiness. Generation after generation passed without it ever being needed or used. Blykad continued tradition by ensuring it was ready should the day arise. Unbelievably, the facility was now in use. Blykad continued to watch as the chosen females battled for the title of Empress. The competition was now down to seven. In very short time, order would be restored and Annunaki everywhere would have a new leader.

Blykad reorganized the soldiers guarding the rearing facility and ordered additional reinforcements. Alliance ships were continuing to patrol the area and the new Empress needed be protected at all costs. The underground facility was impossible to attack by air. She continued to watch as two more females were killed. In a matter of days, her species would celebrate the arrival of a new Empress.

Chapter 17

"We've been flying around this planet for two days now. It sure would be helpful if we knew what we are looking for," Vincent said as the Santa Maria searched from the skies above Tanas. "Look at the Annunaki on the ground below. It appears they are in some kind of formation," Andy said. "That does seem out of place. The other Annunaki we've seen on the ground have been wandering aimlessly for the most part. Bring us lower; let's have a closer look," Vincent ordered. As the Santa Maria closed on the ground position, two additional Annunaki emerged from an underground entrance carrying something. Before anyone could utter a word, the ship was rocked by an explosion. "Get us out of here, they're launching missiles from the surface!" Vincent yelled.

The Santa Maria quickly accelerated and gained altitude. "Captain, they are firing again!" Julia shouted. "We're out of range. Those aren't the same missiles the Annunaki use for space combat. Damage should be minimal," Andy stated. "Goddammit, that was a surprise. Computer, provide a damage report." "There is minor damage to the engine and in the cargo bay."

"I think we may have found the rearing facility. Should we fire?" Julia asked. "No, not yet. Andy do we know what's underground?" Vincent asked. "Scans indicate a shaft extending deep into the planet. The depth of the shaft is extreme and we are unable to determine where it ends or what it leads to," Andy replied. "The Annunaki went to a lot of trouble to hide this facility and it's well guarded. Send the information to Commander Evir and set a course for his location. Let him know minor repairs are required."

"Are any of those unusual Annunaki children talking yet?" Vincent asked as he approached Commander Evir. "We've tried everything without success. Excellent job finding the rearing facility. It's going to buy us more time. We've destroyed all the technology and infrastructure in this solar system, but we know the Annunaki have conquered other worlds and solar systems. After we destroy the rearing facility the Alliance will travel to worlds outside this solar system and continue to destroy their ability to wage war," Commander Evir reported.

"What's the plan to destroy the rearing facility?" Vincent asked. "It should be quite easy. We'll eliminate the ground forces and clear the shaft. Once the shaft is clear, we'll lower explosives to the bottom and destroy anything living. I've sent a drone to monitor the area and to provide video in the event anything changes." "When are you planning on doing this? We might be running out of time. From what Tony told us, a new Empress could emerge at any moment." Vincent asked.

"The mission is planned for tomorrow. A few logistical issues need to be taken care of before we can proceed. Right now, I need to prepare for Zabu and the arrival of her family.

Monique prepared to land her vessel and couldn't ever remember seeing so many troops gathered in the same location. "Damn Alixias, you must have some powerful friends," Isabella remarked. "I told Kizak that if Zabu wasn't properly protected we'd turn around and leave." "It appears your message was received very clearly," Patrick remarked. "Bring us down; it's pretty obvious where Evir wants us to land," Monique ordered.

Patrick, Alixias and Zabu prepared to exit the ship. "Zabu has been assigned a security detail of thirty Alliance soldiers. The personnel chosen are exceptional at what they do. Your child will be well protected," Monique said. "I don't care how good they are. If there's any danger, we will leave immediately."

Vincent observed as the security detail carefully escorted Zabu toward the facility. Snipers positioned on top of the building scanned for threats as Zabu and her parents were led down a path separated by hundreds of soldiers. "Welcome to Tanas," Vincent said as Zabu and her family approached. "Thank you, Vincenzo. We have work to do. Let's get to it." Zabu said.

Vincent and Monique's crews were present for the briefing. Alixias, Patrick and Zabu listened intently as Commander Evir spoke. "Your task is very straightforward. Make contact with the Annunaki who choose to defy the Empress. Find out why they do not follow the Annunaki custom of embracing and serving their supreme leader." Evir said. "I've been informed the rearing facility has been located. Please give me an update on that situation," Zabu requested calmly. "The rearing facility will be destroyed in a matter of hours. Final preparations for destruction of the facility are being made right now," Commander Evir replied.

"You must not destroy the facility. The new Empress must be captured, not killed," Zabu said surprising everyone. "The Tactical Council has advised us to destroy the facility. We will abide by their wishes," Evir replied confidently. Zabu countered the Commander's orders. "Has the Tactical Council considered the option of capturing the new Empress? What is in the best interest of the Alliance? Capturing, imprisoning and controlling the Empress or having a new Empress emerge on an unknown world free to rally her species? Please forward my request to the Tactical Council and delay your attack on the rearing facility. Your orders will likely change. I will prepare to make contact with the Annunaki children in this facility." And with that, the meeting adjourned.

Blykad was trying to maintain order. Word spread and hundreds were trying to come down the shaft to learn who would be their new Empress. There were three combatants remaining and one was severely injured. The weak and injured female slowly circled and tried to attack. She was swiftly and savagely killed by the two remaining enemies. The contest would be over soon. Two combatants remained and they were covered in blood, entrails, and royal jelly. Both were determined and passionate. Blykad would have the rare privilege of watching the new leader kill her last remaining challenger. A new Empress would be anointed at any moment.

Evir led Zabu and her security detail out of the meeting room. Everyone else gathered in the lobby of the alien building to relax and eat. Tulari quietly excused herself and exited the facility. "Zabu is pursuing a reckless course of action. We must destroy the rearing facility as soon as possible," Patrick said. "I disagree. Capturing and controlling the new Empress will give the Alliance valuable intelligence. If the new Empress can be captured, we will be able to control the entire species. It's a plan we must follow," Vincent replied. "In the end, it doesn't matter. We'll follow the advice from the Tactical Council," Monique said. "Unless the advice endangers Zabu," Alixias concluded.

Tulari enjoyed spending time with Tony's friends and was happy knowing he was able to associate with such good people. He was dead because of the Annunaki and her hatred of the species continued to build. She lost her mate and Olanion was decimated. As she explored the Annunaki home world, she concluded that the Alliance was wrong. The immoral existence of the Annunaki needed to be extinguished. A new Empress couldn't be allowed to live. Tony prepared, trained and planned day after day to end the Annunaki once and for all. She wouldn't allow a new Empress to rise.

Her lover completed what everyone thought couldn't be done. Tulari was not an Overlord, but she knew as much about the Annunaki as anyone. She found the weapons locker onboard the Santa Maria and selected two lethal guns. The first was a long-barreled rifle that silently fired projectiles, or it could be modified to fire small grenades. The second was a short barreled, rapid fire, plasma gun. She left the ship, found a two-wheeled ground vehicle and traveled toward the newly discovered rearing facility.

Tulari entered a rural area and found a group of Annunaki clustered together. She fired the plasma gun and was pleased with the results. The grouped aliens died a gruesome hot death as she passed. Her adrenaline flowed as she increased the speed of the vehicle. The landscape flew by and soon she spied another group of Annunaki ahead. Tulari raised her weapon and fired.

"Are you sure she won't be in danger?" Alixias asked. "The Annunaki are being held within a protective shield. Her security detail will be present as well. We can't make it any more secure than it already is," Commander Evir assured the fearful mother. "Very well, but I will pull her out of the room at the first hint of danger."

Zabu was nervous. She'd only been in contact with friendly minds and didn't know what to expect from the Annunaki. She approached the protective shield and was completely ignored. "Which one spoke?" she asked Commander Evir. The Commander pointed and Zabu prepared for her task. She focused on the individual alien and opened her mind. The alien resisted, but Zabu forced her way in and sent a powerful message.

Yuzotak was committed to her fate. She was deemed unworthy and would be fed to animals. Somehow, she was considered a threat to Empress Zovad. After she was born, her connection to the Empress was immediately terminated. There hadn't been any other communication until this new, strange creature entered her mind. Yuzotak approached the shield.

"You have reached my mind. Why do you wish for me to communicate? We are here to die. The Empress has rejected us. We will not serve you," Yuzotak said emphatically. "If I wanted your servitude, I would invade your mind. You would give it freely if I unleashed my power. I'm not here to demand your allegiance to my species or the Alliance. In your mind, I saw the hatred you have toward the Empress and this society. We can give you the opportunity to leave and live independently from the Empress and the rest of the Annunaki. You can all live freely for the rest of your lives," the small alien offered.

Zabu waited as Yuzotak considered her offer. "Our purpose is to die. There are no other options. The Empress will torture all of us for the rest of our days if we defy her." "Empress Zovad is dead. Do you think we'd be here if she were still alive?" Zabu asked. "You lie. The Empress cannot be killed!" Yuzotak replied. "Explore my mind," Zabu invited the young alien into her consciousness.

The strange alien opened her mind. Yuzotak couldn't believe it! Empress Zovad truly was dead. She quickly closed the connection. The information was disturbing and overwhelming. "I will speak to the others about your proposal. We have much to discuss and to take into consideration. I will let you know when we've reached a decision," Yuzotak said.

Zabu left the room with her security detail in tow. Commander Evir led her to a meeting room, but nobody knew what to say. "Do you really have the ability to demand the servitude of these Annunaki?" Patrick finally asked. "I don't know. It's possible my species could control them in the future, but it's not a moral solution and it won't be attempted." "Can these Annunaki be turned against a new Empress?" Commander Evir asked. "Not soon. They must be given space and an opportunity to learn what they can accomplish working together. We must keep them hidden from the new Empress and give them time to grow and flourish. For now, I think it's a clever idea to generate some good will. Please provide the prisoners with better food and some entertainment."

After half a day, Tulari arrived at a distant hillside overlooking the rearing facility. She killed many Annunaki with the plasma weapon and now it was time to concentrate on her precision. The long-barreled rifle was sleek and smooth in her hands. She selected a target and fired. The weapon silently unleashed a lethal round. A soldier guarding the entrance was struck and collapsed to the ground. She took aim at the next target and fired. The shot was accurate and the hated alien

355

also fell. One of the soldiers fired a missile in her general direction, but the shot wasn't even close and the soldiers didn't know where she was. Tulari took aim and fired again.

"Commander Evir, we have activity at the rearing facility," a technician reported. "What's going on?" Evir asked. "Several Annunaki near the entrance have been killed. They are firing missiles haphazardly and are still under attack, but I can't determine where the attack is originating from," the technician replied. "Move the drone and search for nearby lifeforms!" Evir commanded. After several minutes, the drone zoomed in on the shooter. "That's the Olanion from the Santa Maria. Get Vincent in here now!" Evir commanded as the alien female fired and killed again.

"Can you explain why your guest from Olanion is attacking the rearing facility, Captain?" "I don't know. She has suffered extreme personal tragedies, but she didn't say anything to me about attacking the rearing facility," Vincent replied. "Get aboard your ship and take care of the situation. An attack against the rearing facility has not been authorized," Commander Evir ordered.

Vincent quickly gathered his crew. Monique arrived as well. "What are you doing here?" he asked. "I'm not going to miss this. Besides, you might need me

to prevent you from doing something stupid again."
"Andy, bring us to the rearing facility as quickly as possible," he ordered.

Tulari continued to fire, but the Annunaki she killed were quickly replaced. A missile struck dangerously close to her position. She switched to grenades and launched one toward the opening. All Annunaki in the area were killed instantly. She mounted her vehicle and raced toward the underground entrance. As she approached, a dozen Annunaki quickly emerged from the entrance. She fired her plasma gun killing all of them instantly.

"Tulari is approaching the entrance and has eliminated all surface resistance," Andy reported. "Get us down there! Park the Santa Maria on top of the entrance. I don't want her going down to that facility," Vincent ordered. Andy quickly complied and parked the Santa Maria. Vincent was waiting when Tulari arrived. "What in the hell do you think you're doing?" he asked. "This isn't your battle. Move your ship!" "I will not. You can get onboard my ship willingly or we can do it by force," Vincent said. "I won't get on your ship and you can't stay here forever. I'll wait as long as I have to," Tulari replied stubbornly. "That's what I thought you'd say," Vincent said as Monique stunned

Tulari with an electrical weapon from the doorway of the ship.

"You were brought to Tanas as our guest. You are now interfering with Alliance operations," Vincent said to her as they brought her aboard and restrained her. "You're all traitors to Tony. He died trying to eliminate the Annunaki race!" Tulari screamed at everyone. "Tony was our friend. He told me he was going to kill the Empress. I never heard him say he wanted to wipe out Annunaki everywhere. Did he ever tell you he wanted to eliminate the Annunaki as a species?" Vincent asked. "Well, not directly, but it's logical to assume that's what he really wanted." Tulari angrily replied. "I don't think that's what Tony wanted. I'm bringing you back to your home world. You can try to defeat the Annunaki from there. Set a course for Olanion," Vincent ordered.

Zabu rested as Patrick and Alixias shared a meal. "She's made some bold statements. I think this all might be too much for her. She might be intelligent, but she's still very young and immature. Her confidence is not tempered by experience," Alixias said. " You're probably right; however, she's given these unusual Annunaki children something to think about and has them talking. She's doing her best to protect her species and the Alliance," Patrick said optimistically.

"Yuzotak has requested the presence of Zabu," Commander Evir interrupted as he walked into the room. "We must prepare Zabu. We will be there when she is ready," Patrick replied.

Zabu looked at herself in the mirror. What she was doing would define the path of her species and the Alliance for a long time. "Mom, do you think I'm doing right?" she asked. Alixias was surprised by the question. Her daughter never expressed any self doubt. "I think you are, but you must be careful; overconfidence can be very dangerous. You must always look for threats," Alixias cautioned.

Yuzotak was waiting when Zabu arrived with her security personnel. "Have you decided to embrace freedom?" Zabu asked. "Our species is not accustomed to freedom. The concept of a life without serving the Empress is foreign to us." "There is a reason you exist and you have a purpose to serve, but your species will not survive if you don't adapt. If you truly wish to serve, you must ensure the survival of your species," Zabu said. "Our species will survive with or without us. Our existence means nothing." Yuzotak replied grimly. "The Empress is unwilling to adapt to change. Your planet is out of resources. I will ensure your race becomes extinct if you fail to accept my offer and you will be the first to die. Prepare to deactivate the shield and fire on my command," Zabu ordered emphatically.

Her security detail raised their weapons. "We accept your terms, but I must insist we be placed on a world out of this solar system," Yuzotak said. "A wise decision. You will be informed when arrangements have been made. I recommend you begin making plans to ensure your species can exist in peace with the Alliance. My guards wouldn't have fired on you. I just thought you needed some motivation," Zabu said with a smile.

The meeting between Zabu and Yuzotak was broadcast on all Alliance frequencies. Vincent wanted to be there. Unfortunately, the trip to drop off Tulari on Olanion delayed the Santa Maria. He watched the meeting en route to Tanas with his shipmates. "Damn, Zabu doesn't screw around," Monique commented. "I can't figure out if she's bluffing or not. I'm glad her species is on our side. We're approaching Tanas. Prepare to land," Vincent said as Andy carefully guided the ship to the surface.

"Commander, we've received a response from Rabanah. The Tactical Council agrees with Zabu. They advise that we try to capture the new Empress. We are to kill the Empress only if were unable to successfully capture her," the communications officer reported. "We're running low on time. A new Empress will be declared very soon. Tell the extraction team to send the gas cannisters down the shaft. I want every Annunaki unconscious when our team goes down there," Evir ordered.

Too much time was passing. Normally his orders were carried out quickly and Commander Evir was growing frustrated. "What's the problem? Why haven't the cannisters been sent down the shaft?" he asked. "The shaft has been blocked. Our instruments indicate a series of steel plates slide out horizontally throughout the shaft. The Annunaki at the bottom of the shaft are monitoring the situation and blocking it. The first steel plate has been activated," his aide reported.

"Drill through the damn thing!" Ever replied. "Yes, Commander. We estimate there are over one hundred plates protecting the shaft. It will take a great deal of time. We must be precise, or the shaft will collapse," his aide relayed. "No, it won't take a great deal of time. Find a powerful laser drill and get it done. Start immediately. Station troops on the ground outside the entrance."

The room quickly filled with Alliance personnel. Zabu noticed very few looked in her direction. "The Annunaki in this facility have agreed to relocate and live independently from the Empress. We must find a suitable planet and a way to assist them in their new endeavor. In the future, the Annunaki rebels might displace the Empress and bring morality to the species," Evir stated.

"I recommend planet Vandi," Vincent said. "The Volmer told us we are no longer welcome on the planet," Evir replied. "I'm a friend of their leader, Gly. I believe they will allow the Annunaki to live on the planet after a short negotiation. Tulari informed me that all Volmer have advanced mental abilities, so it's possible they could help guide the rebels."

"Captain, bring the Annunaki children to Vandi, but do not allow them on the planet until you've successfully negotiated an agreement with the Volmer. Am I understood?" Commander Evir asked. "Yes, Commander. I believe the Volmer will help our cause. They assisted in the liberation of Vandi and I believe their recent involvement has opened their eyes to the Annunaki threat. We will leave at once."

"What is the status of the drilling?" Commander Evir asked. "We've drilled through approximately seventy-three percent of the steel plates. Within the next half day, we'll be able to drop the gas cannisters rendering the Annunaki unconscious," his aide replied. "What about the rest of the Annunaki on Tanas? Have there been any observable changes?" Evir asked. "Nothing we can detect. The Annunaki are still unorganized. They're doing little more than eating and sleeping," his aide reported. "That will change if we don't get down that damn shaft pretty soon. Send a few cannisters down now. There may be Annunaki hiding in side tunnels," Evir replied testily.

Volmer were not a jovial species. Existing in solitude and peace was all they desired. A very rare celebration took place when Gly learned Tony killed the Empress and lost his life in the process. Days later, Gly still marveled that the unique human and Keeras were successful.

Gly sat on the edge of an ice shelf eating the Piszen he spent hours chasing through the ocean. The light of the setting sun suddenly dimmed more than it should have. He looked up and saw a ship approaching. With the death of Empress Zovad, he believed his species would finally be left alone. Apparently, he was wrong. The ship landed and a familiar human approached. Gly continued to sit and eat his kill.

Vincent knew it was Gly. He could tell by the distinguishing injuries. The leader of the Volmer ignored him and continued eating. "Gly, I've come to speak with you," Vincent said. "I'm sorry your friend is dead. What he accomplished was extraordinary and we are grateful. An agreement was reached before you left, so why have you returned? We only wish to be ignored and left alone," Gly asked as he finished his meal and stood up.

"You know the threat the Annunaki pose to all of us who wish to be free. On Tanas, we found a group of young Annunaki who were rejected by the Empress. In time, they might oppose the Annunaki leader. A new Empress will arise any day now. We must keep these rebels safe, so they can flourish and find a course of change for their species," Vincent replied.

"There are no Annunaki who defy the Empress. What you speak of is impossible. I've seen into the mind of Zovad and I saw no such information," Gly responded. "These young Annunaki were garbage to her. Others like them were killed and fed to animals on Tanas. When you shared minds with Empress Zovad did you take note of all the trash she disposed?" Vincent asked. "I still don't believe there are Annunaki capable of opposing the Empress. Unless you can change my mind, it's time for you to get on your ship and leave." Vincent grabbed Gly's arm and gently turned him towards the Santa Maria. "The young rebels are aboard my ship. I suggest you come and make contact with one,"

If it weren't for Tony's accomplishments, Gly wouldn't have bothered. He reluctantly boarded the strange ship. Vincent led him to the group of young

Annunaki. He opened his mind and was surprised. The young were scared and confused. Their mental connection to the Annunaki and the Empress was completely severed. He was surprised by Yuzotak's mind. Gly did not want the Annunaki to become powerful and dominant again, so he grudgingly decided to help.

"You may leave these Annunaki on Vandi providing you follow my conditions," Gly said. "What are your conditions?" Vincent asked. "Yuzotak must make regular journeys here. I will need to advise her and ensure these young Annunaki are not led astray. A Strithu will be assigned to bring her here. In addition, the young Solian Zabu must visit and meet with me as soon as possible."

"How do you know of Zabu and why do you want to meet with her?" Vincent asked. "I learned of Zabu from the mind of Yuzotak. She is a Solian and is powerful like Keeras; however, she is too young for what she has undertaken and requires solitude and training. Zabu must also be involved with these young Annunaki. In time, they will view her as their liberator."

"I agree to your terms, but Zabu is quite busy now. When the current crisis has concluded, I will escort her here personally," Vincent said. "Her mind is powerful. She is making decisions that are too important without proper training. These young

Annunaki have established a bond with her. If they are to challenge the new Empress, Zabu must be involved," Gly responded.

"I understand. She will be brought here as soon as possible. Her parents will insist on accompanying her." "That will be fine. After they speak with me, they will insist on leaving." Vincent escorted Gly off the ship and was preparing to leave. "Are we returning to Tanas after we drop off the Annunaki?" Andy asked. "We're not leaving quite yet. I have one more thing I need to ask Gly," Vincent replied as he left the ship.

"I believe our business is concluded," Gly stated as Vincent approached. "I have one last question. Tony had a companion known as Tulari. She told me you bonded and made a telepathic connection with Tony. His body has not been found. Is there any chance he survived?" Vincent asked. "I'm sorry, his mind has gone silent. I do not detect his consciousness, you must accept his fate."

Vincent found a suitable area to relocate the rebel Annunaki. "This lake has fish and abundant wildlife. Make shelters and survive. Meet with Gly and listen to his wisdom. Be a leader for your species and prepare for peace." Yuzotak looked around in awe of the surrounding landscape. "This is more beautiful than I could have imagined. I didn't know such places existed.

We will attempt this new existence and I will listen to the wisdom of Gly."

Chapter 18

A stalemate was the worst possible scenario and occurred only a few times in the past. There were rare instances when the last two females killed each other and the process started all over again. Blykad couldn't believe one of the two females hadn't died by now. Both were severely injured, wouldn't give up and currently resting. With any luck, one would die while sleeping. The moment either moved, the other awoke.

Time was growing very short. A new Empress was needed to rally those on the surface and Annunaki everywhere. The Alliance would soon break through the last remaining defenses and both females were in danger of not ascending to the position of Empress. Blykad glanced at one of the ceremonial blades on the wall and contemplated the unthinkable. It was forbidden to interfere in the contest. Soon there would be no alternative. He took an ancient blade off the wall and prepared himself to enter the forcefield and join the females.

"Do you know why Gly was so insistent on meeting with Zabu?" Monique asked as the Santa Maria traveled back to Tanas. "I didn't press him on the matter, but it was very important to him. He believes the rebel Annunaki will view Zabu as their liberator and savior. I think he's more interested in seeing the Annunaki defeated than he's willing to admit. If we lose and Vandi is invaded again, the Volmer would eventually be wiped out. Especially after Gly's assistance with the battle for the planet," Vincent replied.

"The war with the Annunaki has been ongoing for a long time. After what's occurred over the last few months the Alliance is finally making real progress. If the rebel Annunaki on Vandi can survive and flourish, the species will likely never be a threat again. The Alliance has never inflicted such severe damage to the Annunaki up until now," Andy said. "We must not let up. Any mistakes we make will be amplified exponentially in the future," Vincent replied.

Alixias, Patrick and Zabu joined Commander Evir in the makeshift operations center. "Are we through yet?" Patrick asked. "Just a few more minutes. We're drilling through the last plates now," Evir replied. "What's going to happen on Tanas after we capture the Empress?" Alixias asked. "Tanas will become an occupied planet of the Alliance. We are in the process of constructing military facilities across this world. The Annunaki will not be imprisoned. In fact, they will be allowed to move around freely. We will, however, withhold all technology and if any decide to fight they will either be killed or imprisoned indefinitely," Evir replied.

The females were awake and combat resumed. The stalemate dragged on with no end in sight. Both were fighting defensively hoping the other would eventually die. There were no longer any options. The facility would soon be completely breached. Blykad briefly turned off the shield and stepped inside with his weapon. Combat stopped and both combatants looked at him curiously.

Only one was the true Empress. Blykad didn't know which one to kill, so he decided to kill the female who was fighting the most defensively. Surely an Empress would be bolder. He raised his blade and pierced the heart of the weaker female. She screamed and glared at him with pure hatred as her life faded.

"Congratulations, Empress. You are now our new leader. We are in great danger. What do you wish to be called and how can all Annunaki serve you?" Blykad asked.

She was angry, confused and in great pain. "I am Axxon. What have you done? You have violated tradition!" she demanded. "There was no choice. I knew you would be victorious and simply sped up the process to defeat those who wish to oppress our species. Your leadership is vital and needed right now. How can

I serve you?" Blykad asked. Empress Axxon was robbed of her ultimate victory by a fool. "Give me your blade and kneel before me," Empress Axxon commanded. As her subject complied, Axxon plunged the blade through Blykad's neck with her last useful limb. She reached out with her mind and connected with all her subjects.

"Commander, we've disabled all defenses at the rearing facility. We can drop the gas cannisters at your command," his aide reported. "Drop them now and inform the extraction team. Instruct them to activate their respirators. We need to secure the facility and capture the new Empress. Tell the team not to take any action until the new Empress is anointed," Evir ordered. The gas cannisters were finally dropped. He watched with Alixias, Patrick and Zabu as the extraction team entered the shaft. Each member of the team descended in slim pods which had thrust for descent and ascent.

"There is new activity near the rearing facility. All Annunaki in the area are converging on the site. Many are approaching in ground vehicles with weapons," his aide reported. "Get all of our ships into the area. Do we have any more gas cannisters?" Evir asked. "We have a very limited number. It will not be enough to fend off the Annunaki traveling to the site," his aide reported. "The enemy is organizing. It appears there is a new Empress. Inform the extraction team and tell them to get the new Empress out of there as quickly as possible."

Uliantra was in command of the extraction team and was the first to enter the facility. All Annunaki were unconscious except for one. A shielded room prevented gas from entering and a lone and bloody Annunaki female glared at him. "You are weak. Conquering your species will bring me boundless joy," the female hissed.

"Why hasn't the new Empress been captured and brought to the surface?" Evir asked. "Uliantra reports she is guarded by a shield. We cannot extract the new Empress until the shield has been disabled and we need to send down a specialist to disable it. Thousands of Annunaki are now descending on the site," his aide reported. "Prepare to defend the site at all costs. Instruct all available vessels to converge and fire at will!" Evir ordered.

"I must confront the new Empress. Send me down the shaft," Zabu insisted. "Absolutely not. The risk is extreme. I will not allow you to place yourself in such danger," her mother said. "If the Alliance wishes to capture the Empress alive, sending me is the only choice," Zabu explained. "There are always other alternatives. You are my child; I will not allow you to enter such a dangerous situation."

"What are your orders?" Zabu asked Evir. "Proceed to the shaft. You will be the next to descend." "I forbid it! Zabu is not allowed to go down!" Alixias screamed. "Zabu is the current leader of her species. According to Alliance regulations, her choice supersedes your role as parent," Evir replied. "Enough, Mother. Get me down there now!"

Her subjects would come to her defense and she'd be revered as their new Empress. It was only a matter of time. The Alliance wasn't aware of how far out her species had spread and conquered. She recalled vessels from other solar systems and instructed everyone on the planet to defend her. Victory would only be delayed. Empress Zovad was overconfident; she would not make the same mistake. Battle left her severely injured. The injuries would heal and be a reminder of what was required to become Empress.

Zabu knew there weren't any choices left. "I'm going and if you try to stop me I'll have my security detail detain you. I'd prefer for both of you to accompany me and support my decision," Zabu said to her parents. "Jesus Christ, I guess we don't have any choice, do we?" Patrick replied. Alliance ships fired on arriving Annunaki as Zabu landed and disembarked. "You must be damned important. We've been ordered to defend this mission at all costs," a soldier said. "Get us down to the Empress right now," Zabu demanded.

Axxon knew she would become a powerful Empress. It was only a matter of time before the aliens on the surface were defeated. Her subjects would give their lives to ensure she would survive and with each passing moment she grew more confident. The shield would last long enough for her subjects to defeat the enemy. She vowed to become the Empress who would finally defeat the Alliance.

The long trip down to the facility put Zabu on edge. She tried to refocus her thoughts before the confrontation. Now was not the time to be distracted or show any weakness. She entered the royal chamber and found a bloodied and severely injured Annunaki female standing before her. Zabu took a deep breath and reached out with her mind.

Empress Axxon nearly lost consciousness. Her body was in pain and now her mind was under attack. She instinctively fought back as the intrusion grew stronger and her mind was forced open. What felt like an eternity was only a few seconds. The mind departed.

Axxon turned and found a small child standing outside the shield. "You are not the true Empress," the child said with conviction and Axxon suddenly felt less confident. "Who are you? How dare you invade my mind! You will be the first alien to die under my rule!"

Commander Evir was quickly becoming worried. Annunaki everywhere were traveling toward the rearing facility and he was out of gas cannisters to drop. "We need to get the specialist down there right now to disable the protective shield. Tell the ships in the area to start firing missiles on approaching Annunaki. Send a message to Patrick and Alixias and let them know Zabu must do something now or their lives will be in serious jeopardy."

Patrick received the transmission and it angered him to the core. He hated putting so much pressure on his child. "Zabu, you must sever the connection between the Empress and her subjects. We're all in extreme danger." "I understand father. I'll try my best."

Her subjects were getting closer and would soon arrive in overwhelming numbers. Empress Axxon knew she would soon be free. The alien child approached. "You did not ascend to the position of Empress by the rules of your own ancient tradition. I've seen the doubt in your mind. You did not defeat all your enemies by yourself and required help to ascend to the throne," the child said. "It no longer matters. I'm the leader of my species. The sole purpose of my subjects is to worship me and do as I demand. All Alliance worlds will eventually be mine!"

Empress Axxon barely finished speaking when her mind was invaded again. Her resistance was ineffective. Everything went black and she lost consciousness. Zabu gasped and sat down. "That was not a pleasurable experience," she said. "Are you alright?" Alixias asked with concern. "I'm fine. Just give me a few moments to recover. I require complete silence."

"The Annunaki have stopped their approach and appear disoriented. Zabu must have done something to the Empress," the tactical officer reported. "She did Sir, we just received a report from Patrick. The new Empress is currently unconscious," the communications officer reported. "This is our chance; tell the specialist to get the damn shield disabled now. We need her in custody as quickly as possible. Have a doctor standing by prepared to sedate the Empress. We must keep her unconscious," Evir commanded.

Empress Axxon awoke and found the alien standing over her less than an arm's length away. She instinctively reached out and the child flinched as her attempt was blocked by the shield. If it weren't for the shield, she would have killed the alien child. Her mind was not completely her own. She felt the presence of the alien child and she was no longer connected to her subjects. With her last remaining energy, she stood up.

"We've been ordered the rearing facility. Prepare to fire weapons. According to the latest update from Commander Evir, the Annunaki are no longer approaching. If they reengage, we have orders to fire," Vincent said as the Santa Maria returned to Tanas. "What else did the update say?" Julia asked. "The new Empress is protected by a shield and it's caused an unexpected delay in her capture."

The specialist was finally close to disabling the shield. "How much longer will it take?" Patrick asked. "Just a few minutes and we will have her out shortly," the specialist replied. "Is there anything I can do to help?" Patrick asked. "Yes, stop talking, stay out of my way and let me do my job!"

The power of the young alien's mind constituted a new and unknown threat. Empress Axxon shared the child's thoughts. "My consciousness is more powerful than yours. If it weren't for my physical injuries, I would have overpowered you the moment you arrived. I've seen into your mind as well. You plan to imprison me and keep me from my subjects." she said. "Your species is an immoral abomination. We will do what we must," Zabu replied. "As will I. You may have been correct. Tradition was not followed and perhaps my final opponent was supposed to lead my species.

You've blocked my mind and I'm unable to connect with my subjects. The fact is repulsive, but true. My subjects won't be coming and you are moments away from capturing me. I can't believe a true Empress would be so easily defeated. Tradition must be followed and a proper Empress will soon rise," Axxon said as she walked across the room.

"No!" Zabu softly whispered with her eyes closed. Empress Axxon could feel the alien trying to overpower her mind. The child was growing weary and less powerful. She picked up the blade she used to kill her opponents and sat down. With careful precision she thrust it into her chest. She withdrew the blade and sliced open a vein in her neck.

"Son of a bitch! We need to get her out of there and up to a medical chamber now!" Patrick said. Alixias couldn't believe what was happening. Zabu stopped moving and slowly slumped to the floor unconscious. "Zabu! Wake up!" Alixias picked up her child and slapped her across the face. "That wasn't very nice. I'm tired mother, let me sleep. She's going to die now." Zabu responded and quickly fell unconscious.

"We need that fucking shield down now!" Patrick yelled at the specialist. "It will be deactivated in approximately twenty seconds," the specialist replied. Patrick sent an update to Commander Evir as he watched Alixias attend to Zabu. "Is our child going to

378

be alright?" he asked. "She needs medical attention, but her vital signs are still strong," Alixias replied.

Vincent and the rest of the crew listened to the report from Patrick. "Inform Commander Evir we are landing. Tell him we will get the Empress into our medical chamber as soon as her pod arrives on the surface. Ask the Commander to send another ship with proper medical facilities for Zabu," Vincent ordered.

Andy landed the ship as close to the shaft as possible. Vincent quickly opened the hatch and everyone exited. Isabella and Julia brought a robotic stretcher. "Dammit, too much time is passing. We need to get the Empress into the medical chamber!" Vincent said. He wasn't sure how much time passed when a pod finally emerged from the shaft. When Monique quickly opened the pod, blood and entrails spilled out. What was left of Empress Axxon was placed on the robotic stretcher. An automated medical tube suddenly appeared and was inserted into her mouth and her vital signs were promptly displayed on a small display. Isabella and Julia brought the Empress to the medical chamber. "It doesn't look good. She's nothing more than a slab of meat," Monique said. "We've been surprised by the medical ability of the Alliance before. She might survive," Vincent replied as they boarded the Santa Maria.

Empress Axxon was placed into the chamber as quickly as possible. The translucent lid closed and everyone waited for the report. The diagnosis took much longer than normal. "All major biological functions of the patient have stopped. Resuscitation is not possible. The patient is deceased," the computer reported. "I knew she was too far gone. The only successful thing she accomplished was her own suicide," Monique remarked. "Son of a bitch! All that work for nothing. Please send the bad news to Commander Evir and tell him we'll be there shortly," Vincent instructed Isabella.

Alixias and Patrick watched over Zabu as she received treatment. "All vital signs are stable and the patient requires no treatment at this time," the computer relayed. "I don't agree. She requires rest. That was one hell of an ordeal," Alixias said. "She's sleeping now. I'll tell everyone to stay out of here until she wakes up on her own," Patrick replied.

"So, the Empress chose to take her own life? I guess we need to begin searching for another rearing facility," Commander Evir said as the crew of the Santa Maria arrived. "I think we were fortunate to find the last one and from the little we know about the Annunaki, the next location could be anywhere. In the past we know young females have been reared in caves, open fields and just about anywhere else. It's possible the location might not even be on Tanas," Andy replied grimly. "We'll look and hope to get lucky again. I just received a report that Zabu should be fine. She just needs some rest. I thought you'd want to know," Evir said.

"What's going to happen now?" Monique asked. "We go back to the original plan. We didn't capture the new Empress, but she is dead. It buys us more time to find Annunaki on other worlds. That said, our war strategy has changed. The stalemate is over and the Alliance will actively search for pockets of Annunaki resistance. Speaking of which, it's time for you to go back on duty. Continue searching Tanas for a rearing facility," Evir ordered. "Let's go. Please send a message to Patrick and Alixias. I would like to speak with them after Zabu has fully recovered," Vincent told Isabella. "We will return to our ship as well. At least we know what to look for now. Maybe we'll get lucky again," Monique replied optimistically.

Chapter 19

The Santa Maria joined dozens of other Alliance ships and began searching Tanas again. Three days passed without any progress. "Captain, we're receiving a message. I'll put it on the screen for you," Isabella said as Patrick and Alixias appeared. "How is Zabu doing? Has she fully recovered?" Vincent asked. "She is fully rested and back to normal. Thank you for asking," Patrick replied. Vincent suddenly felt awkward and wasn't quite sure what to say. "That's good to hear. I probably overstepped my bounds and should have consulted with you first, but there is a situation that requires your assistance," Vincent said.

"You're not making much sense Captain. What are you talking about?" Alixias asked. "When we brought the rebel Annunaki to Vandi, I promised Gly he would have an opportunity to meet and speak with Zabu. I was required to agree to his terms in order to relocate the rebel Annunaki on Vandi." he said. "Captain, you didn't have the right to make such a promise. There are Annunaki on Vandi. The species now considers Solians as their greatest threat and Volmer are unpredictable. It sounds like you're trying to place our child into another dangerous situation," Alixias replied. "The small number of Annunaki rebels are harmless and are on one of the continents far from where we will meet. Gly and the rest of the Volmer have proven they are true allies. There will be no threat to Zabu," Vincent stated emphatically. "Please give us a moment to discuss your proposal," Patrick said diplomatically.

The audio went mute as Patrick and Alixias discussed Vincent's proposal. After a few minutes the audio resumed. "The Volmer don't appear to be a threat; we will allow Gly to meet with Zabu. I must insist we accompany Zabu along with her entire security team. Gly must be alone and if any other Volmer are nearby we will leave the surface immediately. Are these arrangements acceptable and understood?" Alixias asked. "They are. I will contact Commander Evir and request permission to escort you and your party to Vandi."

"Why did you agree to such an arrangement in the first place?" Commander Evir asked when Vincent explained his plan. "I was required to compromise in order to get the rebel Annunaki on Vandi. Gly is an ally and I believe he wants to meet with Zabu to fulfill a greater purpose. I have faith this meeting will be beneficial for the Alliance," Vincent explained. "We're not making any progress here. Your request to accompany Zabu to Vandi is approved. When you are done on Vandi you and your crew are to return to Earth." "For what purpose?" Vincent asked.

"Reinforcements are arriving to relieve crews that have recently engaged in combat. You and your crew are being rotated out for now," Evir replied and ended the transmission.

"Is he saying we get a vacation?" Julia asked. "I think so. Some down time will be nice," Vincent said. "It's likely we will be off duty for an extended period. We should have been replaced by another vessel quite some time ago according to Alliance protocol," Andy stated. "I think our time off has been well earned. Let's pick up Zabu and go meet with Gly," Vincent happily ordered.

The Santa Maria cruised in open space toward Vandi. Vincent watched the stars pass outside the window in his room. He knew he should be sleeping but was transfixed. The communication console flashed. He walked over and played the message. Monique appeared. "We've been replaced and ordered back to Earth. Commander Evir told me you will return when you're done on Vandi. We haven't been able to spend much time together with all that's happened. Find me when you return and we'll change that. I love you."

Vincent paused the message before it could end and stared at the image of Monique. He didn't understand why he was so lucky. She supported him in everything he did and rarely complained or criticized. The only time she called him out was when it was absolutely necessary. She appreciated him and he appreciated her. He resumed gazing at the stars and looked forward to returning to Earth.

Alixias and Patrick were in the command center when the Santa Maria returned to Vandi. "We've arrived at the coordinates you provided, Captain," Andy said. "I will speak with Gly to make sure he understands the conditions of this visit. Please have Zabu ready when I return," Vincent said. "Make sure he understands the conditions clearly, Captain. We won't put our child in danger again," Alixias replied sternly.

For once, the sound of the approaching ship was welcome. The human was fulfilling his part of the agreement. Gly waited anxiously as he approached. "I'm here to complete my end of our deal and have brought Zabu. As I anticipated, her parents insisted on coming. She has a large security detail accompanying her. You must meet with her alone. Her guards will sweep the area. If any other Volmer are found, we will leave immediately," the human said. "I'm alone. Do what you must. I will meet with her in the cave," Gly replied.

"We're all set. You can deploy your security detail. Gly is waiting for us," Vincent said as he boarded the Santa Maria. The security detail quickly departed the ship and swept through the area and the cave. A perimeter was made outside the entrance.

Vincent led Patrick, Alixias and Zabu inside for the meeting. They found Gly sitting in front of a small fire and joined him.

"My species prefers solitude. On this occasion, I thank you for coming. Solians have the most powerful minds my species has ever been in contact with. The mind of Keeras was undisciplined and chaotic which is understandable considering he had very little contact with anyone as he developed," Gly said as he stared intently at Zabu. "What do you want from me?" Zabu asked. "I wish for us to share minds and for you to learn what Tony and Keeras shared with me. It's important to know if your mind is more disciplined and less chaotic than that of Keeras. You are now the leader of all Solians and I must know how you plan to guide your species."

"Zabu was recently in contact with the mind of Empress Axxon. The experience was very exhaustive and put her in danger. I don't think this is a good idea," Alixias said. "This experience will be much different. I will offer no resistance and if anyone is in danger, it will be me. Her mind is much more powerful than mine." Gly responded. "It's fine mother. I wish to gain knowledge and have nothing to hide." "I will not resist. Relax, and make contact when you are ready," Gly said and closed his eyes.

Zabu was hesitant. The last experience left her traumatized. She tentatively reached out and made contact. The mind of Gly was peaceful and welcomed her. She learned about his species and how Volmer helped to liberate Vandi. She delved deeper and learned about Keeras. What he was forced to endure saddened Zabu. His mind had been troubled, tumultuous and in need of guidance. Tony was a truly remarkable human who transformed into something else entirely. He was determined to overcome any obstacle to kill Empress Zovad. Zabu was grateful Gly opened his mind. She learned much from the introverted alien.

The power from the mind of Zabu was greater than that of Keeras; it was more orderly, logical and focused. Gly learned of her plan to guide the Solians. In time, she planned for her species to become the most powerful within the Alliance. He detected a profound sense of morality and desire for prosperity and peace. Through her eyes, he witnessed the battle with Empress Axxon. Gly was stunned the young Solian overpowered an Empress at such an early age. If Zabu was older, wiser and more disciplined, she would have easily been able to capture Axxon.

"Should it last this long?" Patrick asked. "Neither of them appears to be in pain or distress and both are breathing normally as far as I can tell," Vincent replied after thirty minutes passed. "She's coming around,"

Alixias said as her daughter opened her eyes and stood up. Zabu smiled, ran to Gly and gave him a hug. "Thank you! I learned so much and I'm so glad we came to see you." she said. "The experience was very gratifying and you are on the right course. Trust your instincts and embrace your vision. You must prepare for the unexpected."

Vincent was happy the meeting went well and Zabu was safe. He decided to speak with Gly one last time. "You've been invaluable to the Alliance. Are you sure we can't relocate some of you to your ancestral home world of Ganymede? There's a beautiful view of Jupiter," Vincent asked. "I'll see if anyone is willing to go, but if any of my species chooses to relocate, the world must be left to us completely. For now, I must speak with you alone. Everyone else is free to leave. Vincent will remain for a brief time," Gly replied. Zabu and her parents walked back to the ship with the security detail.

"What do you wish to discuss?" Vincent asked as Gly motioned for him to sit. "I didn't want to say anything in front of the child or her parents. The Alliance must protect the Solians at all costs. The war with the Annunaki will end provided the Solians can flourish. This should be as important to you as killing the Empress was to Tony. It's critical in the long term," Gly advised. "I will make it my mission to ensure the

Solians are protected. Is there anything else?" Vincent asked. "Yes, I have one more suggestion and it will cause me personal turmoil. The Solians must spread throughout the galaxy. As they grow and mature, send some to this world. If any species can figure out what's going on with the rebel Annunaki, it will be the Solians. There must be a reason the Annunaki rebels exist. I believe the Solians will find the answer. Until then, I will do what I can with the rebels."

Vincent was stunned. "Let me get this straight. You're inviting a species onto this world? I never thought I'd see the day," he laughed. "It will only be the Solians. I don't want to see any of your kind here. Your much uglier than the Solians and you produce unnecessary drama," Gly said and made a strange sound. Vincent couldn't tell if the alien was laughing or not. "Very well. I will advise the Alliance of your invitation. If there's nothing else, goodbye my friend." "Take to the skies in your ship and remember what I've said. You're no longer needed here." Gly sat on the ice shelf and watched as the ship flew into the night sky.

"What was that about?" Patrick asked when Vincent returned. "We briefly spoke about some of the Volmer returning to Ganymede. How about we get out of here and go home? Set a course for Earth," Vincent ordered. "Do you mind dropping us off first, Captain? Alixias asked. "Oh sorry, I almost forgot. Set a course

for Mars. Are there any other ships in the area?"
Vincent asked. "Negative Captain, were you expecting
any?" Andy asked. "No, but you can never be too
cautious. The Solians must be protected," Vincent said
as he glanced at Zabu.

Chapter 20

The trip to Mars was uneventful. Vincent cherished the peace and quiet after recent events. As the daily report was broadcast on the viewscreen, it appeared a new Empress would emerge sometime soon. The Alliance still hadn't located the new rearing facility. "I wonder where it is?" Julia asked no one in particular. "It doesn't matter. The Annunaki will never rise again," Zabu replied determinedly.

The broadcast ended and a distant planet appeared on the viewscreen. "Andy, I thought I ordered us to Mars, not Earth," Vincent said. "That is Mars," Andy replied. "Please enlarge the image," Vincent ordered in disbelief. The planet suddenly appeared much larger on the screen. "My God, it's beautiful. There are only traces of red and orange now," Julia was incredulous. "I guess we missed quite a bit. I'd stay for a while, but I've got a date on Earth," Vincent said as the ship descended.

He made a promise to Gly and planned to keep it. Zabu departed with her parents and the security detail. "Goodbye for now. Thank you for all you've done. I guess we don't need the security detail anymore," Patrick said as the ship landed. "I've made arrangements with Chief Administrator Kizak. The security detail will remain with Zabu on Mars. She is the leader of her species and must be protected at all times," Vincent replied. "Thank you, Captain. A wise precaution," Zabu said as she disembarked with her parents and the security detail. "Andy set a course for Earth, let's go home," Vincent ordered.

The enormous lake was beautiful and surrounded by mountains. Isabella was hot. The sky was clear and the summer sun blazed down. It took three days to arrive by car and when she finally arrived and knocked on the front door there was no answer. "Dad?" she said as she opened the door and entered. After going upstairs, she still didn't find him. The sliding glass door facing the lake was open and she walked outside and found her father. He was at the end of the dock as close to the water as possible.

Enzo pounded away on the antique keyboard, stopping for a moment to take a swig of his beer. "You know, most people don't actually use those things anymore. How old is that laptop anyway?" a voice from behind him asked. He stood up and gave Bella a kiss on her cheek. "I don't follow the rules. It's much easier to do what you're comfortable with. I'm so glad you could make it. So, what happened?" Enzo asked.

"We won," Isabella said simply. Enzo listened and took notes as the story was told. "You've done well. Continue asking questions and remember to keep an eye on everyone. The Alliance doesn't know it, but they need people like us. I'm so proud of you. The guest house will always be here for you. When you get married and have children I expect all of you to come here often. For now, we will have pizza for dinner."

The pounding on the door was way too loud. Monique couldn't understand why someone was knocking so loudly. "Who is it?" she asked crossly. "It's the CIA. We're here to arrest you for all the horrible crimes you've committed," a voice said. "Very funny," she replied as she opened the door. Vincent came in and gave her a long, passionate kiss.

"We should get married," he said. Monique wasn't expecting a proposal. "You're not even on your knees and you don't have a ring. I suppose you want some huge fancy wedding with all of our friends?" she asked and waited as Vincent began to mumble a reply. "Just stop. It sounds like too much trouble. I won't marry you right now. I'd rather skip to the honeymoon."

Monique never failed to surprise him. "That's not the answer I was looking for, but it's good enough. Should we go somewhere?" he asked. "No, I think the temporary housing the Alliance provides in the middle of a field is very romantic," Monique replied sarcastically. "Where would you like to go? I'll take you anywhere." he said. "I've always wanted to visit China. Let's go to the Huangguoshu Waterfall." Monique kissed her lover and led him to the bed.

There were very few things in life Monique enjoyed more than the smell of food in the morning. Vincent returned to the bedroom with a plate of eggs, bacon and hash browns. "When our vacation is over, you will not be returning to your ship," he said as he handed her a plate. "Since when did you start doling out duty assignments?" she asked. "I've been discussing the Solians with Chief Administrator Kizak and you've been assigned to my team. We've been tasked with safeguarding the Solian species," Vincent explained.

"I don't understand. The Solians are simply a new species within the Alliance. Why do they need protection?" Monique asked. "In time, the Solians will become the most important species within the Alliance. The Solians will end the war with the Annunaki." he replied. "If you think it's important, I will join you."

Vincent took hold of Monique's hands and looked into her eyes. "If it weren't for the Solians we'd be dead right now. Even with his unique abilities, Tony couldn't kill Empress Zovad on his own; he needed help from Keeras. If it weren't for Zabu, we would have been overrun by the Annunaki on Tanas. The Solians will end the war once and for all. It's our job to make sure the species survives," Vincent explained. "So, the Solians are the key to peace?" "Yes, they will become very powerful and bring peace and morality. We now have the most important job within the Alliance." Monique smiled and handed Vincent her empty plate. "You do need me. Somebody has to make sure you don't screw this up."

"Depressurization will commence in fifteen seconds," a voice announced through the loudspeaker. "I never thought this day would come," Dalton said incredulously. "We will be among the first to breathe the new Martian atmosphere. Get ready, here we go!" Patrick replied excitedly. A sudden gust of wind swept through the entire Martian community as depressurization occurred. Everyone cautiously stepped outside to breathe the Martian air.

Zabu walked with Alixias and Patrick through the light rain, taking note of the parents who came outside holding infant Solians. "It's time to move into the countryside and become one with our world. To think we almost lost this world to the Annunaki. Everything came so close to ending," Alixias said. Zabu looked to the horizon as the sun broke through the clouds. "The adventure of my species has just begun."

Epilogue

The battle was difficult and gruesome. Ajal secured the spoils of war and returned to the Scalga Pyramid. His job was to ensure all treasure made it to Pharaoh Quarcius. The all-seeing eye stared at him from above. "We have defeated our enemies. The treasures are vast and the Gods will be happy," Pharaoh Quarcius declared. "We lost thousands in battle and will not be able to fight again soon," Ajal replied. Pharaoh Quarcius laughed. "We've defeated all our enemies! There will be no more battles and I will reign unopposed until my death."

"I can't believe you've finally travelled outside our solar system. It took a unique opportunity like this to finally get you away from Mars," Vincent said. "Explain to me what we're doing again. I'm still a bit fuzzy on the details," Dalton asked. "We're travelling to a planet called Corvus and will briefly meet with a local leader. Subjects of Pharaoh Quarcius will load our ship with artifacts and treasure collected in battle. We will then travel to a predetermined location where the subjects of Pharaoh Quarcius will offload the treasure. You'd already know all this if you took the time to read the mission briefing from Chief Administrator Kizak. Just follow my lead; I'll do all the talking," Vincent said.

"So, we're hiding their treasure for someone on their planet to find it in two or three thousand years?" Dalton asked.

"I suppose you could simplify it like that, but there's more to it. When we arrive, the Alliance bots and equipment on the surface will be taken away. Legends about the all-powerful "Gods" who briefly graced their species will spread and in time, as the species grows, there will be questions. Doubts will arise about these "Gods" and some will start asking questions and digging for answers, just as we did. The species must advance and learn how to be self-reliant," Vincent replied. "It sounds overly complicated. There has to be an easier way," Dalton was baffled. "This is the way the Alliance has proceeded for thousands of years. If you can think of a better way, tell Chief Administrator Kizak."

Pharaoh Quarcius fell asleep listening to the surf in her royal encampment near the shoreline. With recent victories, she would never be challenged as leader within her lifetime. She slept well until a sudden noise startled her. She gasped as two large Gods stood before her. The Gods were hideous, but she didn't dare show any disrespect. "You are to bring our tribute to the Scalga Pyramid in six days. Arrive at sundown and bring six of your subjects to load our tribute. Do not fail us," one of the Gods said. "I pray we are worthy and our tribute is acceptable," Monarch Quarcius replied as the Gods departed.

"Members of that species sure are short and have very strange bodies. What's with the three legs and short arms?" Dalton asked after returning to the ship. "If you would have done your research, you would know that one of the legs is actually a short tail. Much like a kangaroo, it helps with balance and can help get them moving quickly when necessary," Vincent explained. "What are we supposed to do for six days?" Dalton asked. "We explore and relax. The planet is sparsely populated, but it won't be in the future."

The chariot was lit by bright fire as it descended from the heavens. Pharaoh Quarcius issued one last instruction to her subjects. "Do not dare approach or speak with the Gods if you wish to live."

"Damn, I didn't know this ship had so many lights," Dalton said as the ship landed and he clumsily fell out of his seat. "We need to put on a big and glitzy show. Jesus, try to pull yourself together and be a little more Godlike. I'm about to open the cargo bay, so try not to stumble and fall down the ramp," Vincent replied as he exited the ship.

"Instruct your subjects to load our tribute quickly," Vincent commanded as he and Dalton watched the strange aliens scurry about. Two hours later, the cargo bay was full and Monarch Quarcius boarded the ship with her subjects. Vincent deactivated both his and Dalton's translation application, so they could speak privately. The Santa Maria approached a snow-capped peak halfway across the planet. The side of a hidden pyramid suddenly slid back. "Damn, it's just like Old Snowy Mountain!" Dalton exclaimed.

"Yes, it is. It will take this species a long time to find it," Vincent replied as he guided the ship into the pyramid. The tribute was quickly offloaded and Vincent set a course back to the Scalga Pyramid. The Santa Maria graciously landed minutes later. "It's bewildering none of them saw you trip and fall over the ramp. I'm going to speak to Alliance medical personnel about you," Vincent said. "What for?" Dalton replied. "I think a tail might improve your balance."

She was nervous. Her tribute was safely offloaded and the Gods continued to speak only in their divine language. Pharaoh Quarcius worried the tribute was insufficient and she would be punished or killed. She would soon know her fate as the ride in the glorious chariot was about to end. The Scalga Pyramid appeared on the horizon.

As her subjects departed, one of the Gods approached. "Pharaoh Quarcius, your tribute is acceptable. You are the leader of your kingdom and you must expand your empire and instruct your subjects. Those with knowledge should instruct those who have none. Find subjects with intelligent minds and embrace their proposals. Surround yourself with the wisest of your subjects. If you follow my commands, you will prosper. This will be the last time you see one of us in your lifetime, Pharaoh. Use the knowledge we have given you. We have assisted you in building this empire with our mechanical devices. The devices are now gone and you are on your own. Help your subjects prosper and learn." the God turned and boarded the chariot.

"That was fun. I wish we could have kept some of the artifacts. It looked like there were some interesting pieces from this species," Dalton said. "The treasure is unique to their society and culture. It will always be more valuable to them, than to us," Vincent said. "We began our quest on Earth to prove Maria was right about ancient Egypt. It all started with her and you've proven her right and honored her memory," Dalton said. "Everything worked out. I'm glad I could share this moment with you. The species from this world will join the Alliance in a few thousand years and add their uniqueness. Let's go home. We must watch over the Solians."

Thank you for reading my story and supporting independent authors. If you enjoyed the story, please share with your friends! I truly appreciate all the fans of the Lost Sols Trilogy.

All my work is currently available on Amazon or you can receive updates at:

JamesKirkBisceglia.com

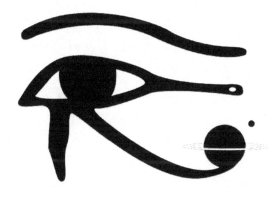

Made in the USA
Columbia, SC
13 March 2019